CONJURING CHAOS

DYSTOPIAN FANTASY

SANCTUARY, BOOK TWO

ANN GIMPEL

CONTENTS

CONJURING CHAOS

SANCTUARY, BOOK TWO

Dystopian Fantasy

By
Ann Gimpel

**Tumble off reality's edge into a broken world
fueled by lore and despair**

Copyright Page

If this were a normal nightmare, I'd wake up, dust myself off, and forge a path. Nightmare, yes. Normal, not so much. After the world imploded, none of the usual rules applied.

They say finding your roots is freeing. In my case, it was like nailing a coffin shut. Everyone has a few rotten relatives. Mine created me to serve their purposes millennia ago. Except nobody bothered to tell me, not until my world shattered. When I rebelled, they labeled me extraneous, so now I'm on the lookout for them along with every other evil thing that's risen to populate Earth.

All the mortals seem to be dead. In theory, those like me, mages, survived, but outside our small group, we haven't stumbled on any of them beyond a lone skinwalker. Rhys is a bright spot. Who'd have thought I'd find love amidst the ashes of civilization. Sometimes, I want to cling to him and run away, but Earth needs us.

And there it is. Along with love, I'm coming into the full extent of my power. The more I push it, the brighter it burns.

We tried to alter the cataclysm that ended everything. It didn't work, but we haven't given up. Between Rhys and an eldritch griffon tasked with protecting me long before my birth, we'll tackle my masters. Everything points to them blowing up the world.

If we could figure out why, we might turn the tides in our favor.

AUTHOR'S NOTE

This series has been percolating for months. I finished writing *Promised*, last of the Bound by Shadows books in early June, 2023. It was slower than expected because I'd begun penning chapters for *Alive, Surviving Modern Oncology*, my passion project aimed at helping other cancer patients navigate challenging waters. It took far longer than I'd anticipated. Here it is mid-August already, but *Alive* is loose in the world, and I'm ready to return to my first love: fiction.

Many of my other series feature a dystopian near future. Bitter Harvest and Earth Reclaimed are the two that jump to the forefront. *Icy Passage* is a standalone novel with a similar dystopian cast.

I'm excited to jump back into my comfort zone. Bits and pieces of this series have been rattling around in my head since I wrote the blurb a couple of months back.

<cracking knuckles> Let's get to it, shall we?

CHAPTER ONE, ALIA

I checked the gas gauge once more. We weren't quite running on fumes, but almost. Ever since we abandoned the cave system outside Sedona, we'd been on the move. Seven isn't all that many people, but we split up a couple of weeks ago. The shifter sisters, Karen and Moriah, wanted to take to their wolf forms and hunt. Nola, a weak-as-dishwater witch, is holed up in a farmhouse in southwestern Nevada where the previous owners, now dead, had laid in enough food to sit out eternity.

Their cellar reminded me of advertisements for the Doomsday crew. Who would have guessed Armageddon would play out in our lifetimes? Some days, I'm used to the status quo. Others, not so much.

Mostly, we've been in survival mode. We have yet to meet a mortal who escaped destruction. All their abandoned cars and trucks have come in handy, though, since the highway system is mostly intact. Enormous cracks and potholes have blocked roads in some spots, but nothing a determined four-wheel drive can't manage.

The engine sputtered. I'd hoped for five more miles, but it wasn't going to happen.

From long habit, I pulled to the side of the road while the wheels were still turning. It scarcely mattered since no one else was likely to come along. Chanting from the back seat suggested Rhys was conducting one more interminable magic lesson. I swear, that man has the patience of a saint, but we are improving.

Not that I need more magic. I don't. My problem is a surfeit that's mostly out of control. Too much when I don't need it; too little when I do.

"What's up?" Connor called. He's a dark-haired hawk shifter with blue eyes and pretty levelheaded.

"Out of fuel."

Rhys cut the flow of his lesson. "Odd. I was certain we'd have enough to hit the next town."

I grabbed the paper map sharing the front seat with me and stared at it. After the wolf shifters defected, group consensus had been to head north. We weren't breaking any speed records as we meandered up a north-south highway spanning the eastern escarpment of the Sierra Nevada mountains.

Towns were few and far between. That would change once we crossed into Nevada, for a while anyway, but it hadn't happened yet.

I flipped the ignition to off and pushed the driver's door open. Rhys, Connor, and Joss, a druid, piled out of the back of the white Toyota 4-Runner. It was the middle of the afternoon; a chill wind battered me. Shading my eyes with a hand, I scanned the skies for my gold-and-brown griffon sidekick but didn't see him.

Bound to me by eldritch Sumerian enchantment, he chose to use his wings to travel. Being confined in vehicles made him uncomfortable. The era that spawned him had used oxen, horses, and carts to get around.

I wrapped my arms around myself. We needed to find a clothing shop and stock up on warmer garments.

"Grab whatever you don't want to leave," Rhys instructed. "I'll move us away from here."

The only possession not on my back was the map. I reached into the cab and retrieved it. Nearly every gas station had them, but who knew when we'd find another? My useless cell phone was a weight in my jacket pocket, but I couldn't bring myself to throw it away.

Stupid, huh?

Above us, the clouds turned gray and menacing. Rain spit in violent bursts pushed by escalating wind. I zipped my faded green jacket to the chin and wished for a hood.

An eerie howl was followed by several more. Great. Was a wolf pack bearing down on us? Not that I couldn't immobilize them, but I hated to. Unless they were werewolves, but we hadn't seen any of them since leaving Sedona.

No vampires, either.

Surprisingly, we hadn't run into any trouble. It was one reason Karen, Moriah, and Nola had cited for jumping ship. They'd downplayed the dangers we faced to convince themselves it would be okay to pretend things weren't as bad as we feared. So, what else was new? They'd been reluctant recruits from the moment our world imploded.

I jammed my hands into my pockets before my fingers froze.

"Alia." Rhys's tone was tense.

"Yeah?" I scuttled to his side.

"Try a jump spell."

I angled a sidelong glance his way. "Uh, why? What happened to yours?"

"For god's sake, woman, for once do what I ask without questioning it."

Oops.

Whatever was going on wasn't good. Not that Rhys couldn't be temperamental, but his comment was uncharacteristically strained. With thick ice-blond hair and blue eyes, he was tall, well-muscled, and lean. He was also my partner and lover, although we'd had precious few moments to ourselves.

I still harbored reservations—big ones—about the lover part. We're so different, and he's like a bazillion years older than me. Although, apparently, I'm far older than I'd thought since the Sumerians kept me in some sort of unnatural stasis until they tucked my essence into a human woman so she could birth me. I'm still unsure what all that means. It's kind of like a "next life rebirth" gig but on steroids.

I cleared my head and focused power into a simple jump spell, one designed to move us a few miles north. Not so far we needed the usual journey channels, which had been perverted by evil, but away from here and nearer the next town.

The men pressed close. I goosed my casting, fully expecting it to take off.

We didn't move. What in the hell? After forcing vision through my third eye, I tried again.

And ended up with the same results. An old saying about doing the same thing and expecting a different outcome being insanity swatted me broadside.

"Not good," Rhys muttered. "Same thing that happened to me."

"Then why'd you set me up?" My tone was testy, but worry gnawed a hole in my guts.

The look he skewered me with made me feel about an inch tall. "Don't be so edgy. This wasn't a setup. Christ, Alia. I wouldn't do that to you, but I was hoping a different style of magic might turn the tide."

"So, the bottom line is we're stuck walking?" Joss asked. He tossed flame-red hair over slender shoulders. "If so, we'd best get to it. Nightfall is only a couple of hours away."

The pain in my midsection intensified. Night brought vampires and werewolves and god knew what else. We needed shelter. Even the car was better than nothing. Maybe we should stay put.

"I'll fly reconnaissance," Connor offered and started to strip off his clothes.

"Good idea." Rhys gathered the discarded garments and slung them over an arm.

Eh, guess we weren't remaining here.

Connor's hawk spread shapely brown wings and took to the skies. We plodded north. I spread magic all around hoping it would provide some level of warning since we were terribly exposed. The only living things around.

"Where's Cleyn?" Rhys asked, referring to the griffon.

I shrugged. "Not here, but it's not unusual."

"Don't you have some kind of link with him?" Joss asked. His blue eyes were narrowed against the wind.

I did, but it wasn't as if we were connected at the hip. "Doesn't mean I know where he is," I replied. Rain had settled into a steady drizzle. Cold leached every scrap of warmth from my body. My feet were turning into chunks of ice. I started to shiver. Worse, weariness dragged at me, made it hard to think. Despite walking, I was having a tough time not falling asleep.

What the hell? I'd slept decently the night before cradled in Rhys's arms. Because my eyes were at half-mast, I stumbled and would have fallen if he hadn't grabbed my upper arm.

"Are you all right?"

Trying to form words was a struggle. By the time I managed, "Not even close," Rhys had spun me to face him. He placed a hand on both sides of my face. The familiar touch of his power flooded me. It was a wakeup call, but after an initial jolt, I slithered back into the pit.

"What's wrong with her?" Joss's voice came from a long way away, which was odd since he stood next to me.

The shrouding I'd erected to check for bad shit folded around me, effectively rendering me blind and deaf. Rhys and Joss were there, but I could no longer sense them.

I should have been terrified, but all I wanted was to lie down and shut my eyes. Peace would reign. All would be well. No more running with an eye over one shoulder. No more struggling.

"Alia..." It sounded like Cleyn, but then that faded as well.

A vision of an oblong ball of light filled my visual field. Crystalline with pale pink and lavender highlights, I knew that sphere. Realization punched me in the guts; I twisted from side to side. The light coffin was where the Sumerians had dumped me—or my essence. I'd lived out millennia within its clutches. Guttural moans ripped from me. Wrenching my head out of Rhys's grip, I vomited onto the asphalt.

Someone was shaking me. A short, wicked blade materialized in my hand. I still couldn't see through my earth eyes, but my third eye was functional. I ended up in a crouch, head whipping from side to side and knife at the ready. The reek of puke was strong in my nostrils.

Rhys glowed where he'd surrounded himself with something. Joss did too. Why were they protecting themselves, but not me? And then it dawned they'd erected a barrier I couldn't penetrate.

Were they abandoning me to my fate?

Did they know about the crystal coffin that had held me prisoner between my making and when the Sumerians decided my time to serve had arrived? I made a grab for anger; it eluded me. The same thick, sticky mud I'd been drowning in returned with a vengeance.

My stomach burned, throat too. Dry heaves racked me, but my stomach was empty. Despite how cold I was, foul-smelling sweat beaded on my body and trickled down my sides.

Ghouls circled, staring with empty eyes. I recognized them. Watchers. Servants of the Sumerian gods. Was that what this was about? Were they sick of my insurrection and forcing me home?

I had to fight this, but when I hunted for motivation, it scuttled away. Simpler to sink into the crystal and let it take care of me as it had for many a long year. No more hunger. No more thirst. No more cold...

"Alia." The voice in my head was hypnotic, mesmerizing. *"We'll take over now."*

"Leave this place. Immediately," Rhys thundered in one of his many languages, except I sort of understood this one. No wonder. On closer examination, it was Sumerian.

Something must have swatted him, since he flew through the air. The next glimpse I caught of him, he ran toward me, fists swinging. I did my damnedest to marshal words to tell him there was no hope, not for me, but he could save himself if he left now. Joss too. At least Connor was safely away, flying somewhere above this mess.

I tried, but nothing beyond a squeak emerged from my throat.

The shining crystal edged nearer. I wanted its gentle confines, its nurturing. My longing horrified me. I shuffled away, fighting its pull. A goddess-like figure formed behind my third eye. She might have been the same woman I'd seen deep underground. She carried a lantern. Her silvery eyes were warm, inviting as she herded me toward the crystal.

If it reached me, I'd never escape.

Fight this, a faint inner voice cried. *You cannot give in. You know what awaits if you do.*

Of course, I knew. Why didn't I care more?

Had I been drugged? I didn't see how. Our last meal had been canned peaches and tinned bread scrounged from the remains of a small market in Independence, a tiny town squatting in the shadow of enormous mountains.

Thinking about the food inserted a ray of objectivity. It wasn't the food. How could it have been? No. This was about running out of gas. Someone had finessed it, and they'd done it in a specific place. This area must house a gateway or a power point amenable to their control. It also explained the griffon's absence. Either he couldn't break through, or they were holding him prisoner.

The latter explanation broke my heart. Cleyn had lost everything on account of me. I'd be damned if he'd add suffering to the mix.

The crystal coffin wasn't more than a foot away. How had it come so close? Breath burned my abraded throat. I finally understood what I had to do to break free. Could I manage it?

"Distance," I panted, but the word emerged so garbled it was unrecognizable. No wonder our jump spells hadn't worked. They'd been tainted right along with the Toyota.

"Got to get away from here." I reverted to mind speech.

"I'm trying," Rhys gritted.

Somehow, I was on my feet but disoriented. How broad a net had the Sumerians cast? No one's magic is limitless. I couldn't go back toward the Toyota. Pushing ahead on the road didn't feel right, either. Running on instinct, I forced myself into a shambling run at right angles to the highway into sand and sagebrush.

At first, it was impossibly difficult. The lantern goddess blocked me, except I stepped through her. Whoa. Hadn't expected that. Ghouls brushed against me. I ignored them and kept moving. They'd attacked Cleyn, but so far they'd let me be. If I were right, the horridly debilitating exhaustion would lessen as I inserted space between me and the highway.

If I was wrong, at least I'd go down swinging. I did not want to drag Rhys and Joss into the muck with me. Wings swooshed past just before talons closed around my shoulder. Their sharp points made me yelp, but they also pushed the fog around my brain back a little.

"Nothing is out there," Connor squawked. "Keep moving, Alia."

I'd suspected as much. We'd been waylaid and done the expected: walked in the same direction as we'd been driving. Shit. How had we been so stupid?

Not stupid, complacent. My inner wise woman was back, and she was right. In the absence of werewolves and vampires, we'd let our guard down as if they were the only bad things in the world.

Awk. Bad things. Where was the coffin?

Staring through my third eye, I still saw it, but it was maybe twenty feet away. I felt like crowing. It wasn't about to snatch me into another dimension. Not today.

"Damn straight," I muttered and plodded on.

Manzanita branches tore at my pants. I was soaked to the skin and had passed beyond being cold to numbness, but I was moving more easily. Relief sluiced through me. I'd guessed right. Emphasis on *guessed*.

This could so easily have gone another way.

Another 500 paces, and I felt more like myself. The crystal orb and the amorphous goddess had vanished. Connor still rode on my shoulder offering moral support.

"Thanks," I murmured. "I'm good."

Rhys and Joss caught up. Connor fluttered to the ground and shifted. Rhys dropped a pile of garments in front of him, and Connor grumbled about how wet everything was as he dressed.

"At least you still have clothes," Rhys told him. "I could have left them back where you dumped them."

Connor cracked a grin. "Thanks, man."

"Bet your jump spell would work now," I told Rhys. "But I'm worried about Cleyn."

"You can help him from anywhere," Rhys pointed out. "We need shelter. Maybe only half an hour before nightfall."

I glanced skyward. Crap. He was right. How had I burned through a couple of hours trekking due east? Because I'd been moving with all the speed of a land tortoise until about half an hour back.

Power surged, illuminating the droplets around Rhys. "I need to hear everything," he said, "but not just now."

His words were so typical I smiled. He was far better at triage than me. Aiming at the problem burning brightest.

"Liked it better as a hawk," Connor mumbled as he wrung water out of his pant legs.

"Don't take us too far," I urged. "Bishop is the next town

on the map. We were only about five miles away when the Toyota broke down."

As Rhys worked on his casting, I shielded my eyes with a hand and stared at the skies. Where was the griffon? Since Plan A hadn't worked, were our erstwhile masters holding him hostage and planning to use our link to force my cooperation?

More importantly, would they ever leave me alone?

When the answer, a resounding *no*, came, my spirits drooped. I'd considered separating myself from Rhys and the others more than once. Trouble dogged me; no reason to drag the others into my personal hell.

"No fucking way," blasted through my mind.

I snorted. Ever the consummate mage, Rhys could craft a spell and track my thoughts without breaking a sweat. Before I dredged up a snappy reply, the sagebrush shimmered and vanished. Moments later, we stood on the outskirts of one more trashed town. Rows of cars and trucks were promising as was a mostly intact Quonset hut that had once housed a tire business.

Too burned out for subtle, I focused a blast of power at the hut to ascertain if anything living bided within.

"Well?" Connor arched a dark brow.

"We're good," I said and led the way toward a side door hanging open on bent hinges. If we got lucky, there might be a can or two of food. Anything fresh would have long since rotted.

After a bit of hunting, I located a small kitchen off a work area. The others pushed in after me. It was a tight fit for four of us. Joss, our *de facto* cook, rustled through cupboards.

Rhys turned me to face him. "Strong work."

My damp face warmed. "Thanks, but more like a strong guess."

He shook his head. "Nope. You followed your intuition."

"Score!" Joss cried and held up a box of Triscuits and a round of some kind of hard cheese. Bits of mold grew along the edges, but those could be cut off.

My more-than-empty stomach growled. I'd eat and then address myself to the missing griffon. Rhys wouldn't want me outside at night, but leaving the beast to whatever fate awaited didn't sit well. He'd have come after me if he could. I'd be damned if I abandoned him.

Rhys took a cracker with cheese layered on top and handed it to me. "If Cleyn isn't back soon, I'll help you find him through your link."

The day had been rougher than I expected; my eyes filled with tears. I brushed them aside hoping no one noticed. Sorrow was an old-world luxury; my tears wouldn't help Cleyn—or anyone else.

Connor had been rifling through cabinets. He set a can of tuna on the counter, followed by a jar of what looked like home-canned pears. At least our bellies would be full.

Faint scratching drew me to my feet, head cocked to one side as I pinpointed the noise.

"I heard that." Connor shot upright, nostrils flaring much as his hawk's might have.

"Not magical," Rhys said as he, too, stared at a spot on the far side of the kitchen and added a drawing spell to the mix.

Because the creature couldn't help itself, a smallish gray rat scuttled forward, whiskers twitching.

"How'd it survive?" I blurted as it edged toward a pile of moldy cheese Joss had left next to the sink. Rodents are smart. Somehow, it knew not to dive into the round we'd fed from. At least, not while we were here.

"Good question," Rhys muttered. Power surged as he tested our temporary home, searching for whatever it is mages hunt for. I'm still new and green. Ambivalent as fuck about my ability despite Rhys's lessons.

Nowhere near dry from hours in the rain, I prepared to trade our shelter for somewhere safer. Joss wrapped the cheese in a chunk of butcher paper. Connor returned to the cupboards to see if he'd missed anything. Our uninvited guest hunched over the cheese scraps eating methodically.

Colors swirled around Rhys, blues and violets, before he reeled in his spell. "We're good," he announced.

"Good how?" Connor stopped searching long enough to eye Rhys.

"Energy fields coalesce around this area," he explained. "It's what saved the rat, and probably a bunch of his relatives."

"Could it have spared any people?" I asked.

"Good question," Rhys said. "Let's look, shall we?"

"Maybe we shouldn't be eating their food." Joss put the cheese back in the cupboard.

"Premature until we know there's actually a *them* out there." Rhys flapped a hand his way and started out of the kitchen.

If we did anything, we should be hunting Cleyn, but I

didn't call him back. Instead, I activated my link with the griffon and held it wide open.

Please let him be there. Please.

It was selfish, but I'd lost so much, even one more defeat was unacceptable.

CHAPTER TWO, RHYS

T he caves where we'd initially taken refuge hadn't proven all that safe, but it didn't mean other protected places didn't exist. At least in theory.

Alia had put me through the wringer earlier. I've rarely felt as helpless. She couldn't hear me or see me. Worse, she'd drawn a weapon against me. Except it hadn't been her. Not really. Given her lack of sensory input, perhaps the blade hadn't been meant for me—or Joss.

Her power is untrained, and I'm unsure about the limits of its ability—or if it even has limits, since she's growing so rapidly. We'd spent half a minute in my guild house in the Old Country. Returning there to have others from my order assess her would be useful, but it was unlikely to happen.

For one thing, we'd have to leave Joss and Connor. When the other women had been part of our group, I'd have been more inclined to do so, which was stupid since they'd added very little to the magical spectrum. More part of the problem than part of any solution. Compounding the predicament were teleport channels that had been perverted by something wicked. Traveling back in time to an earlier point when they were clear solved that problem, but it added to the time we'd have to be gone.

Regardless, we'd been drawn to this Quonset hut for a reason, perhaps because it contained built-in protection. It damn near had to, given the surviving rodent still munching cheese rinds.

I hustled out of the small kitchen intent on searching the place for survivors. Midway down the long central wing, I stopped. What would I do if I unearthed anyone? We were scarcely in a position to provide aid. Hell, I hadn't been able to keep our group of seven in one spot.

Altering strategy, I sent beams of gentle seeking enchantment spinning outward hoping for a Pied Piper effect. Sure enough, about twenty rats sashayed forth along with a couple of large ginger-colored cats. Apparently, they'd established détente, since neither cat took off after the rats.

I focused my attention on one of the cats. *"Is anyone else here?"*

A muted yowl was followed by the creature hissing and writhing as it tried to escape the pull of my power.

"You're hurting him. Stop this instant." A short, round woman took shape and lumbered toward me. Brown hair was pulled into an old-fashioned bun. A dirty long-sleeved red dress fell to ankle level. Even standing tall, she barely reached the middle of my chest.

I could have probed, dug into the meat of who she was,

but the woman quivered with indignation. Jabbing her with still more magic wouldn't help the situation.

"You're a Brownie," I said, not turning it into a question.

"And you're a sorcerer. So what?" She made a face and shrugged. "This is my home. You must leave. Now." The cats and rats created a protective arc around her.

"What the hell?" Alia joined me.

"You can leave too," the Brownie shouted. "Don't need your kind here."

Alia took a step closer. Hackles raised the length of the cats' spines. The rats bared yellow fangs and squealed. "What exactly is *my kind?*" she inquired.

"If you don't know, I'm not the one to tell you, missy."

Alia fell back until she stood next to me.

"How'd you get here?" I asked the woman since Brownies and Leprechauns were native to the Old Country.

"Does it matter." She made shooing motions. "Leave. Find your own place."

"What is she?" Alia asked me. "I sense weak power."

The woman rolled her shoulders back. "I. Am. Not. Weak."

"Fine," Alia muttered. "Poor choice of words."

Connor and Joss trotted close. "You found someone," Connor said.

"Epic," Joss tossed out. "We can help each other."

The woman flapped her hands in the air. "Impossible. Go away."

"She's a Brownie," I answered Alia. "They're household Fae that usually only come out at night. Mostly, they enjoy domestic tasks—"

"We do not enjoy them," the woman screeched. "Mortals are pigs. We like things neat is all."

It did not answer how she'd gotten here. "Have you always been in this spot?" I asked.

"What do you think?" she shot back.

"I think no. Whatever happened to Earth opened channels, and you ended up here through no specific efforts of your own."

"This is still my place," she bristled. "I was here first. You're stealing from all of us." Reaching down, she patted the cats who stood on either side of her.

I turned my hands palms outward. "We'll go, but first I need to know if you traveled through broken gateways."

"What difference does it make," she mumbled sullenly.

"A whole lot," Connor dove in. "If portals that kept mages in a single spot crumbled, it explains why we've run into vampires and werewolves."

"Weres were always here," I said.

The Brownie's bright blue eyes rounded. "Vampires? They never leave the Old Country."

"Neither do your kind," I inserted dryly.

She made a hissing sound not unlike one of her cats, as the reality of my insinuation sank in. Gathering herself, she glared balefully. "You still need to leave."

"Are there more like you?" Alia's question was soft and laced with subtle compulsion.

"Of course." The Brownie's reply may as well have been, *What planet were you born on?*

"Here. I meant here," Alia clarified.

"There's usually only one per household," I murmured. "They don't care for competition."

"You know nothing," the woman snarled.

We were getting nowhere fast. "Answer my question, and we'll leave you in peace," I said.

When a minute ticked past, followed by several more, I considered my options. I could dredge through her mind. Wouldn't take long, but it violated several aspects of a pact that bound magic-wielders together—the good ones, anyway.

"I went to sleep in Northern Ireland," she gritted. "When I woke, I was here. 'Twas well over a month ago, give or take."

Intriguing. "Did the cats and rats come along for the ride?"

"Found them here. Poor little creatures, clinging to life by a thread. I saved them."

As if to corroborate her statement, they hugged her sides, clearly ready to do battle to save their mistress.

"Did you try to return?" Joss asked.

"What kind of stupid question is that?" she growled. "Of course, I did. It's impossible."

"Are you certain you want us gone?" I skewered her with a direct gaze.

"Yes. Safer if 'tis only me. As you"—she aimed a gnarled finger Alia's way—"noted, my magic is barely discernable."

"We could help—" Alia began.

The Brownie hooked two fingers in a sigil against evil. "Help from your kind never bodes well."

There it was again. *Her kind.* What did the Brownie

sense? They might not be strong magically, but they're intuitive as all get out. Plus, they're extremely long-lived.

"What's your name?" I asked.

"Ha. Like I'm about to tell you."

Her persistent negatives grated on my nerves. Out of patience, I skimmed the surface of her mind.

Yelping, she grabbed her head. "Stop this instant."

It was an empty threat, empty words. She and I both knew she was out-manned and out-gunned enchantment-wise.

"Nice to make your acquaintance, Gretta," I said, emphasizing her name.

She cringed; I felt like a cad, but I'd never use her name to damage her. She had no way of knowing that, however. In her world, she'd become doubly vulnerable.

"Do you mind if we spend the night?" Connor asked.

"We'll leave with first light," Joss corroborated.

Gretta drew back. Most of the animals joined her. One of the rats slithered toward Alia, followed by a second. She knelt, and they positioned themselves near her hands.

"Come back this instant," Gretta ordered.

Alia stroked two gray-furred heads. "Animals like me," she murmured. "No harm will befall them."

"We'd take it as a great kindness if we could shelter here till morning." I layered a soothing spell into my words. "Evil things stalk the darkness. We'd be vulnerable."

"How'd you get here?" she asked.

"We had a car. Didn't plan well, and it ran out of fuel," I replied.

Gretta's dark brows pinched together. "That's not everything."

"No, it's not," Alia spoke up. "The same ones who crafted Armageddon have been after me. They set us up when the car ran out of fuel, and then they attacked. It took all my magic and a bunch besides to extricate ourselves. This was the closest town. We used a jump spell to get here."

"I see. Why this hut?"

"When I tested it, it seemed empty," Alia told her.

"Would it have stopped you if it weren't?" Bitterness lined the Brownie's words.

"We're not the enemy," I said softly.

She laced her fingers together. "Everyone is the enemy."

She hadn't expressly said we couldn't spend the night, so I motioned my crew close. After a final head pat, Alia shooed the rats toward Gretta and joined us. Before I said anything, she murmured, "I have to hunt for Cleyn."

"Who's that?" Gretta asked. Still standing in the same spot, she wasn't yielding any ground.

"My griffon," Alia replied.

The Brownie's eyes rounded. "So the old tales are true."

"What old tales?" Connor asked.

Good thing he asked, so I didn't have to.

Gretta poked a gnarled index finger in Alia's general direction and recited in a singsong voice: "Set to watch over, set to guard, griffons herald the beginning of the end of everything."

"Where did you hear that?" My tone was sharper than I'd meant; the tiny woman flinched as if I'd whipped her.

"Does it matter?"

"It does to me, or I wouldn't have asked," I murmured.

"Didn't you grow to magehood listening to tales? That was one of the oldest."

Before I could question her further, she twisted and walked through an invisible portal. One moment she was with us, the next she was gone. Cats and rats scattered in every direction.

If I ever returned to my guild house, I'd look up griffons in our library.

Alia started toward the far end of the Quonset hut, intent on locating Cleyn.

"Wait up," I called, but she didn't even slow down.

"We'll be in the kitchen," Joss told me.

He and Connor retraced their steps. I took off after Alia at a dead run, not catching up until I was outside the hut. At least the rain had quit, replaced by a chill wind.

"Bad idea," I panted. On the hunt for enemies, I painted the area with seeking magic.

"I have to look for him," she protested. "He's been missing for a long while."

Switching gears, I asked, "Where will you start?"

She turned to face me, her lovely features with distinctive cheekbones illuminated by moonlight. Spreading her hands wide, she said, "That's the problem. I have no idea where to begin. I've been searching for our link, and it's as if someone chopped through it."

Oh-oh. "You can't sense him at all?"

Alia shook her head. Strands of blonde hair fell across her face. Almost as tall as me, she has a waiflike appearance with a slender build. Hazel eyes changed color with the light.

"When's the last time you could feel him?"

She pressed her mouth into a tight line. "When I was fighting the goddess and the crystal coffin."

First I'd heard of them. "After we abandoned the car?" I sought clarification.

A curt nod. "It felt like he was trying to break through to me, but from a great distance."

"How about now?"

Alia raised her hands. Power swirled around her in shades of lavender and teal. I heard her mind voice, but no reply. Despite lacking her direct linkage with the beast, I reached for his distinct essence.

And ran into a wall. Still, I kept trying.

"It's no good." Alia's voice was a dull ache. "They have him."

"What did you see?"

"Nothing from this effort, but before, when I was trying to escape."

I wrapped my arms around her thin shoulders and held her against me. She was shivering. "From the goddess and the coffin?"

A mute nod.

"Did you know them?"

Another nod, followed by, "It's the same place they kept me all those years in stasis. The goddess might have been the same one with the lantern I ran into underground."

"So, the Sumerians have Cleyn?"

Her shivering intensified. She tilted her head. Gaunt features regarded me. "It's my first guess. We have to get him back. He lost everything on my account. This isn't fair."

A tear escaped the corner of one eye and ran down her cheek.

I cradled the back of her head in a hand and held her against me. Nothing about any of this even remotely resembled *fair*. Pointing it out would be cruel, though.

"Come back inside." My voice was as gentle as I could make it. "First thing tomorrow, we'll go after him."

"How? For all I know, they dumped him in the coffin."

"You're not thinking, Alia. After all the years you spent within its confines, you have a link with it too. Come on. Let's go inside before we have to fight our way back to Joss and Connor."

She let me herd her through the door at the far end of the hut. The muted glow of mage lights flowed through the door into the tiny kitchen. When we entered, Gretta was perched on a stool chattering away with Connor. The shift in her mood vanished when she laid eyes on us.

"Och, you again." She made a sigil against evil aimed dead center at Alia.

"Stop that." I stepped between them.

"We were explaining how Alia was just like us, a student at Rhys's sorcery retreat," Joss said.

"She was pretending," Gretta mumbled.

Matching her Gaelic, I said, "No, she was not. Try a truth spell if you don't believe me."

"Never mind that." Alia strode forward and positioned herself in front of Gretta's stool. "If you know something about me, spill it."

"Why would I do that?" The Brownie snorted.

"Because I know next to nothing," Alia retorted.

Softening her tone, she added, "Please. We went to Rhys's guild house on the Isle of Skye, but we weren't there long enough to learn much. Until the world slewed sideways, I had no idea I was dealing with anything beyond unwanted magic."

Gretta tilted her head to one side. "Unwanted? No magic is ever unwanted, child. Why would you say that?"

"Because I was raised by mortals."

"She knew nothing about her origins until the world turned upside down," I cut in.

"I see." Gretta raised a glass to her mouth and took a long drink.

Alia unzipped her jacket and hung it over a hook near the door before grabbing a cracker and a thin slice of cheese.

Curious about what the Brownie might know, and frustrated she wasn't more forthcoming, I debated ways to extract the information but couldn't come up with anything that wouldn't permanently alienate her.

Alia leaned against a wall and shut her eyes. Dark circles etched beneath them. Now that I knew more about what she'd faced today, her weariness was understandable. She'd come up against what had to be one of her worst fears: being trapped by the Sumerians to sit out eternity.

Gretta jumped off the stool and carted her glass to the sink. I expected her to walk out of the kitchen. Instead, she turned to face us and crossed her arms beneath her breasts.

"I suppose I can tell you what little I know. No harm will befall me for speaking the truth."

Alia's eyes flew open. She dashed to where the Brownie stood and gathered her into a hug. "Thank you."

Gretta wriggled. "Let go of me."

Alia did. "I'm sorry. My griffon is missing. Maybe something you say will help me find him."

"Don't see how, but here goes. In olden times, Sumerians ruled the other pantheons. They were stronger magically, and canny when magic alone wouldn't do the trick..."

CHAPTER THREE, ALIA

I'd allowed Rhys to guide me back inside, but what I really wanted was to expand my hunt for Cleyn. If I'd had even an inkling where to look, I'd have summoned power and been gone, night and evil creatures be damned.

Was he in some subterranean grotto like the one I'd been dragged into the first time I'd met the lantern goddess? If so, finding him could prove impossible. Could I jump backward in time to when Sumerians ruled the magical world?

Even if I could, they'd scarcely be glad to see me. A renegade from the crystal coffin they'd stuffed me into. In truth, I had no idea which part of me had dwelt in that space. I'd also had no memory of it until the thing showed up in the desert.

A shudder racked me. Why in the hell wouldn't they leave me in peace?

Because they created me for a specific purpose, and I

haven't been especially compliant, my inner wise woman piped up.

Surprise straightened my spine when we walked into the kitchen and saw Gretta sitting on a stool and chatting up a storm with Connor and Joss. Her good mood faded the second she saw me.

Not in a mood to play games, I asked her point-blank what she knew about me. When she blew me off, I resorted to begging. Pride's never been one of my vices. Hell, I've been so busy shielding my ability from the world, tripping over my own ego never came into play.

At first, I figured she'd sashay out of the kitchen. Instead, after a lengthy pause, she began talking. After a primer on Sumerians and their superior magic, she added, "One of their seers was quite the icon—"

"Do you mean Tevys?" Rhys cut in.

Gretta nodded. "The same. Did you know him?"

"No, but his prophecies were famous for their accuracy."

The Brownie came as close to smiling as she had since I first laid eyes on her. "That they were. I only knew about him because several of us were summoned to tidy up that section of Mesopotamia."

Rhys's fair brows shot up. "I had no idea you ever left the British Isles."

She placed her hands on her pudgy hips. "Probably many things you don't know about us, mage."

Frustration beat a track through me. Rhys and his curiosity weren't bringing me any closer to the truth about myself. Rather than telling him to shut up, I made a come-along motion with one hand in Gretta's direction and urged, "Please go on."

"Like I was saying"—she squared her shoulders—"my households included Tevys's and the two neighboring homes, except in those days they were more like stone huts with thatched roofs and dirt floors.

"Tevys was particular about when I was present. Normally, I clean at night, but those were his scrying hours, so I ended up there midday when he'd retired to his bed."

She rolled her dark eyes. "Couldn't disturb that one or I saw the rough side of his tongue. I'd have gone home, except I didn't have enough power to travel." Pausing, she leveled her gaze at me. "That's why I told you never to regret your skill. 'Tis rare there's too much. Usually, too little."

Patience, never my long suit, was wearing thin. "What did you find out about me?"

Gretta glanced away. A flush crept up her fair cheeks. "Don't usually do this," she mumbled in her thick Irish accent, "but he got off on my wrong side with his yelling and his rules and treating me like unpaid help."

Bristling, she laced her fingers in front of her, creating a steeple. "I had me a bit of a look around while he was asleep. Not that I had any idea at the time he meant you," she went on, "but pages and pages of vellum talked about a cataclysm.

"Not a natural one, mind you, but one visited on Earth by Sumerian wrath."

"Did he say why?" Rhys cut in.

"Not exactly, other than he foresaw widespread disaster visited on Earth by mankind. Like all mage-ilk, they'd set up shop on a couple of other worlds. Still, they considered Earth their first home. I couldn't make out some of what he'd written, but the gist was they'd approached the other pantheons and been turned away. No one was willing to sign on with their scheme."

"Which was?" I prodded.

"World dominion." Her lips parted in a snarl. "As if that sanctimonious bunch of whiners had a prayer of a chance. Give me a good Celtic god or goddess any day."

"Still not seeing where I fit in," I murmured.

"Och, and I left that part out. Sorry. Talking about my stint at indentured servitude always riles me. They planned to gather blood and magic from Innana and her sister Ereshkigal to form a new being. She'd be held in abeyance until they launched their plans."

"Did this Tevys say why?" I prodded.

"Not exactly. What I gathered was he assumed this would occur so far in the future they'd need someone to interpret modern ways."

"I don't get it," I muttered. "Interpret them to whom? No one is left."

"Things might have changed," Gretta said, "but naught I read indicated the plan was to annihilate mankind."

"So their spell did go off the rails," Connor said.

"Figured as much," Joss added.

Breath rattled from my constricted lungs. "How did you make the connection between whatever you read in Mesopotamia and me?"

She shot me an incredulous look. "Why, child. You're fairly bleeding Sumerian magic. Anyone with the ability of a hedge witch would have picked up on it. First I've run across their brand of enchantment since I was shuttled back to Ireland after the kings and queens of magic decided they could force mortals into service. Presumably, they wouldn't talk back or question orders."

A sidelong glance at Rhys confirmed his discomfort with her assessment since he certainly hadn't picked up on my heritage, but then I'd become proficient at shielding my enchantment, a trait I'd brought into the sorcery retreat.

Disappointment slumped my shoulders. She hadn't told me anything I didn't know. "Were there notations about a griffon in those pages?" I pressed.

Gretta frowned, drawing her forehead into a mass of horizontal lines. "Now that you mention it, aye. They planned to set a beast to watch over you, protect you until you came into the full extent of your power."

The Brownie jabbed me with a shot of something-or-other. "You're still growing, missy."

"Why'd you refer to me as *your kind?*"

She shrugged and glanced away. "I was upset at being disturbed. Been rough since I ended up here through no doings of my own. Being confronted with the fruit of Tevys's foreseeing was damned unsettling too."

"Is there any way we could help you?" Connor asked.

A corner of her thin mouth twisted downward. "Aye, you can leave."

"We will, come morning," Rhys reassured her.

"Bed down out there." She pointed at the door. "I need to clean this part of my home."

"Thank you for trusting me enough to talk with us," I said. "And apologies for barging in."

"Be gone by the time I'm up."

"We'll try our best," Rhys said and motioned for us to follow him into the long wing of the Quonset hut.

A hasty search turned up cardboard and a stash of clean coveralls, no doubt provided by a laundry service the tire store had used. We each set about laying down materials to shield us from the grease-stained concrete floor.

I lay next to Rhys, but sleep eluded me. After an hour of tossing and turning with my mind racing a mile a minute, I rolled to a sit.

"Wait until dawn to search for Cleyn," Rhys rumbled in his deep voice.

"I can't. Something terrible is happening to him. I feel it in my bones." By now, I was on my feet. Connor and Joss, who'd taken up positions a few feet away, didn't stir.

Rhys scrambled upright and tossed an arm around my shoulders. "Do you have a plan?"

Grateful for darkness to mask my overheated cheeks, I mumbled, "Best I can come up with is to use myself for bait. If they take me, I'll have a better chance of finding Cleyn."

The arm around me tightened. "If you do that, I'm coming with you."

I shook my head. "If you're with me, they might not snap me up as readily. Besides, you can't leave the others. I'll find my way back if I can."

Before he argued me out of my poorly made-up mind, or lassoed himself to me via magic I couldn't cut through, I visualized the highway and sent myself there. Cold cut through me the second I left the hut. Warm winter clothes would be a plus, but I wouldn't need them if my plan worked. I had a feeling the Saudi Arabian region that had housed Mesopotamia was always too hot.

To avoid Rhys coming after me anyway, I built wards on top of wards, located an abandoned Jeep with the keys dangling from the ignition, and jumped inside. The stench of rot gagged me. Opening the passenger door, I shoved a decomposing corpse into the street.

The engine started on the first try, and I chugged into the night.

"Alia. Don't do this," Rhys pleaded. Somehow, his mind voice penetrated my shielding.

"I have to. Wish me luck."

If I heard his voice again, I might cave, so I thickened my warding and floored the Jeep to put distance between us. The highway stretched ahead, devoid of people and cars. Would I ever get used to the wreckage of the world I'd once taken for granted? I rather doubted it. In the distance, the mournful howls of a coyote pack were reassuring. Not everything was dead.

I wished Gretta had known more, but perhaps there wasn't anything further to glean. I'd been an afterthought, something to grease the skids of a transition, except they didn't exactly need me the way things had turned out.

That's the trouble with plans. They have a way of blowing up in your face.

I'd reached the northern end of the small town of Bishop. Since I was unlikely to locate Cleyn from the Jeep, I pulled it to the side of the road and jumped out. A cursory search of the back seat yielded a down jacket. It was a bit small, but I put it on anyway and drew the hood over my head. It smelled of decay, but beggars can't be choosers.

Standing in the middle of the highway, I stretched my magical antennae to their fullest and searched for Cleyn. Unlike my earlier efforts, a faint scratching impacted the northern edge of my casting.

Was it the griffon? Was the lantern goddess falling for my trap? Or was it something totally unrelated like a vampire on the hunt for warm, pulsing blood? They're sensitive to expended power.

I pushed harder and called Cleyn's name.

The scratching intensified. Cold night air seared my nose and throat; my breath made plumes when I exhaled. My fingertips were growing numb, but I couldn't spare power to warm them. Who knew what I might need in the hours to come?

Two choices. I set a jump spell to bring me to the scratching. Or I kept on hunting. Door number two wasn't likely to yield any further information. If I sprang through door number one, would I ever make it back to Rhys?

"Stop. Just stop," I muttered. The sound of my voice steadied me. I'd run out of the Quonset hut like a house afire. Had I done it to chicken out now? A visual of the griffon with his golden-brown eagle's plumage and tawny lion's hindquarters filled my mind. He'd lost everything on my account. I refused to compound his losses by leaving him to whatever doom had claimed him.

Holding the direction of the scratching front and center, I built a careful casting, one with an open back door. Maybe it was a sick joke pitting my paltry ability against those who'd made me, but I'd play with the hand I'd been dealt.

The distinctive feel of Rhys's magic was closing fast.

If I was going to do this, it was now or never. Not that he couldn't track me, but I wasn't about to wait around for him, either.

Keeping a vision of Cleyn clearly fixed behind my third eye, I engaged my jump spell. The ruins of Highway 395 vanished, replaced by vibrating darkness. The scratching intensified. I did my damnedest to home in on its precise location.

"Turn back. It's a trap," was followed by a heart-wrenching howl.

Fuck. What were they doing to him?

Rage pounded through me, igniting fire, my strongest element. I'd burn down the world and everyone in it who'd harmed a feather on Cleyn's head.

Out of nowhere, my mini travel channel imploded, leaving me standing on a grassy plain that stretched in every direction. The air had an odd smell, dry and burnt. Fire danced between my hands as I searched for something, anything to pulverize.

Where in the fuck was I? A quick check validated my back door—presumably an exit to where I'd left the Jeep— was intact.

On my second scan, the sky developed a glittery aspect about ten feet above me and off to my right. Sure enough, a portal took shape. Open, inviting, it practically screamed at me to dive through.

Ha. Compulsion flooded from it. No wonder I was drawn.

"What you seek lies within." A deep voice grazed my mind.

Crap. Did they take me for a total fool?

I rolled my shoulders back and tossed my hood aside. For whatever reason, it wasn't cold here. It also couldn't possibly be Mesopotamia. Not with scrub oak and sagebrush.

"Prove it," I bellowed, proud my voice didn't so much as quiver.

I took a tentative step toward the gateway and stopped. If I got too close, maybe some sort of eldritch tractor beam would snag me. The thought made me smile grimly. Too many *Star Trek* episodes colored my reality.

"What you seek lies within." The same disconnected voice repeated the same words, almost as if they were embedded in a tape loop.

I reached for the griffon, activating my link with him. At first, nothing happened. The same sensation of our bond being severed persisted. Until it blew up in my face, and I felt Cleyn as cleanly as if he stood next to me.

A low growl filled my mind, followed by piteous moaning.

I'd saved him before. I could do it again.

An idea took shape. I clung to my restored linkage and tossed pieces of a bridge in place. Each portion was banded with fire to strengthen it. The growls intensified.

Suddenly, the portal changed, closing in on itself.

Time's up. Now or never. In a single fluid motion that

probably left me vulnerable as fuck, I shot my bridge through the rapidly closing hole, shouting, "Grab on."

And then I tugged with all my might. The bridge didn't budge.

I tried again.

And a third time.

By now, the hole was barely big enough for the griffon to crawl through. It might hurt him, but I had no choice. I chased fire with still more to free the track I'd stuffed through the hole.

Flames flickered and flared, but my channel was moving, goddammit. I held on to it and on to my link with Cleyn. Breath churned raggedly. Skin sloughed off my hands, burned by the heat.

In a flurry of feathers, magic, and rage-filled yowls, Cleyn burst through the hole just before it snapped shut, holding my working captive.

He looked like crap. Wounds crisscrossed feathers and fur. I'd deal with that later. I cut the flow of power to my bridge, draped enchantment around Cleyn, and activated the back door I'd built into my jump spell.

The beast sagged against me. I wrapped him in my arms and prayed my return casting would hold true. Somehow, against all odds, I'd done it. We were together. If I had my way, we'd never be separated again.

"Makes two of us," he purred deep into my mind.

The return trip was taking longer than I expected, but I'd blown through scads of magic with my rescue effort. To be on the safe side, I held an image of the empty highway, the Jeep, and Rhys.

I had little doubt he'd be waiting for us.

"You can do this, mistress," the griffon said.

Huh? Did I need a vote of confidence? Guess so. My eyes had been drifting shut. I clamped teeth over my lower lip. Pain jolted me to full awareness. No wonder my spell wasn't tracking straight. Neither was I.

Finally, when my magic was dwindling to wisps, the Jeep wavered and came into view. It was still pitch black, so I couldn't have been gone as long as it felt like.

"Thank fucking god. When I tried to follow you, I got slapped down." The sharp tones of Rhy's voice reassured me I was really back.

"We can talk later." I was so tired, my words slurred together. "Help me get him in the back of the car."

Rhys did me one better. He bundled Cleyn and me into the Jeep. I held the griffon in my arms. "You're not allowed to die on me."

"I don't plan on it." A cross between avian cawing and feline yowling filled my heart with joy. Maybe Gretta would recant and let us stay long enough for me to ensure the worst of Cleyn's wounds were tended to.

Weaving in and out of consciousness, the last thing I remembered was the sweet sound of the engine as Rhys drove us back to the Quonset hut.

I only stopped long enough to tell Connor and Joss where I was going before I raced out of the hut after Alia. She was long gone. I linked a tracer to her energy and initiated a jump spell. It spit me out next to a black Jeep with the engine still warm.

When I reached for signs of her beyond the Jeep, information fragmented. One message pointed north, another southwest. Testing each for relative strength didn't help.

Nothing for it but to follow first one and then the other.

Naïve of me to expect it could be that simple.

I pushed toward the southwest. A wave of my own power boomeranged back and slapped me hard enough to push me into the dirt. Getting smarter by the minute, I warded myself and tried again.

Same result, except I was ready for it and managed to remain upright. My next effort aimed northward. For the barest of moments I thought I might punch through. Throwing caution to the winds, I poured power into my working.

Rookie mistake. The problems from my initial effort intensified by a factor of ten, and I ended up not only in the dirt, but fifty yards away.

Oooph. I picked myself off and slogged toward the Jeep.

The Sumerians—assuming it had to be them—had my number or the signature feel of my magical ability. It's simple enough to turn power back onto the maker, but it's considered dirty pool.

Much cleaner to fight back directly using one's own ability rather than purloined goods from your assailant.

What to do next?

After a few deep breaths, I cleared my mind of everything but Alia, the feel of her, the sense of her presence. This time, four paths opened before me.

Crap. So much for clearing the decks of extraneous data.

Someone knew I was here—they'd known all along.

Presumably, they also expected Alia to attempt to rescue her bonded beast. They'd set a trap, and she'd walked right into it.

Goddammit. I drove a fist into the side of the Jeep. Pain had a salutary effect, but it underscored how helpless I was, how incapable of breaking the barrier to wherever the trail of breadcrumbs had led Alia.

Why in the hell hadn't she waited for me?

Because her magic is as strong as my own, an inner voice noted.

Yes, but she's untrained.

Great. I was answering myself.

Alia might lack training, but she had good instincts. I paced circles around the Jeep, determined to keep trying at intervals. Maybe I'd locate a chink in their armor, a moment when they assumed I'd given up. Magic isn't limitless; it wouldn't take much for them to relax their vigilance.

A quarter hour passed. I tried again. This time I picked the westerly track since four possibilities still presented themselves. My power still reared up and slapped me, but not as hard as before.

It gave me hope they were tiring.

The night was cold; it cut right through me. I ignored it. Least of my problems. I was born in an era long before the advent of central heat. Huts in the British Isles were usually cold and damp, or smoky from peat fires.

I waited through ten more minutes, determined to marshal my best shot soon.

Because I was tuned to it, I noticed an alteration in Alia's energy. It pulsed stronger, brighter. Was it wishful thinking on my part?

I reached for her. Suddenly the multiple paths dropped away. Only the one to the north remained viable. Ha. It had to be where she was. Gathering the remnants of my last jump spell, I was about to launch when she tumbled through a rough portal with her arms around the griffon.

I vaulted to the two of them, relief streaming through me.

"Thank fucking god. When I tried to follow you, I got slapped down." My tone was far brusquer than I'd meant, but she didn't seem to notice.

"We can talk later. Help me get him in the back of the car." Alia was so trashed she could barely walk; her words bounced against one another.

With an arm around both of them, I guided the duo to the Jeep and tugged a back door open. First, I lifted her inside, and then tucked the griffon next to her. Long cuts scored his chest and flanks, but he was breathing.

Questions bounced from one side of my brain to the other, but they could wait. The soft sound of Alia murmuring to Cleyn was reassuring. I flipped a U-turn and drove us through Bishop's silent streets until we reached the Quonset hut. We had a few hours yet until dawn. Hopefully, enough time to prepare Cleyn for travel.

He'd have to stick with us from now on, no matter how he felt about vehicles.

I'd no sooner brought the Jeep to a stop than Connor and Joss burst through the door and ran to us.

"You found her!" Connor exclaimed.

"Where was she?" Joss called out.

I pushed the driver's door open and walked to the other side where Connor and Joss were helping Alia and Cleyn out. "I don't know any more than you do," I told them and wrapped an arm around Alia's shoulders. Connor and Joss supported the griffon. We retreated inside.

Getting out of the wind was a small gift. Alia had found a down jacket somewhere. At least it would have kept her warm.

"Where to?" Connor asked.

"How about the kitchen?" I suggested. "We'll have running water to clean Cleyn's wounds."

I expected the griffon to countermand my suggestion. He didn't. Connor and Joss had just hefted him onto the table when Gretta bustled into the room. She stopped dead, eyes widening.

"Och and I thought sure you were nattering on about him." She pointed at Cleyn, who clacked his beak weakly.

Alia flipped the taps, bent, and sluiced cold water over her dirty face. When she straightened, she flicked droplets into the sink and walked to Cleyn. "Nope. He's quite real," she told Gretta and ran her hands over the beast.

"He's beautiful," the Brownie murmured as she joined Alia. "Let me help you."

I'd never known Brownies had healing ability, but then I knew very little about them.

Cleyn remained still under their ministrations.

I didn't realize Connor had left until he strode back into the room buck naked and dropped two rabbits in front of the griffon. "More where they came from," he said and turned to leave. Presumably, he'd been hunting in hawk form.

"It's enough for now," Cleyn squawked and snatched one of the rabbits. It vanished down his gullet mostly whole.

"Are you certain?" Connor asked. "Hunting is good in the before-dawn hours."

"Maybe one more," Cleyn said around what passed for marginal chewing of rabbit number two.

I heated water on the propane stove for tea while the women worked on Cleyn. Joss divided leaves among several mugs, handing one to Connor when he returned with three more rabbits. This time, he was dressed, so he must have stopped wherever he'd left his garments.

"I think we're done," Alia murmured.

"Almost," Gretta said. "Just this one wee last bit here."

I handed steaming mugs all around. Cleyn jumped down from the table and hunched over the fruits of Connor's efforts.

Alia flopped into a chair and drained half her mug.

Gretta clucked as she glanced around her sullied workspace.

Curiosity and worry ate at me. "What happened after you left here?" I asked, not willing—or able—to wait longer for information.

"Cleyn holds the front end of this tale," Alia replied. "Even I'm not sure how he was captured."

The griffon straightened from where he'd been scarfing down rabbits. "You mean captured again," he snarled.

"How did it happen?" Alia pressed.

The beast spread its wings until they ran against the sides of the kitchen and roared. Gretta brushed fingertips over the feathers nearest her. "Poor, wee beastie. 'Twill be all right."

Another roar before Cleyn reared on his hindquarters and folded his wings across his back. "I was tracking your car from the air, until I wasn't. There was no warning. One minute, I was flying, the next I'd been sucked into a travel spell not of my making. I fought with everything in me, but they were too strong. I ended up in a cave lined with crystals that sapped my power and occluded efforts to reach out.

"It was clear from the onset they weren't interested in me. No, I was but a means toward an end. I called to Alia, tried to warn her."

"Some of it came through," she reassured him.

"I attempted to escape," Cleyn went on, "but it was impossible. They used my own power to shackle me. I reached for my kinsmen in hopes some remained, but it wasn't until Alia arrived and added her magic to the equation I was able to break free."

"How exactly did that work?" Alia asked.

"You and I are the same, but not," Cleyn replied. "Some of the magic that made you is repeated in me, but much isn't. When you mingled your enchantment with mine, it gave me what I needed to push through the bonds of my prison. That's all of my story."

"Guess it's my turn." Alia drained her mug, plucked tea leaves off the tip of her tongue, and sighed. "After I'd nearly cleared town, I got out of the vehicle I'd stolen and hunted for Cleyn. My only clue was a faint scratching at the edges of my seeking spell. I focused power that way and went for it."

"You'd have had an easier time since it was you they wanted," I muttered.

She snorted. "Ya think? At one point before my spell cleared, I thought I heard you"—she patted Cleyn—"warning me, but it was too late to go back, not that I would have.

"I emerged on a high desert plain with scrub oaks and sagebrush. The air smelled odd, dry and burnt. Fire played between my hands, fire I'd raised to mow down anyone who tried to stop me."

Another heart-wrenching sigh. "I had the presence of mind to hold a trap door open at the back of my spell. Figured if I found Cleyn, we'd need to force a hasty retreat.

Once I was there, I activated our link, determined more or less where he was, and sent a metaphorical ladder through a hole that had conveniently opened in the ether."

"It gave me what I needed to fight harder," Cleyn cut in. "The hole they'd opened to lure Alia started closing the second she tossed me a lifeline."

"Scared the crap out of me," Alia murmured. "I poured power toward Cleyn and urged him to scuttle through while he could. The second he squeezed through, I jettisoned the bridge and beat a path for home."

"Smart of you to keep a back door active," I said.

Her mouth twisted into a wry grin. "Flying by the seat of my magical pants, don't you mean?"

"Does it matter?" I countered. "What you did worked." Admiration for her sheer guts swelled through me.

"This time," she said. "Eventually, they'll be wise to my tricks."

"Then you'll come up with better ones," Joss said, followed by, "Does anyone want more tea?"

"Maybe hold it until later," Connor replied. "We haven't had much of a night's rest."

I glanced at Gretta, who'd edged toward the door. "We promised to be gone with daybreak. Is it all right with you if we remain a few more hours? Just until we get some rest and Cleyn is ready to travel."

The Brownie nodded. "How could I refuse. The lass is one brave woman."

Color flooded Alia's cheeks. "It's not brave when you're doing what you must to survive."

"Aye, but it is," Gretta retorted. "Courage is grace under pressure."

"I'll just close my eyes for a moment," Cleyn squawked and tucked his head beneath a wing. Nothing remained of the pile of rabbits, and his wounds were visibly smaller. He was well on the way to a full recovery.

I stood and extended a hand to Alia. She took it and we walked into the long wing of the Quonset hut to where we'd arranged cardboard and coveralls into bedding for us. Though only a handful of hours had passed since then, each felt like a day or better.

She knelt before lying on her side. I positioned myself behind her, body curved around hers. "You gave me quite a scare."

Turning in my arms, she faced me and wrapped an arm around my back. "You understand why I couldn't risk bringing you, right?"

I nodded. "I do now. Every time I tried to follow you, something sabotaged me."

"Yeah, and if you'd been with me, we'd never have broken through."

"Understanding doesn't mean I have to like it." I tightened my hold on her.

She tucked her head into the hollow between my neck and shoulder. "Will they ever leave us be?"

I flirted with a polite lie, but she wouldn't have believed me. "That's rhetorical, right?"

"Wishful thinking," she murmured. "I didn't mean to scare you, but I was terrified. If I hadn't just pushed through, if I'd stopped to think about it, I would have been immobilized."

"But you weren't." I stroked hair back from her face.

"I'm responsible for him." She lowered her voice.

"He feels the same way about you. It's what bonding is all about."

"I wish there was a place he could go, maybe return to his clan, except they're all dead."

"Hush." I cradled the back of her head in a hand. "He wouldn't leave even if you ordered him away. Rest now. You're where you're supposed to be. So is he."

"But they hurt him."

"Or maybe he hurt himself trying to escape."

"Does it matter? What about next time?"

"There won't be a next time, since he's going to remain with us." It was a nice premise, but so far I'd done a piss-poor job keeping any of us together. My thoughts scattered as I wondered how Nola, Karen, and Moriah were getting by.

"Not your fault they left," Alia murmured.

I chuckled. "Told you thought plucking is a two-way street."

She scooted closer. I tugged extra coveralls over us for warmth. "Where do we go from here?"

"Not sure. How about if you hold that thought until everyone's awake."

Suddenly, she pushed against me, trying to sit.

"What is it?" Alarm beat a track through me.

"Cleyn. He needs to be here. With us. The kitchen is too far."

"It's all right. I warded the hut. Gretta probably did as

well. It was why you couldn't sense her when we first came upon this spot."

Alia stopped struggling and lay against me. "Not sure I can do this. Any of it." She trembled in my arms.

"You're tired." I kneaded tense muscles in her back and shoulders.

"Doesn't matter. I'd feel the same way if I were fresh." After a pause, she added, "Oh god, that feels heavenly."

I added a smidgeon of healing to my massage. "You'll get by the way you have been. One moment at a time, one hour at a time, one day at a time."

Maybe what I said made a difference. Her body relaxed against mine. Soon the even cadence of her breathing told me she'd fallen into a well-deserved sleep. We needed another spot to hole up and lick our wounds. A place the Sumerians couldn't breach.

As I kept watch over Alia and everyone sheltering in the hut, an idea took shape. I'd float it past the group once we were awake. The more I turned it over in my head, the better I liked it. Somewhere along the way, I set my wards on autopilot and closed my eyes.

Without rest, my magic wouldn't fully recover. The way things were going, I'd need every shred of ability to pull off our next moves.

CHAPTER FIVE, ALIA

Tired of feeling helpless and hopeless, I aimed for deep relaxation. Looping the threads of my astral self around Cleyn was reassuring. At least I'd know the second he stirred so much as an angstrom from his position in the corner of the kitchen.

I'd been honest with Rhys about my fears, but tomorrow I'd paste on my brave face and keep on keeping on. What choice did any of us have? The temptation to retreat to the past, to a time before any of this had occurred, was overwhelming, but it wasn't an answer, not really.

All it would do was stave off the inevitable.

And what precisely is that? Even my inner wise woman sounded trashed.

I took it as a sign to pack it in, but quieting my mind wasn't simple. I kept telling myself I had no idea what the future held—for any of us. We had as good a chance at prevailing as my erstwhile makers. Probably a better one, since we knew the modern version of Earth better than they did.

We'd dropped into the past once with the intention of confronting them and forging a different outcome. It hadn't gone well, but we'd made a commitment to return and try again. This time, we'd talked about hitting up various mage groups with information about what their future held and soliciting assistance. Surely, a critical mass of magic would be sufficient to derail a few Sumerians who hadn't poked their heads out of the sand in thousands of years.

Next to me, Rhys's solid presence was warm, reassuring. I narrowed my focus to the few square feet where we lay and matched the cadence of my breathing to his.

It worked because when I opened my eyes light flooded the interior of the hut through dirt-streaked windows. Meant I'd caught a few hours' rest.

"About time, sleepyhead," Rhys murmured.

I tangled my fingers in his hair. "You could have woken me."

"Nah. Nothing is critical enough to justify that. Besides, Connor and Joss are just now getting up."

I reached for Cleyn, reassured he hadn't budged from the position he'd taken up last night.

Rhys pressed his lips to my forehead before rolling away and getting to his feet. I still felt fuzzy headed, but not nearly as wiped-out as I had the night before. After a trip into a small bathroom where I splashed icy water on my face and hands, I joined everyone in the kitchen and stroked the griffon's silky plumage.

He clacked his beak and leaned in to me.

"Thank you again for letting us stay another few hours," Rhys told Gretta.

"Least I could do," she murmured.

Joss heated water for tea. "What will you do when the gas runs out?" he asked Gretta.

The Brownie shrugged. "Tank was almost full. Cooking doesn't use much. I turned the water heater off. Don't worry about it." She made a wry face. "There's always the old-fashioned way with rocks and fire. Someone dug a pit out back. The store half a block away has bundles of kindling and bags of charcoal."

I smothered a smile. Gretta may not have been here long, but she'd scoped out local resources.

"Do you want to return home?" Rhys asked.

The tiny woman's eyes grew rounder. "Of course, but I'm getting by."

I glanced at him. Something was percolating in his mind.

He took a mug of tea from Joss and blew on it before sipping slowly. The familiar feel of his power settled around us as he sealed the kitchen from prying ears.

"Now, you wait a minute." Gretta pressed against the sound shield. "Never agreed to be—"

"I will not harm you," Rhys spoke over her. "I do need to ensure no one overhears what I'm going to propose. We had problems with Watchers in the last location where we remained for a while. It complicated our strategies, since they were reporting to their masters."

"We think they were," I tossed out. "Never knew for certain."

"Watchers? As in Anunnaki?" Gretta folded her arms

beneath her breasts. At Rhys's nod, she muttered, "Impossible. They never left Mesopotamia."

"You're not supposed to be here, either," Rhys reminded her. He set his cup down. "My proposal won't take long. I'd like to transport us to Mount Shasta. There's an extensive cave system beneath the mountain. It used to house a substantial city."

"I thought that was a myth," Connor said.

"Are you saying Lemurians are real?" Joss added water to his pot and turned the flame up.

I racked my brain. Lemurians. The name rang a distant bell, but I wasn't connecting the dots.

"Quite real," Rhys said. "When I was through there last, the entire place was deserted. Felt as if it had been abandoned, so we should be safe enough for a while. There could well be an entry point to special journey channels there, which was why I asked Gretta if she wanted to go home."

"Not seeing the connection," the Brownie said. "You could teleport and bring me with you."

"Something evil has taken up residence in the usual teleport channels," Rhys said.

It reminded me of something. "I teleported to find Cleyn," I said. "Nothing amiss stood in my way, so perhaps whatever it was has moved on."

"Or maybe whoever used Cleyn as bait did something to ensure you'd pass through unharmed," Connor murmured.

I shook my head. "Nope because I was able to retrace my steps uneventfully. If there'd been a way to intercept us, force my hand, we'd never have returned."

"Not necessarily," Connor said. "What if whoever polluted the usual channels is on the outs with the Sumerians?"

Gretta cleared her throat and addressed her words to Rhys. "What you're suggesting is I accompany you to this Mount Shasta. If—and you're not certain—an entrance to journey portals exists, we'd teleport back to Ireland."

"Something like that." Rhys nodded.

Gretta drew her brows together. "'Tis tempting, but I will remain here. The wee beasties depend on me." She stabbed a finger at a window. "Not safe out there for them."

I resisted stating the obvious. The only reason her entourage was alive and kicking was because they'd been within this structure when the worst of the destruction hit. For whatever reason, the hut hosted positive energy.

"I respect your decision." Rhys bowed his head in her direction.

"And 'tis grateful I am you considered diverting magic to rescue me."

"What do the rest of you think?" Rhys's gaze settled on each of us in turn.

"How will Mount Shasta be better than the Sedona caves?" Joss asked.

"Not certain it will be," Rhys replied. "I'm hoping residual magic from the Lemurians will have kept their city clear of taint. We'll drive as close as we can get. Shouldn't take more than a day or so."

"I'm game," I said grateful for something new and different. If Rhys was correct, and Mount Shasta held access to transport channels, perhaps we could work on our plan to activate a network of mages, so it wasn't just the four of us against the Sumerian gods and goddesses.

"I've met Lemurians a time or two," Cleyn squawked. "They sent envoys to my people long ago."

"They seem to have moved on," Rhys reminded him.

"Why would they abandon their home?" Gretta asked. "No one does that willingly."

"No idea. Perhaps we'll unearth a clue or two," Rhys replied.

The two cats from yesterday strolled into the kitchen. One jumped onto the ledge; the other took up a position next to Gretta.

I rose from where I'd been crouched next to Cleyn. "Past time for us to get moving."

"I could make breakfast," Gretta offered.

"Thanks, but we've made enough inroads into your supplies," Rhys told her.

Joss doused the flame beneath his pot and proceeded to collect cups that he placed in the sink.

"I'll take care of them," Gretta said. "Not much else to do. I'd welcome the work."

After a flurry of goodbyes, we walked out into a sunny day. It was cold, but the wind wasn't blowing. I still had the down jacket I'd borrowed from the back seat of the Jeep, and I was grateful for its warmth.

Rhys had started toward the Jeep, but changed direction. It would have been a tight fit with the four of us and Cleyn. After checking several abandoned cars and trucks, he trotted to where we stood.

"How about this?" he suggested. "We'll take two

vehicles. Alia, Cleyn, and me will be in the Jeep. Keys are in the white Toyota and the blue Subaru."

"I hate to split up," I said.

"I could fly but stick really close," Cleyn offered.

"Nope. Not after what happened yesterday," I told him.

Connor loped to the Subaru with Joss behind him. "This will work," Connor said. "We'll caravan and travel right next to each other."

"Fuel up before we leave town," Rhys called.

I opened one of the back doors. Cleyn crawled in, tucking his various appendages against his body. He didn't look very comfortable. Maybe we could swap the Jeep for something larger like the Toyota we'd abandoned.

Rhys got in and waited for me to climb into the passenger seat. "What is it?" he asked.

"Could we find something where Cleyn fits better?"

"I'm good," the griffon growled.

"Sure. We can be on the lookout for something with keys. Maybe a pickup. He could ride in back."

"No. I want a roof over him."

Connor and Joss pulled away from the curb. We followed them to a gas station and convenience store. While Rhys magicked up a gas pump so it would spit out fuel in the absence of electricity, I rustled through the remains of the store.

Joss joined me and started pulling boxes of crackers and bags of cookies off shelves. "Lucky this side of the building wasn't crushed."

"Lucky, indeed." Food had been scarce lately, so I filled my arms with junk and carted it back to the Jeep. "Hold up,"

I told Rhys as I returned for one more trip. This time, I grabbed soda, mineral water, and deli cheese and salami packets. They had so many preservatives, they'd probably not have rotted.

Once we were underway, I tore open wrappers and handed food across the console to Rhys. Reaching back, I offered salami to Cleyn, but he refused, squawking, "How can you eat that? It's not even food."

Rhys chuckled. "Out of the mouths of beasts."

"I'm kind of sorry Gretta didn't join us," I said around a mouthful of crackers and cheese.

"Brownies are a lot like cats," Rhys said.

"What do you mean?" I cracked the top of a can of soda and placed it in the cupholder closest to him.

"They develop attachments to places. She might not have been there long, but she's already made it her home."

I switched topics. "What made you think about Mount Shasta?"

"Not sure. It came to me before I fell asleep last night."

"You've been there before?"

A nod. "Several times. It's one of those power points scattered around the world that I mentioned to you."

"Remind me who the Lemurians are?"

He levied a grin my way. "Not part of your college curriculum, eh?"

"Nope. I'd have had to sign up for mythology. Not part of my major."

"What was?" he asked as he munched through a bag of Cheetos.

"Environmental engineering."

"Planning to save the world, were you?"

"Nothing quite so grand. I was hoping to slow its demise. I'd asked about the Lemurians," I reminded him.

Something poked into my back as Cleyn stretched a leg into the seat.

"Okay," Rhys said. "Here goes. Lemurians originally lived on Mu, the fabled sunken continent of Lemuria in the Indian Ocean. It included a land bridge to India and was one of the ways ancient mortals traversed from continent to continent. Millions of years ago, Mu sank into the ocean.

"At that point, it's unclear how its inhabitants migrated, but the next place they showed up was Mount Shasta. Of course, that was centuries before mortals populated the western coast of the United States. Lemurians are quite tall and hermaphroditic, but produce very few offspring since they're so long-lived."

"They're gentle," Cleyn squawked. "Never got along well with my masters for that reason."

I digested what had been said. "What do you suppose happened to them?" I asked Rhys.

"Not sure. They could have simply been gone when I last stopped by maybe fifty years back, but it didn't feel that way."

I hoped something wicked hadn't chased them out but kept my thoughts to myself.

Connor and Joss had been following us. The Subaru pulled in front and stopped by the side of the road.

"Wonder what's up," I murmured.

Rhys stopped behind them. I opened my door. Before I jumped out, Cleyn said, "My door too."

Of course, he'd want to unkink his legs and wings.

Connor trotted over to us. "My hawk is uncomfortable. He senses something."

Oh-oh.

I kicked myself for letting my guard down while Rhys and I ate and chatted. Before I could deploy an arc of seeking magic, Rhys said, "I'll do it."

White light surrounded us as he deployed power.

Cleyn clumped close. "I feel it too."

"Could you two be more specific?" My voice shrilled with worry. The highway stretched through rolling hills dotted with evergreens and bushes. I'd been paying attention to signs. The last one mentioned the turn-off to Sonora Pass was soon. Perhaps we'd rolled right by it.

"Not really." Connor raked fingers through his matted dark hair. "But this vague pins-and-needles sensation just kept getting more annoying. I told Joss, and he suggested we stop and sort things out."

Joss.

"Where is he?" I asked.

"Still in the car. Or not." Connor's sharp blue gaze zeroed in on the Subaru. It was empty.

Fuck. I hustled to the other car, magical antennae on full alert, and tugged the back door open. Breath swooshed from me.

"What?" Joss glanced up from rooting through an assortment of junk food.

"I, er, we... It didn't look as if you were here."

He tapped a window. "They're darkened. You can't see in. Geez, Alia. Lighten up."

By now, Connor had joined us. "Where were you?"

"Here. In the back seat." Pushing past where we hovered near the door, Joss got out.

"Back in the cars. Now," Rhys shouted. He jumped into the Jeep and gunned it until it practically mowed us down. "Hurry," he urged.

Not a time for questions.

Connor and Joss lunged for the Subaru. I pushed and prodded Cleyn back into his prison-like enclosure.

"Stay with him," Rhys instructed. The Jeep lurched down the road. I made a grab for the back door to secure it.

"What the hell?" I asked.

"Hang on," he said. "We may have run out of time."

The Jeep passed sixty then seventy then eighty. It wasn't designed for speed, and we swayed from side to side. Muted booms reached my ears. At first, I thought it was the Jeep ratcheting this way and that over rocks, but then I recognized it was coming from outside.

A glance behind us showed the Subaru right on our bumper. It was far more maneuverable than we were.

"I want out," Cleyn announced. "I'd rather die with my wings spread than when this hunk of metal crashes."

I sort of felt the same way, absent the wings part, but I remained silent. Asphalt flew past. Soon we passed a huge lake on our right.

"Almost," Rhys muttered. "Almost."

We cleared the north end of the lake, and he pulled off the road. Behind us, what had been muted explosions grew far louder. He peeled whitened knuckles off the steering wheel. Breath rattled from him.

Outside the Jeep, Connor pounded on my window. I rolled it down and then opened the door. "What in the fuck?" he demanded.

"Seismic disturbance," Rhys wheezed. "If we return, it won't be by road. A half mile section fell in."

"I'm guessing this wasn't a natural phenomenon—" I began.

"Let me out. Now." Cleyn's voice was strident.

I moved to one side. The griffon shot forward as if he'd been propelled by a cannon. Wings spread, he took to the air and scribed circles around where we'd parked, cawing balefully.

Joss walked close. "A spot of warning if you plan to do that again, please."

Rhys opened his door and got out. "Sorry, everyone. We outran the problem. This time."

I was the only one left inside, so I swung my legs over the side of the back seat and exited.

"What problem?" Joss was asking.

Rhys shook himself from head to toe before answering. "When I searched for what might have alerted Connor's hawk, I found an oddness beneath us, cracks that were spreading out and up."

"Any idea who's behind them?" Joss asked.

"No. It might be aftershocks from the initial destruction."

"But that was weeks ago," I protested.

"Sure, but the destabilization could have persisted."

"So this might not have been targeting us, specifically?" Connor arched dark brows.

"Seems remote," I muttered. "We're the only things out here."

"If everyone's good, we need to move." Rhys skirted my observation by ignoring it. "Find a spot to hole up for the night."

The griffon yowled a protest.

"We'll hit a city in maybe half an hour, according to my map," I said not knowing if it was a plus or a minus.

Cleyn skidded to the ground and folded his wings. "I do not want to get back inside that thing."

"We'll trade it for something bigger as soon as we can." I aimed for reassuring. It bought me a sour look.

The noise of distant explosions had ceased.

"Feel like driving?" Rhys asked and ushered a snarling Cleyn into the back seat.

It was my first clue how rattled he was. I got into the driver's seat and started the engine. Maybe another hour until full dark. Meant we needed to be somewhere vampire and werewolf proof.

Just because we hadn't seen any since leaving Sedona didn't mean they weren't a threat.

"You okay?" I asked Rhys.

"Sort of. Something latched onto my magic back there. It let go, but it was odd. Like having an unwanted passenger."

"So much for your theory we weren't in someone's gunsights."

"We might not have been. Power calls to its own. Some entity might have sensed my seeking spell and glommed onto it. The two don't have to be related."

Typical Rhys explanation, but I wasn't mollified.

The outskirts of one more deserted town came into view. Thinking we might be better off here than in the town proper, I slowed and began hunting for a likely place to sit out the hours of darkness.

"Over there." Rhys pointed at a motel that had somehow escaped annihilation. A falling-down sign mentioned a café. Meant a kitchen with food. Cheese and crackers only go so far.

I turned off the highway and drove to the far end of the motel's parking lot, waiting for the Subaru. Once we were all in the same place, I killed the engine, got out, and opened the door for Cleyn.

"Feel like hunting?" Connor asked as he stripped out of his clothes.

"Thought you'd never ask," the griffon cawed.

I picked up Connor's discarded garments and cast a worried look skyward. They were together, which was somewhat reassuring.

"Don't be gone long," Rhys called after them and walked to the closest room. A small bit of magic forced the lock. We walked inside.

"Oh look, the rooms are adjoining," Joss said and picked the deadbolt leading into the neighboring suite.

"Here." I handed him Connor's clothes. "Take these."

The bed looked inviting as hell, but I started back outside.

"Where are you going?" Rhys asked.

"Kitchen. Come with me. Maybe we'll find something dinner-worthy."

The clomp of his boots sounded behind me as we set out

to make the best of yet one more home for the night. So long as I kept myself front, center, and present, it was tolerable.

"No point borrowing trouble," he said, having clearly helped himself to my grim thoughts.

For some reason, it struck me as funny, and I started to laugh. In between gales of graveyard humor, I choked out, "No need for borrowing; it finds us just fine."

CHAPTER SIX, RHYS

Orpses littered the walkway as we neared what had been the café. They'd been dead long enough, the stench was manageable. Alia was laughing, not because I'd said something funny but to cut the tension that had taken up residence as I'd fled from whatever wreaked havoc beneath us.

The door leading to the lobby was propped open.

Alia stopped abruptly and sent visible bands of power forward. She could have saved herself the effort.

"No one in there," I said as I caught up.

"How can you know?"

"Already checked."

"You could have said something," she mumbled and skirted a body as she walked inside.

I hooked a hand around her upper arm. "When will you start trusting me to protect you?"

She stopped long enough to lean into me. "It's a nice thought, but when I'm vigilant, I feel more in control."

"Fair enough."

We found a kitchen behind the small café. Whoever had been responsible for purchasing hadn't been invested in healthy food. Cupboards full of canned goods were untouched, as were packages of pasta and rice.

Joss joined us and whistled, long and low. "Great. I can make dinner. Not supposing Connor or Cleyn will want anything." Pushing around us, he plucked cans of tomato sauce, sliced mushrooms, and green beans from the pantry.

I'd assumed we'd ferry foodstuffs back to the room, but this made more sense.

"Can I help?" Alia asked.

"Nah. Small space. How about if you and Rhys grab seats out there. This won't take long."

I backtracked into the café and hauled two bodies outside. Because I had time, I sent exploratory threads into the best preserved corpse to determine what had killed the man.

Alia knelt next to me. "What are you checking?"

"We never did determine what killed everyone."

She rocked back on her heels. "Do you know now?"

"Two of the vessels in his heart blew out."

Alia swiveled and laid a hand on the other corpse, this one female. She shuddered. "Something about touching them is disconcerting, like I'm trespassing or something."

After a pause, she added. "Blown valves here, too. What could have caused it?"

"Pressure changes."

"Someone was manipulating the atmosphere? Seems remote."

I got to my feet and extended a hand to Alia. "From what little we know, this was targeted destruction, specifically aimed at getting mortals out of the way. Animals were likely collateral damage. Mostly, I was curious how they'd accomplished it."

"Surely not one person at a time," she protested.

"Of course not. The Sumerians came up with something that would make a clean sweep of things."

Back inside the café, we sat at a table close to the kitchen. I kindled a mage light and sent it to hover off to one side. The aroma of dinner was enticing.

"Sure you don't want help?" Alia called.

"Just dishing up," Joss replied.

"Stay put," I told Alia and headed for the kitchen to ferry food to our table. Joss had made a spaghetti-esque dish with noodles, sauce, and vegetables. Clumps of parmesan cheese sat on top.

Joss followed me with three tumblers full of water. "There's pop, too, or I could make coffee or tea."

"This is perfect," Alia said. "I'm surprised there's still water."

"The cold tap works," Joss explained as he slid into a chair. "What's in those glasses came from bottles, though. I overheard you talking," he went on. "I don't care how efficient the Sumerians were, there have to be a few mortals they failed to steamroll over. Maybe younger people with robust constitutions."

"Logical," I said, "but we have yet to find anyone."

"If I were them, I'd be deep in hiding," Joss said between bites.

"Speaking of finding people," Alia cut in. "Connor and Cleyn have been gone for a long time. Been full dark for the last half hour."

I pushed my empty plate to the side. "I'll hunt for them."

"We all will," Joss said. "Give me a second to toss these dishes in the sink. Already cleaned the pot."

We retraced our steps through the office. This time, I shut the door behind us. The night was cold. We could take bedding from one of the other rooms to augment what was on the beds.

Alia stopped, head tilted to one side. Even absent eavesdropping, my bet was she was talking with Cleyn.

"Everything okay?" Joss asked.

She placed a finger over her mouth and flashed five fingers. As we waited, I scanned the immediate area. Connor and Cleyn were definitely heading our way. I exhaled sharply. I didn't want to make prisoners of them, but I'd been concerned ever since they took to the skies.

"They'll be back soon," Alia said. "Maybe a quarter hour."

"Where were they?" I asked.

"First hunting, but then they found...something."

If I'd had hackles, they'd have activated. "As in what?" I growled.

"A band of mortals. According to Cleyn, they've gone to ground in an abandoned silver mine to the east of Carson City."

"Makes sense," Joss mused and motioned us toward the

rooms we'd staked out. "We were just talking about how some people had to be left."

"Did they make contact?" I asked Alia.

"I don't think so." She pushed on the door. It opened, and we stepped inside.

Joss perched on one of the beds. I searched the skies and left the door propped open.

"Brrrr," Alia murmured.

"Sorry. I'll be in once they're back." After kicking the door closed, I waited outside the room. While I was at it, I locked both cars. Silly of me. Anyone with magic could make short work of any lock. The world was full of abandoned vehicles.

The whirr of wings snapped my attention upward in time to see both griffon and hawk circle to land. Cleyn dropped several rabbits that had been dangling from the talons on his back legs before touching down.

Connor shifted midair and somersaulted to the ground where he scooped up the rabbits.

"We're in here," I said and pointed at room 124.

"I feel so much better," Cleyn squawked as he lumbered after Connor.

I sealed the door behind us and added a sound shield.

Alia had wrapped a bedspread around herself. Joss did the same. It reminded me of my idea about filching more bedding from other rooms.

"Be right back," I said. "Don't start without me."

A few minutes later, I returned arms laden with extra blankets. Connor had dressed. The rabbits were stacked in a neat pile on the table next to the defunct television.

"What'd you find?" I asked.

"Probably a group of humans," Connor replied. "We had power deployed to make hunting as efficient as possible when Cleyn alerted me to a spot in the hills maybe five miles east of Carson City."

"Why do you believe it was mortals?" Joss was on his feet, bedspread flapping as he paced.

"We saw smoke," Connor said.

"Until we got closer, and then it stopped," Cleyn added.

"Probably posted sentries," I mused.

"We thought the same," the griffon said.

"It could be a mage encampment," Alia suggested. "Using magic to stay warm burns through a lot. Any idea how many were living there?"

The griffon shook his head.

Alia glanced my way. "Should we approach them?"

I considered the pros and cons. We'd talked about retreating to the past, before the cataclysm, and warning groups of mages about what was bearing down on them. The assumption being if we developed a critical mass perhaps we could stave off the disaster.

"Rhys?" she prodded.

"Other than assuaging my curiosity, I don't see much point."

"Shouldn't we at least determine who's there?" Joss asked.

"If it is mortals," I told him, "they'll be running scared."

"Petrified is more like it," Connor mumbled.

"That too," I agreed. "Presumably, they're figuring out

how to survive. If it's some iteration of mage, we're probably not going to join forces with them."

"We'll pass within a few miles of them on our way north," Alia cut in. "I say we stop long enough to figure out who they are."

"We can firm up that decision come morning. I'm going to turn in," Connor said.

"We're in the next room," Joss told him and led the way.

Cleyn waddled to the table with the rabbits. "I'll take these and be outside."

Alia joined him. "How about if we open another room for you?"

"I prefer outside."

"You're safer within," she insisted.

He spread his wings. They ran into walls on both sides. "I will be outside this room. Consider me your sentry."

Grumbling under her breath, Alia scooped up the rabbits and followed him out. "Do not leave this area," she adjured before shutting the door.

"You can't turn him into a prisoner," I observed.

A long, rattling sigh escaped. "I know, but he's vulnerable. They've grabbed him more than once."

"Do you think he's unaware of that?"

"Of course not." She cast a sidelong glance my way. "Your point?"

"He may be bonded to you, but he's still master of his own ship. We have a long haul ahead of us."

Clutching the bedspread tighter around her, she sat on the edge of the nearest bed. "Haven't quite got my mind around the forever part of this yet."

I sat next to her. "Feel like cleaning up a bit? Joss said the water's still running."

"I sound like a wuss, but it's cold."

"The bathroom has a tub. I can warm water for you."

She cracked a crooked grin. "Guess I could do the same."

"You could," I agreed. "Or we could hunt for a natural hot springs. There are several in this region."

Alia snapped her fingers and picked up the paper map she'd been carting around. I hadn't noticed her bringing it in from the car, but she must have since it was in her hands. Unfolding it across the table, she stabbed a spot with her index finger.

"Look here."

I joined her, got my bearings, and focused on the spot she'd indicated. Located north and east of Carson City, the springs were within easy jump spell reach. "We could go there."

Alia nodded. "And kill two birds at the same time. The enclave Connor and Cleyn found has to be fairly close."

Leaving the griffon behind wouldn't set well with him, but an idea surfaced. Beckoning to Alia, I walked outside our room. Cleyn squatted about twenty feet away working his way through the rabbit pile. Blood smeared his beak and front talons.

"A favor mate?" I said.

A rabbit hindquarter vanished down his gullet. "And that would be?"

"Alia and I are going to check out a hot springs that's not too far. Could you keep watch and let Joss and Connor know where we went if they waken before we return."

After a few beak clacks, the griffon said, "We saw that place. Steam was rising."

"Was anyone there?" Alia asked.

"No. Not that we could tell." He narrowed his lidless avian eyes. "You're planning to check on the enclave."

"Not necessarily," Alia replied. "Mostly, we want a bath."

"Still, it's close," the griffon persisted. "If you go, you shouldn't be alone."

As encouragement to remain behind, I said, "We won't disturb the enclave."

"I should come along."

"No need," Alia said. "We'll be back soon, and someone needs to stay with Joss and Connor. Call me if anything happens."

Before Cleyn could launch an argument, I swept Alia into a jump spell I'd been crafting while she was talking. Steamy air surrounded us. Two of the tubs held the remains of corpses. We walked to the rear of the place, away from rotting bodies.

"This one looks good," I said.

Alia knelt and dipped a hand in surprisingly clear water. "Wonder why this pool doesn't have floating bodies?"

"It's nearest the natural spring," I noted. "Most people don't like water quite this hot."

"Perfect for me," she announced and stripped out of her clothes while making a face. "These stink, but I'm not macho enough to put wet things back on."

I toed off my boots. My pants followed and then jacket and shirt before I joined her in deliciously hot water. We'd had precious little time alone together, let alone time when we were both naked. Alia's hair fanned out around her, floating in the water. The tips of her nipples bobbed just beneath the surface.

I scooted closer. "Have I told you how beautiful you are?"

"Not lately, and not enough." She grinned and closed a hand around my errant appendage. "Hold that thought. I want to at least rinse out my hair." Tilting her head she scrubbed water through tangled curls.

After grabbing a handful of sand from the bottom, I slathered it through her tresses. That done, I did the same for my equally filthy hair.

"Gawk. Why did you put dirt in my hair?" Head still tilted back, she worked her fingers through her hair, opening channels for the sand to settle to the bottom.

"Shampoo hadn't been invented when I was born," I reminded her. "Sand has always been an all-purpose cleaner."

"Know-it-all." She made a scrunchy face.

"I scarcely know everything." Done with my hair, I moved behind her, tucking her between my straddled legs, and finished cleaning her hair. The press of her spine against my erection was enticing. We'd said we'd return soon, but five more minutes wouldn't make much difference.

"Why do you think we'll only be a few minutes?" she purred.

"Sneaky wench." I closed my hands over her breasts and rubbed already erect nipples.

"Mind reading is only instructive when you don't know

I'm there," she countered and leaned into my touch. "Damn that feels heavenly."

"Admit it. You had ulterior motives when you lured me to these springs."

"I'll never tell." She rocked against my erect cock; sensation ratcheted through me.

Using the water's buoyancy as an aid, I turned her until she faced me and slid farther onto the stone outcropping I'd taken as a seat. Kneeling, she spread her legs. Holding onto me with one hand, she guided my cock inside. We were well past her virginal days when I'd worried about hurting her. Even then, she'd been an enthusiastic bedmate.

"Mmmm." She kissed my neck and nibbled my earlobe. "We should do this more often."

"In between goblins, ghouls, vampires, and keeping all eyes open?"

"Hush." She crushed her mouth on mine.

I cupped her ass and drove into her. Both of us were hungry. If I had my way, I'd have spirited her to a habitable borderworld and spent the next century swimming in lust.

Still might happen, but not until we had a better handle on Earth's problems.

Her tongue swept the inside of my mouth. I returned her kiss with pent-up need and ferocity. Keeping her close and safe were my number-one priority. Within her body, my cock swelled growing harder, thicker. Her vault tightened around me just before it pulsed in concentric spasms as she came. I hung on, rode it through.

Nails dug into my shoulders as she shuddered against

me. My murmured endearments in Gaelic halted abruptly as she rose off my throbbing member.

"Come back here." My voice was husky with desire.

"I want to do something," she panted and clambered to the side of the pool. "Sit here."

Too aroused to argue, I dropped my butt onto the indicated spot. Alia pushed my legs far enough apart to settle between them just before she closed her mouth over my cock. One hand worked my shaft. The other slithered down and teased the spot just behind my testicles.

I gave myself up to the sheer joy of being pleasured. She brought me close to release and backed off. I buried my hands in her hair, drowning in sensation. Usually, I'd taken the lead in our lovemaking, but turning over control was a sensual gift.

After two more almost orgasms, she swirled her tongue around my glans and nipped the sensitive skin, experimenting as she went. Finally, I couldn't stand it any longer. Control shattered as semen juddered from me, painting her mouth and face with heat.

Somehow, we ended up back in the water in one another's arms panting and moaning. "Amazing," she murmured. "I love doing that. It's like you're alive in my mouth."

"Oversexed hussy."

"Only for you."

"The best part. I'd love to stay here for hours, but we should get back."

"Bet that cabinet has towels." She pointed.

After one lingering kiss, I hauled myself out of the pool

and padded to the cabinet. It was stuffed with fluffy white towels, souvenirs from when the springs were a going concern.

I tossed one to Alia and hastily dried myself. What I'd planned as a five-minute adventure had morphed into perhaps an hour.

"I know, I know," she said. "Time flies."

"With you, it lasts forever."

"Gallant of you." She unwrapped the towel from around her hair and snugged into her jacket.

"Ready?" I asked.

"She might be," a voice called, "but we aren't. Who in the fuck are you?"

The magic I'd been shaping into a jump spell changed venues quickly. I aimed a bolt of defensive enchantment in the direction of the voice and was greeted with an outraged yelp.

"Show yourselves," Alia shouted, power of her own at the ready.

The entirety of my attention was focused on who'd spoken. After a cursory exploration of the hot springs when we'd first arrived, I'd let my guard down. Stupid of me.

"*We should leave,*" I told Alia.

"*Not until we figure out who's here,*" she retorted. The patterning of her power shifted as she added a drawing spell to the mix.

I gave her points for gutsiness. It was one of the many reasons I was falling in love with her. Ready for damn near anything, I waited to see who—or what—came forth.

CHAPTER SEVEN, ALIA

I should have been terrified when that voice came out of nowhere. My body was still alight from Rhys's touch, though, and the best I could gin up was annoyance anyone would have the balls to disturb us.

How long had they been watching, anyway? Were they some sick fuck voyeurs? In a take-no-prisoners mood, I cast a drawing spell. If our uninvited observers were powerful, they'd shrug off my efforts. But one of them—assuming they traveled in packs—had yelped when Rhys fired in their direction. No answering volley of power had zinged our way.

It argued for humans.

I tugged harder, wanting to get this over with so we could return before Cleyn came looking for us.

"Shit. More of those magical fuckers," someone shouted.

"They look human," someone else argued.

Answered one question. I moved next to Rhys and dropped my spell. "Cut your power."

"Could be a trap," he cautioned.

"How? They haven't returned fire."

On the heels of my words, a rifle blast was followed by a bullet zinging by.

"That's enough," Rhys shouted. "We mean you no harm."

Another volley from the rifle. Luckily, they were lousy shots, or maybe anyone would be in the dark.

"That does it," Rhys muttered. He changed up the cadence of the spell he hadn't exactly released. Two decent sized rifles catapulted through the air and landed at our feet along with several rings, a knife, a bracelet, and a necklace.

"Whoa. Color me impressed. How'd you do that?" Stooping, I picked up one of the weapons and engaged the safety. Next, I piled the jewelry and knife on a flat rock.

"Drawing spell for metal," he explained and grabbed the other rifle. "Come down here and get your guns," he thundered. "You're lucky we aren't in a retaliatory mood."

Five minutes ticked past.

"If you don't show yourselves," Rhys yelled, "we'll round you up and feed you to the vampires."

My mouth fell open. "Talk about idle threats," I mumbled.

"They don't know that," he retorted. "If you're correct, and I believe you are, about them being human, they will have had run-ins with the undead."

Rocks rolled downhill as someone approached. Three people, two men and a woman, stopped about twenty feet away. All looked ragged, with wary expressions.

The taller of the two men sported greasy black hair and a

scraggly beard. "You going to give our rifles and other stuff back?"

"If you don't, we're as good as dead," the woman, a dishwater blonde, whined.

"Not seeing it," I tossed back. "Just grab more guns from the shops."

"How do you think we got these?" The other man, who had cropped brown hair, sounded beyond weary. "Your buddies, the vampires, were lying in wait and nabbed three of us. We were lucky to get away with guns and ammunition."

I reluctantly offered points to the vampires. They'd set up shop in a spot humans would go and simply bided their time.

"Rhys was lying about being in cahoots with vampires," I said. "We hate them as much as you do."

"But you're not human." The woman made a sigil against evil.

"Not entirely," Rhys agreed. "Tell us how you escaped the initial carnage, and we'll return your possessions and be out of your hair."

"Are there more of you?" I asked.

The woman nodded. "We were twenty. Now seventeen. It's been rough."

Talk about an understatement.

"Where were you when the world imploded?" Rhys pressed.

"In the silver mine," the first man said.

"Working?" Rhys asked.

He shook his head. "Erm, borrowing ore."

"You mean stealing," I said flatly. "Regardless, your location saved your lives."

"Why don't you want to hurt us?" The woman managed to focus her blue gaze my way.

"Not everyone with magic is bad," I explained.

"We figured maybe you were like us," the second man said. "Until you sent that lightning bolt our way."

"How come you didn't run?" Rhys angled his head to one side. A truth spell clanked over the trio.

"Erk. What was that?" The woman twisted this way and that.

"The kind of magic that keeps you honest," I said.

The first man shrugged. "Dunno. We're sick of being targets. This time we figured we had guns and the upper hand."

I shook my head. "Nah. If you really felt that way, you'd have snuck closer and aimed better."

He hung his head. "Guess we're more thieves than murderers."

"See you stay that way. The mine offers natural protection against vampires. So long as you remain near enough to retreat into it, you should be safe." Rhys let his gaze rest on each of them before reeling in his spell. He set his rifle down next to the jewelry and knife. I did the same, waiting to see how he'd avoid us getting shot as we exited the hot springs.

"So, those myths about silver and vampires are true?" the woman asked.

I nodded. "More than true. A silver stake through the

heart is the only reliable way of killing them. Most can't tolerate direct sunlight, either."

"Good to know." The second man eyed the rifles and pile of loot. "You said you'd be returning them."

Rhys wove his fingers in an intricate pattern. A glowing sphere formed around the rifles and other items. "I am. This spell will dissipate about five minutes after we've left."

The familiar feel of his magic, this time laced with the salt smell of the ocean, encompassed me. The steamy atmosphere dropped away, traded for the strip of asphalt outside our motel.

Cleyn leapt toward us, wings extended. "There you are. Another two minutes and I was going to hunt you down."

"We're okay," I told him. "Come on inside, where we can talk."

Rhys had the door open. I walked through. The room wasn't much warmer than outside. I snatched up the bedspread I'd used before and wrapped it around myself.

"Why were you gone so long?" Cleyn squawked.

"What's all the ruckus?" Connor lurched through the door that led to the next room, rubbing sleep from his eyes.

"Gone where?" Joss chimed in as he trotted after Connor.

Great. Hadn't planned on waking everyone.

"We jumped to the hot springs to take a bath," Rhys explained smoothly. If I dug beneath his words, I was certain I'd find a believability spell. "Mortals are living in a nearby abandoned silver mine. We had a conversation with them."

Joss whistled long and low. "Whoa. How'd they survive?"

"Inside the mine," I said. "It's also what's shielding them from vampires."

"But we haven't seen any since leaving Sedona," Connor protested.

"Apparently, they're here." Rhys shrugged. "Maybe they're city dwellers."

"Makes sense. It's where clumps of people used to be," Joss said, followed by, "I'd like a bath but didn't want to burn through the magic it would take to heat a tub of water."

"Dawn is hours away," Rhys said. "How about if everyone goes back to bed for a while?"

"Did you find out how many humans were left there?" Joss asked.

"They said seventeen. Guess they were twenty, but vamps snared the others."

The druid pressed his mouth into a harsh line. "Damn it. They're sitting ducks."

"What do you have in mind?" I asked him.

"Eh. Nothing. We can't help unless we set up shop here."

"They can't be the only ones who escaped death," Connor reminded him. "Come on. Maybe we'll stop by there come morning."

He and Joss trailed back into their room, pulling the door shut behind them.

Cleyn lumbered near the door and tucked his head under a wing. Perhaps he'd come to the conclusion outside was overrated.

Rhys piled additional blankets on the bed farthest from the window and lay down. I picked my way through the pile and snuggled close to him. Between the covers and our body heat, the space around us warmed quickly. For once, I was able to shut off the circular pattern my thoughts had turned into.

When I opened my eyes, daylight streamed through the windows. Cleyn was where he'd been the night before. No sign anyone else was awake. I snuck out of bed and padded to the bathroom where I splashed cold water on my face and did my best to finger-comb tangles out of my hair. The way things were going, I should twist the curls into dreads and have done with it.

Rhys met me at the bathroom door. Hair spilled down his shoulders, and he kissed me before making his way to the washbasin.

"Guess you're used to not having hot water," I ventured.

"Having piped-in water at all is a luxury," he said, voice muffled by the cloth he was using to wash his face.

"Do you think we should, erm, do something about those humans?"

He turned, arched a brow, and asked, "Like what? They seem to be getting by. That silver mine was an incredible stroke of luck."

"Can't save everyone," I mumbled.

"We don't need to. They managed to save themselves." Rhys joined me and draped an arm around my shoulders as he guided us back into the motel room. "Hell, Alia, we couldn't even do much for our own. I worry about the shifter sisters and Nola out there all by themselves."

"It was their choice," I reminded him.

We sat on the edge of the bed. I made a grab for blankets still warm from our tenure and wound them around us.

"None of this was exactly anyone's choice." His deep voice was reassuring and sad at the same time.

Joss and Connor joined us. "Anyone want breakfast before we hit the road?" Joss asked. "Plenty of instant eggs and canned vegetables in the pantry. Moldy cheese in the cold case too."

Cleyn rustled his feathers and opened his sharp hooked beak in a yawn. "Ick," he pronounced. "I'm going hunting."

"Think I'll sit this one out," Connor told him.

"Your hawk disagrees," the griffon noted.

Connor grinned. It shaved a decade off his rugged good looks. "I promised him we'd hit the skies later."

The griffon pecked at the door, leaving small holes in the wood. I scuttled around him and opened it. "'Don't go far," I cautioned.

"Like you didn't go far last night?" He regarded me with an implacable expression before spreading his wings and gaining altitude.

Joss passed me heading for the kitchen. "This won't take long," he said.

He wasn't kidding. A quarter hour later, he was dishing up food. Fare to fill our bellies but totally lacking in nutritional benefit.

I had to get over my love affair with organically grown

produce, pasture-raised meat, and wild-caught fish. The odds of me ever seeing any of them again were thin.

"You're quiet," Rhys observed.

"It's nothing." I scooped the rest of the glop on my plate into my mouth. May as well shove today into gear.

"Did we make any decisions about the mortals?" Connor wiped his whiskers with a paper napkin.

"I don't see what we could do for them," Rhys replied.

"They weren't exactly thrilled by our presence," I added. "Especially, once they determined we wielded magic."

Connor shrugged. "Tough to do nothing."

I pushed away from the table and ferried my plate to the kitchen sink. No real reason to leave the place clean, but I rinsed my dish and cutlery anyway and stacked them in a drainer. When I returned to the small dining area, Rhys was saying something about picking our battles.

Speaking of which, where was the griffon? He was his own beast and required breathing space, but being separated from him made me uncomfortable in a far different way than being separated from the wolf-shifter sisters and witch we'd left behind.

"I'm going to call Cleyn back," I announced and walked through the office and outside. Today was a shred warmer than yesterday had been, but still chilly. It reminded me about hunting for an outdoor clothing store. Perhaps we'd pass one on our way through town.

No perhaps about it. We would. I reached for my link with the griffon, relieved when it glistened whitely. The creature had been taking care of himself for hundreds, perhaps thousands, of years without my help.

A good reminder to back off.

I stopped in our room and folded three of the blankets. They weren't doing anyone any good here, and we might need them. By the time I walked outside, Rhys had the door to the Jeep open.

"Where's Cleyn?"

"Close," I said and chucked the blankets into the back seat.

Joss and Connor headed for the Subaru.

"You might want to take a couple of blankets," I called.

"Good idea," Connor said and doubled back into the room.

The griffon heaved into view, circled, and landed a few feet away. "What about a bigger car?" he cawed.

Damn it. I'd forgotten that part.

"Simple enough," Rhys said. "Get in, and we'll keep our eyes peeled."

"I'd rather fly," he groused.

"We know how well that went," I reminded him.

"I'd be more careful."

"Please," Rhys said. "Get in so we can leave."

After subjecting us to one of his intense glares, the griffon crawled into the Jeep and folded his wings out of the way.

Connor and Joss were in the Subaru. I covered the distance to the driver's side. "We need to stop two places. A clothing store, and to find a bigger vehicle, one where Cleyn has more room."

"Also need gas." Joss tapped the gauge. It was sitting at a quarter tank.

"So, maybe we prioritize a larger car first," I said. "No point wasting magic gassing up the Jeep."

"We'll follow you," Connor called.

After flashing a high five, I sprinted to the Jeep and got into the passenger seat. The griffon grumbled and hissed his discomfort.

Rhys dropped the Jeep into gear and drove out of the parking lot and onto the highway.

"They need gas," I said.

"Us too," he noted.

"Let's find maybe a Suburban or a 4-Runner," I said.

"Mmph. Is it that bad back there?" Rhys inquired.

A long hissing sigh issued from behind us. I took it as a *yes*.

We passed several small towns before hitting the southern edge of Carson City. "Oooh, look. A car lot." I pointed.

"Convenient," Rhys agreed. "If I recall, there's a Toyota dealer on the other side of the street."

His flawless memory struck again. Once he'd pulled to a stop, I bounded out. Intent on being as efficient as possible, I located a promising SUV, disappointed keys weren't inside.

"What space is it in?" Rhys shouted from a few rows away.

Huh? I glanced at the pavement, surprised to see D7 painted on it.

"Here you go." He loped toward me, a key fob dangling from one hand.

"How'd you know? I didn't answer— Eh, never mind." He'd been auditing my thoughts.

Cleyn lumbered close with his awkward gait and grunted, "Better."

"Maybe we'll trade up too," Connor called from where he'd parked a few feet away. "Might save hunting for fuel."

We transferred the blankets and our few belongings from car to car and rolled out of the lot in two brand new 4-Runners, a blue one and a white one. With the rear seat folded out of the way, the griffon wasn't quite so scrunched.

"Roughly how many miles to Mount Shasta?" Rhys asked me.

I consulted my map that was becoming decidedly dog-eared and added up the small numbers between towns. "Maybe 350 miles."

"Good. We should be there today."

Should being the operative term. If nothing went wrong. "Are you sure you want to get there after dark?" I asked.

"It's either that or spend another night somewhere. Not sure it matters one way or the other."

"You sound tired."

"Thanks for noticing. I hope this location lasts for a while before we have to move on."

"Are you certain these Lemurian creatures are friendly?"

"No, but they used to be peaceful. Things change, though."

On that cheerful note, I bundled up my coat, cranked the seat back, and shut my eyes. We could trade drivers in a bit, and I hadn't gotten much sleep the previous night.

"Awk." I jolted upright.

"What is it?" Rhys jammed the brake pedal to the floor.

Behind us, the other 4-Runner came within an angstrom of our bumper.

"Winter clothes. I wanted to grab better than what we have."

"Damn it, woman. I thought it was a real emergency. Still plenty of town left."

Five minutes later, he pulled into the remains of a Walmart. Half the store had fallen in, but the other half was intact. "This okay?" His tone was gruff.

"Sure." I unbuckled my seatbelt and got out.

Joss and Connor pulled up next to us. "Christ," Connor sputtered. "Nearly rear-ended you back there."

"Sorry. My fault. Let's collect some warmer clothes, and then we'll head north."

Cleyn poked his beak out of a back door. "I'm getting out."

Rhys herded us into a tight knot. "We stick together," he said tersely. "Haven't had the best luck in stores like this one."

After that bitter reminder, I sent power zinging forward and searched the store. Nothing batted back at me, but then I hadn't sensed anything amiss in the spot that had sucked me into a vortex, either. That little episode had spit me out fifty years in the future.

My mouth felt dry. Maybe this wasn't such a good idea after all. Dunning myself for being a ninny, I pressed forward. We'd be in and out in less than ten minutes. It was broad daylight. Vampires aren't much of a problem until dusk. If werewolves were near, I hadn't heard them howl.

Rhys led the way to a side door on the uninjured side of

the big box store. We were within five feet of it when a shattering cry from the griffon spun me around. Searching the skies, I bolted forward.

And came to a crashing halt.

Winged creatures faced off against Cleyn. Smaller than him, they had the upper bodies of women and the lower bodies of some kind of bird, maybe a chicken. Silvery hair cascaded down their bodies, partially occluding bare breasts.

"What are they?" I shouted.

"Harpies," Rhys shouted back. "Do not let them get close to you."

I wanted to ask why not, but it could wait. The critical element now was extracting Cleyn from his face-off with the weird winged women.

"Aello, Ocypete, Celaeno. To me." Rhys ran horizontal to the rest of us while motioning us to stay back.

What? He was on a first name basis with them?

Connor and Joss flanked me.

"What do you know about those things?" I asked.

"Wind spirits," Connor answered.

"They can suck your soul through your mouth," Joss added.

The Harpies abandoned their position near Cleyn and made a beeline for Rhys. Christ, but I hoped he knew what he was doing. He'd told us to steer clear while inviting them to tea.

"Have a little faith," Connor said softly.

"*Return to the cars,*" Rhys instructed while herding the Harpies farther away.

Cleyn dropped heavily to the ground next to us.

"Trouble. Naught but trouble," he muttered. "How did they end up here?"

"Where are they usually?" I cursed my lack of knowledge for the millionth time.

"Greek islands," Joss replied.

Rhys was out of sight. He'd told us to return to the cars. If he was going to sacrifice himself for us, it was the least we could do. Once we reached the vehicles, I said, "Wait here."

"Where are you going?" Connor asked.

"I can't let Rhys face those things alone." How bad could the chicken-esque things be? I'd dispatched vampires. At least these wind spirits couldn't turn me to evil.

The whole soul-sucking thing had to be a myth.

"Get on," Cleyn said. "We'll do this together."

"What about us?" Connor started stripping off his clothes in order to shift.

"You two stick with the cars. Get ready to haul ass out of here the second we get back," I shouted and leapt astride Cleyn. Moments later, we were a hundred feet above the asphalt.

I thought I'd locate them easily from our aerial perch, but they'd vanished. "Fly faster," I cried.

"Won't matter. They left." The griffon yowled mournfully.

"How do you know? Left for where?"

"My first guess is a borderworld, but we'll never find them."

Not wanting to believe him, I reached for Rhys. My spell flashed back and slapped me. Cleyn started downward.

"Oh no, you don't. We're going to scour the area for clues."

"If mistress insists."

Cleyn's tone left little to the imagination. The griffon was certain Rhys was gone and our only remaining task was to wait. It didn't sit well.

"We will look for him until there is no hope left," I said, surprised my voice was so steady. My insides felt like broken glass. My heart beat irregularly.

"Which way?" my steed inquired in a neutral tone.

"Fly a grid. North for five minutes, then east, then south, then back to the west. If we haven't located any clues, we'll widen our range."

Cleyn didn't answer, but he did turn his beak northward.

Compliance was the best I could hope for. Since he was doing his job, I stretched a thread of seeking enchantment forward and imbued it with Rhys's special magical signature.

He couldn't be gone. I couldn't fathom a world without him in it.

Don't think, hunt, one of my many inner voices instructed. Easy advice to follow, since thinking hurt my heart and my soul.

"Do you not trust him to know what he's about?" Cleyn cawed.

I did, but he was gallant enough to trade himself for the rest of us. Panic threatened to swamp me. I reined it in and focused every shred of my attention on my seeking spell.

The griffon turned east; at least he was still flying. I soldiered on, swallowing tears. They wouldn't retrieve the man I was falling in love with.

"How dangerous are these Harpy things?" I asked more to kill time than anything.

"Bad. They should still be on the Strophades Islands in the Aegean Sea. Born of Thaumas and a sea nymph, Electra, they've been naught but trouble since their making."

"Who was Thaumas?"

"A Greek sea god."

Something faint pinged off my spell. Shading my eyes against the sun's glare, I stared into the ether but found nothing.

Cleyn had scribed a square and was once again flying north.

"Go farther," I urged.

"It won't make any difference. We should return to the others. There is strength in numbers."

My fingers curved into fists; nails bit into my palms. After two more full circuits, the bitter taste of defeat coated my mouth and throat. When Cleyn shifted direction and flew toward where we'd left the cars, I didn't call him back.

CHAPTER EIGHT, RHYS

Son of a bitch. Harpies.

Where had they come from? Probably the same wave that had spit Gretta out in northern Nevada had a broad reach. I'd spent time with Aello and Ocypete eons ago when the world was much younger. They'd been half crazed then, but surely they'd remember me and my guild house.

We'd offered them succor when they'd been on the run after some misdeed or other. Not for long. Just until their mother, Electra, could emerge from the sea and ferry them to safe haven.

No matter how recalcitrant offspring are, parents never stop loving them.

Cleyn could hold his own against the women. Not true for Alia, Connor, or Joss. Harpies hated other women. I had to lure them away from Alia. Since I didn't have any better ideas on short notice, I leveraged the power of names and summoned the Harpies.

I hadn't expected my ploy would work, but they wheeled and flew after me. Had they recognized me after all these years? Or were they seeking fresh meat to carve?

I told everyone to return to the cars. The odds of Alia complying were thin, but I prefer my problems one at a time. I felt somewhat confident managing the situation, but not if Alia stormed the castle gates spewing concerns.

To forestall a confrontation, I built a travel spell as I ran.

"Rhys. That is you, isn't it?" Aello cackled.

I turned to face the trio bearing down on me and worked up what I hoped was a welcoming smile. "Of course, it is. Fancy running into you in the Americas."

"Not here by our choice," Ocypete growled.

The three touched down. "Don't get too comfy," I said. "Follow me somewhere more private."

"Och, 'tis private he wants," Aello purred.

Oops. I'd forgotten their proclivity for unbridled sex including all three of them. I'd never partaken, but some of my guild brothers had. They'd spun lurid tales of insatiable appetites.

Too late now. The dice had been cast. "Come with me," I urged and loosed my jump spell. Rather than a spot on Earth, I'd aimed for the closest borderworld. It's always a crapshoot since they move regularly, not sticking in the same spot for more than moments at a time. Fingers crossed I got lucky and landed on one with a breathable atmosphere.

Gaia must have been looking out for me. Or maybe my destination was serendipitous. An ice-crusted plain shaped up around me. Cold wind whipped stunted trees. Judging from how they were bent, it always blew in the same direction.

The Harpies bounced to the ground next to me.

"Brrr. Why choose something this unpleasant?" Aello groused and fluffed her wings around her bare breasted torso.

"These worlds move around," I reminded her. "My aim was something close where we could breathe."

"Aye, afore we freeze," Celaeno muttered.

"How'd you end up here?" I kept my tone conversational.

"Have you not noticed? The world broke." Ocypete's words dripped sarcasm.

I shrugged. "Didn't drag me halfway round the globe."

"Lucky you," Aello hissed and waddled closer. "Keep me warm, sorcerer."

The stench of wet chicken wafted around me. "We won't be here long." I segued into one of the older languages.

"Why bring us if not to play a bit?" Celaeno licked her lower lip suggestively.

"Aye, we can make you forget...everything," Aello smirked. "Even the cold, mayhap."

"You still haven't told me how you got here," I pressed.

"One fine morn we were taking the sun on our island," Ocypete said.

"The sky turned dark. Wind howled." Aello picked up the tale.

"Even worse," Celaeno said, "the very ground began to shudder and shake. Great holes opened."

"The sea raced up the beach, so we took to the air," Aello explained.

"Your idea, bitch," Ocypete shouted.

"Aye, had we remained on the ground, we'd have had a chance." Celaeno jumped down Aello's throat too."

In addition to being oversexed, they bickered incessantly. I'd forgotten that part too.

"Why was ground better?" I smoothed a calming spell beneath my words.

Ocypete turned her ire on me. "I thought you were smarter than that, sorcerer. We're here, aren't we? Freezing our tits off rather than lounging on our beloved beach."

Could they teleport? I couldn't recall. Asking would piss them off further. Instead, I said, "Happy to return you."

The three mobbed me from all sides, the reek of wet fowl so overpowering my stomach clenched in protest. "Och, ye'd do that for us?" Aello demanded in a very early form of Greek.

In answer, I visualized Strophades Island and built a quick spell. "If I craft the casting, can you ride it without my presence?"

"Aye, but why wouldn't you wish to come with us?" Ocypete narrowed silvery eyes.

"I will follow," I said, smoothly ladling magic over the lie so they wouldn't sniff it out. "First, I must alert my companions so they can press on without me."

"You plan to remain with us?" Aello squealed.

"For a time. Till we tire of one another."

To forestall further conversation where they might see right through my duplicity, I draped the edges of my casting around the Harpies and ignited my spell. Their forms wavered before spinning into silvery motes.

Breath whooshed from me. If my plan played out, evil lurking in the teleport channels would feed on them, ensure they never reached any destination. Of course, that could backfire badly.

Well aware they could backtrack along the teleport channel, I visualized the spot I'd left at the northern end of the Carson Valley and jumped off the borderworld. My magic was stretched thinner than usual since a chunk of it had accompanied the Harpies. I'd cut it free, but not until I'd reached Alia and the others.

No one was more surprised than me to find Alia, Joss, and Connor in the cars just as I'd instructed. Actually, they'd congregated in one car. Cleyn divebombed me from the skies.

"How'd you ditch them?" he shouted.

"Where are they?" Connor looked this way and that.

"On their way back to Greece," I told everybody.

"How?" Alia arched a fair brow.

"How else?" I countered. "I created a teleport spell and sent them on their way."

"Are they immune to darkness lurking in the channels?" Joss asked.

I winced. "Probably not."

Cleyn cackled. "I love it. You lured them to their doom. Bitches, one and all. Thaumas should have killed them long since. His spawn. His problem, but Electra called him off again and again."

"We need to get out of here," I said and tested the end of

my casting still linked to the Harpies. Satisfied it was no longer in motion—which could mean a lot of things—I clipped the strands and layered obfuscation over them to ensure no one could trace it back to me.

"Not going to get anywhere near Mount Shasta today," Connor said.

"We'll get as far as we can," I replied. A quick glance at the sky suggested perhaps two to three more hours before we'd need to hole up for the night.

Alia motioned to the griffon. He followed her to the vehicle we'd been driving and hopped into the rear area without complaining. His expression, beak clacking, eyes alight with joy, suggested he was still glorying in the Harpies' destruction.

I wasn't at all sure getting rid of them would be this simple, but I let him gloat unimpeded by facts. The wind spirits were ancient. It would probably take more than the odd demon to derail them.

Connor and Joss got into the companion Toyota.

"Want me to drive?" Alia asked.

"Not yet. I'm good for a while." When I got into the car I noticed a pile of clothing on the seat between us. Concern scoured a hot path through me. "You went into the store, anyway?" I demanded as I pushed the ignition button.

Alia buckled her seatbelt. "Had time to kill. Cleyn came with me. We were in and out in under five minutes." She patted the stack of garments. "Tried to get something for everyone."

Angry words knocked against the back of my throat. I

swallowed them. I'd left, albeit for the best of reasons. Controlling everyone was never going to happen.

"Protecting her is my job," Cleyn chirped from behind me.

Damn, he has more vocalization styles than a hyena.

"Tell me about the Harpies." Alia settled into her leather seat. "How is it you know them?"

"They ran a herd of unicorns half to death on the Isle of Skye," I replied. "The Celts were furious with them and dumped them in our dungeon to await justice."

"Bet that was a long while coming," Cleyn snorted.

"More than a long time," I agreed. "They made such a mess and smelled so bad, our entire guild house because almost uninhabitable. When no one seemed inclined to relieve us of the burden, we extracted a promise from them to behave and bound their compliance with magic.

"After hosing out their cell, we gave them mops and buckets to clear out the filth they'd been living in. That night, they materialized in our dinner hall. Somehow, they'd located clothes to drape around their upper bodies. One plucked a lyre off the wall and sang while we ate.

"They never appealed to me, but they did sucker some of my brothers into sexual escapades."

"With all three of them?" I intercepted an incredulous glance Alia shot my way and nodded.

"Soon thereafter," I went on, "Electra showed up at our guild house and collected her children. They returned a time or two, but I hadn't seen them in centuries until today."

"How'd they end up here?" Cleyn asked.

"Same way as Gretta. Casualties of when the world shifted," I told him.

High desert landscape flashed past as I drove. A sign said Susanville was fifty more miles. Probably as good a spot as any to weather the evening.

"I was scared for you." Alia's voice was quiet, small.

"And I was scared for you," I told her. "It's why I had to get them away from everyone."

"How could you be certain they weren't going to hurt you?" The weight of her stare bored into me.

"I wasn't, but the odds were in my favor. My brotherhood was kind to them, took pity on their plight. We could have tapped Danu and turned them over to Celtic justice. We didn't."

"More's the pity," Cleyn grumbled. "My masters hated them."

"Not much love lost betwixt the Sumerians and any of the other pantheons," I observed.

"Doesn't make the Harpies any better," he said firmly.

Hard to argue with the truth, so I didn't even try.

"Tell me again what you're hoping for with this Mount Shasta side trip," Alia said.

I collected my thoughts. We'd been careening from problem to problem, making it tough to plan too far ahead. When I started talking, the words came slowly.

"We need a spot like what I'd hoped for with Sedona's caves, except safer. A spot our magic can recraft itself. The Lemurians had their own travel channels independent of the ones the rest of us utilized. If they're still whole, perhaps we can traverse to the Old Country to seek clues for how to fix what the Sumerians cast asunder."

I'd lapsed into Gaelic, but she understood me.

"What aren't you saying?" she asked.

I hadn't intentionally left anything out, but she'd picked up on something. Didn't take long to home in on it. "I'm uncertain of our reception—"

"I thought you said the Lemurians were long gone," she interrupted.

"I believe it to be true, but just because no one has laid eyes on them in a very long while doesn't necessarily mean they've left Earth. They were committed to peace. I have no idea what this latest development means to them—if there are any left."

"They lost one world," Alia mused. "That lost planet of Mu, or whatever it was called."

"Could cut both ways," I noted. "Might make them more determined to cling to the life they carved out for themselves beneath the mountain."

"We won't know until we get there," Cleyn said.

"Tomorrow," I told him. "It's only a couple of hours' driving from Susanville."

"Is that where we're stopping tonight?" Alia asked and consulted her paper map.

"It's the only town between here and Mount Shasta, and we're nearly there." A glance in the rearview mirror reassured me Joss and Connor were right behind us. I pulled into a truck stop intent on filling our tanks, so we didn't have to do it in the morning.

"I want out," Cleyn announced. "Need to stretch my wings."

"Okay, but we won't be here long," I told him.

Connor guided the other car to a neighboring pump. Alia jumped out and opened a rear door for the griffon. There might be more space in this car than in the Jeep, but he crept out as if he'd been confined to a coffin. Who knew? Perhaps he viewed it as one step up from one.

After reaching back inside, Alia tugged a flannel jacket from the heap of clothes and snugged into it. After selecting two other heavy coats, she trotted to the other 4-Runner and gave them to Joss.

I'd been half expecting the Harpies to pile out of the sky, fury streaming from them. The more time that elapsed, the easier I was breathing. Perhaps my spell had ferried them all the way home without any fanfare. Unlike Cleyn, I didn't wish them ill, but neither did I want to share space with them.

The gas pump I'd coaxed into life with magic clicked off signifying the tank was full. Shading my eyes with a hand, I scoured the skies hunting for Cleyn. He was nowhere in sight.

"Where's the griffon?" I asked Alia.

"I was just wondering the same thing. We're ready to go, right?"

After I nodded, the air around her turned liquid as she reached for her bonded creature.

Connor came out of what had been a small convenience store that was still standing with his arms full of chips and chocolate. I snatched a couple of bags and bars from him.

Alia turned toward me. "He says five more minutes."

"Did he say why?"

She shook her head and filched a Cadbury bar from Connor's stash. "Should I go back for more?" He grinned.

"No need. I will." Joss was out of the car and loping toward the store where Connor had left the door ajar.

A vague sense of unease assailed me. Rather than scare everyone, I sought the source of my apprehension and came up dry. Was I hyper-alert after my run-in with the wind spirits?

"What is it?" Alia edged closer.

"Not sure. Probably nothing."

"My hawk is nervous," Connor said before dumping his haul into the passenger seat of his car.

It didn't make me feel any better. I scanned the skies again relieved to see Cleyn winging our way. He crawled into the car without prodding, which was unlike him.

"*Oh-oh,*" Alia murmured and followed him.

Joss hustled toward us. In addition to junk food, a case of pop was tucked beneath one arm.

"Not much farther," I told him and Connor. "I'll be on the lookout for a motel like the one where we stayed last night."

"Works for us," Connor said.

Back in the car, I turned the engine over and rumbled back onto the roadway.

"What'd you find," Alia asked the griffon.

"A spot to the east of us felt odd," he said. "So I flew toward it. As I drew nearer, I understood what attracted me. Life flourished in one tiny corner of a vast forest. Birds. Rats.

Mice. Raccoons. Beavers. It was as if every creature in a fifty-kilometer radius ended up squished into the same place."

"Maybe they're like the people we found who took refuge in the silver mine," Alia mused.

"How so?" Cleyn squawked.

"They must have been in a protected spot when the world broke," I said.

"Yes," Alia seconded. "And they didn't venture out until things settled."

Running into pockets of survivors gave me hope, foolish though it was. Protective magic hadn't deserted Earth. Gaia or Danu were doing what they could to preserve survivors.

"Did you talk with them?" I asked the griffon.

"Nay. They were frightened of me. After what happened, magic would terrify anyone."

A small settlement flashed past. Was this Susanville? Seemed too small.

Alia intuited my thoughts. "Keep going," she said. "We have another ten miles or so."

A chasm in the asphalt opened ahead of us. I hit the brakes to avoid falling in, half expecting Connor and Joss's car to plow into us.

It didn't, but the squeal of overworked brakes was loud in my ears.

"Can we go around it?" Alia asked.

Didn't appear so. I opened the door, intent on examining the fissure when a blast of pure evil drenched me in sulfur fumes.

"What is that?" Alia cried and started coughing.

I wasn't certain, but my money was on demons. The

trench stretching across the highway might be a one-way conduit into Hell.

"Get out," I barked. "Grab what you need."

Connor and Joss must have heard me because they exited their car carrying two bags presumably stuffed with convenience store loot and wearing their winter coats.

The sense of wrongness was so pervasive, an icy chill invaded my body. We had to get out of here this second before the denizens of Hell's realm poured through the hole.

"Awk. Look." Alia jabbed a finger at a set of red horns rising above the level of the pavement. Power forked from her upraised hand.

Desperation makes for sloppy spells, but all I had to do was move us away from here. "Get closer to me," I snapped.

"Me too?" Cleyn asked.

"Unless you want to deal with demons on your own."

"Might be fun after being cooped up in the car," he cawed.

The horns were followed by the top of a bald head covered in reddish scales.

No reason to wait around for the rest of him to clear the chasm. Never mind his buddies.

I tied into Alia's magical center, grateful she didn't rebuff me. Once I had a critical mass of enchantment, I engaged a jump spell aiming for the north end of Susanville. It wasn't far enough, but one step at a time.

The griffon chucked magic into the mix.

Even with our combined efforts, the response I'd hoped for was sluggish. The demon was levering himself out of the hole when the cars finally vanished. We floated in darkness.

At least the stench of sulfur retreated. My nostrils would burn for hours. Nothing I could do about it. I fired a mage light.

"Why aren't we out?" Connor mumbled. The shape of his hawk hovered behind him, wings fanning the air.

Good question. My jump spell should have lasted seconds, not minutes.

"Something's wrong," Alia murmured about the time I came to the same conclusion.

"Can you extricate us?" Joss asked.

I could, but was it wise? "Let's ride this out for a bit more," I said.

Alia leaned in to me, breathing heavily.

Switching to my third eye, I scanned our surroundings. We were in a cross between a jump spell and a teleport channel. How had that happened? So long as I had access to the latter, I visualized Mount Shasta and instructed the spell to take us there.

"Erk. What did you do?" Alia clutched at her midsection as the draw on her magic intensified.

Rather than answer her I said, "Believe this will work. Might make a difference."

"Define *this*." Joss's normally calm voice was strained.

"Shortcut to Mount Shasta," I explained and clung to imagery as if it were a life preserver keeping our little band afloat in a choppy sea. Worst case, the darkness that had invaded these channels would force our egress, but until it happened, I'd press onward.

CHAPTER NINE, ALIA

Would we ever catch a break? Not likely. When Rhys slithered into my magical center, I welcomed the feel of him. We made a good team, our magic complementary. Cleyn mumbled something incomprehensible before pressing bands of visible light toward Rhys.

We'd dealt with vampires and werewolves. Were demons about to join the party? How many bad things were there? My magical education was definitely lacking, not a lapse I was about to rectify anytime soon. If we'd remained in Sedona, I could have availed myself of the library Rhys had found in one of the vortex's power points.

Even I'd heard about Mount Shasta. Perhaps it had its own collection of ancient books and scrolls. If so, I made myself a promise to devote at least some time to rummaging through them.

I dragged my thoughts front and center. Something had

to be wrong. Jump spells are over quickly. This one had lasted far too long.

Pain jabbed my midsection. I grunted and stared at Rhys. He must be having a hard time, or he wouldn't have made a grab for still more enchantment from me.

Cleyn draped a wing over my shoulder. *"Steady."* He switched to telepathy.

Rhys said this was a shortcut to Mount Shasta. Must mean we'd stumbled into a journey channel, but how? It wasn't like him to cast one spell and end up with another. That type of shenanigan was more likely to happen to green-as-grass mages like me.

In hopes it might help, I visualized what I remembered of the small town not far from the mountain. Not much to it. A few shops, motels, gas stations.

The channel shuddered as if our presence offended it. Damn it. If we got out of this intact, we needed to go to ground and stay there. Permanently. No matter where it was.

I quieted my thoughts. If any of Rhys's lessons had sunk in, it was the importance of maintaining a positive outlook and a clear focus, not one muddied by negativity.

Light shimmered around Rhys. His blue eyes had darkened to midnight, and his extended hands shook ever so slightly. The tremors in our channel intensified.

Would the tunnel blow outward, taking us with it?

Fuck. *No negatives,* I instructed sternly and wiped my mind clear of everything except a wavery representation of Mount Shasta City. I homed in on a small café that had featured homemade bagels.

The rough sound of Rhys's breathing wasn't reassuring.

Connor's hawk was visible behind him, never a good sign. Joss had clasped his hands in front of him and shut his eyes.

"Get ready," Rhys growled. "This transition will be rough."

The tug on my guts intensified tenfold. I swallowed a yelp and resisted an overpowering urge to slice through the spot Rhys was joined to me. He'd never hurt me on purpose; his need must be great.

In my limited experience, travel channels burst outward. This one did the opposite and folded around us, squeezing tighter and tighter. Panic gripped me like a vise. We'd be crushed, and that would be the end of things.

"Visualize light." Rhys's voice cracked with strain.

I didn't have a better idea, so I added waves of white light to my fledgling vista of Mount Shasta City. I was panting, dredging oxygen out of air that had turned dank and stale. Sweat dripped down my forehead and sides.

Rhys had been chanting. He shifted to pointed words that flayed the skin off my bones. With no warning, the walls holding us prisoner shrieked and moaned before long rents formed.

Cleyn drove his beak through panels that fell away.

Icy air whooshed past, but I could breathe again. Air also provided an element I could weave into a cushion to break my fall. I looked about seeking the others, but it was dark. No extra magic for a mage light. Not until I was on the ground. In that moment, I realized Rhys was no longer connected to me.

Where was he?

Had the last spate of words drained him of something

fundamental? They'd sure as hell done a number on my head. I started to reach for him but held back. Ground first. Then I'd get my bearings.

Wings whooshed past. The welcome feel of Cleyn's magic was reassuring. He plummeted downward. I followed more slowly since I lacked wings to break my fall.

"*Alia.*" Rhys's voice blasted through my mind.

Thank all the fucking deities that ever walked. "*I'm okay,*" I sent back, swimming in relief.

I'd no sooner answered than the ground rose up to meet me. I rolled to my feet and pulled the jacket I'd stolen from the big box store more tightly around myself.

Cleyn was already on the ground fanning his wings.

Rhys landed next to me and drew me against him, murmuring in Gaelic, "Are you all right? I didn't hurt you, did I?"

I wanted the comfort of those arms, but we weren't yet whole. "Where are Connor and Joss?" I asked, sidestepping his question about hurting me. What was done was done. He'd broken free of the magical deathtrap. It was all that mattered.

"Here," a pair of voices called. The crackle of underbrush told me they were closing on where we stood.

"What in the hell happened?" Connor demanded as he clawed through a break in thick bushes.

"Not sure I know," Rhys admitted. "My jump spell shunted us into a teleport channel, but it didn't feel normal to me."

"Why'd we stay in it?" I asked, my voice on the shrill

side. Adrenaline still coated my throat and tongue with an acrid taste.

"I hoped it would bring us closer to our destination."

"Did it?" Joss asked.

"Yeah, where are we?" Connor tossed out.

The air around Rhys developed a liquid aspect. He'd kindled a mage light, but I hadn't noticed until now.

"Hang on," he murmured and shut his eyes before adding, "Not bad. Not bad at all."

"Not bad, what?" I pressed.

"We're about two miles from where I'd hoped to come out. Come on. We can talk while we move. It's too cold to stand still for long."

"I'll fly," Cleyn announced and jetted skyward.

I didn't call him back. Walking was far from his forte.

We set off at a brisk pace. My feet felt like bricks of ice, and my fingers had grown numb. "Why didn't you shift?" I asked Connor.

"My hawk wanted to in the worst way, but I'm sick of going through clothes. Didn't want to waste time hunting down more."

"Did something lure us into the teleport channel?" Joss asked.

"Not lured so much as was waiting," Rhys replied. "Whatever it was, it reacted rather slowly. We were nearly to a point where I was going to commute the casting when the walls started trying to crush us."

"Have you ever had that happen before?" I asked.

He shook his head. "Whole new set of universal rules are in play."

"Wish someone would pony up instructions," I muttered.

A cottage that had miraculously escaped destruction flashed past on our right. I ground to a halt. "How about stopping there for tonight?" I suggested and scanned the place to ensure it wasn't boobytrapped.

"Gets my vote," Joss said.

"Probably best to tackle Mount Shasta in daylight," Connor seconded.

Rhys circled back to where the three of us stood. Power flickered as he tested the area around the log-and-stone hut. "Seems safe enough," he pronounced.

I didn't bother to tell him I'd already checked. Directing my attention skyward, I spoke to the griffon. *"Cleyn. We're stopping short of the mountain. Join us, please."*

He must have been tracking us from directly above because he glided into the clearing and landed next to me. A brisk squall blew out of the north, pelting us with large, cold raindrops. It was the incentive we needed to close the fifty yards between us and the cottage.

Built from stones with a metal roof, it appeared old, out of place in what had been the modern world. Alert for threats—after everything we'd been through, I scarcely trusted my earlier assessment—I searched for anything alive. Faint tracings suggested someone had lived here long ago, years before the world cleaved in two.

Rhys stood at the front door. Made of wood with rounded upper corners, it slotted neatly into the masonry walls. His particular brand of magic flickered and flared as he worked on the locking mechanism.

I pushed around the griffon, Joss, and Connor to stand by Rhys. "Someone lived here long ago."

"Aye, maybe not all that many years. The enchantment holding this lock has been replenished recently."

"How can you tell?" I recalled my earlier commitment to learning more about magic in general. May as well glean what I could.

"Look through your third eye. See the colored threads wrapping around the padlock?"

I'm not nearly as quick as he is shifting from one vantage point to another, so it took me a couple of minutes before I said, "Yes, I see them."

"Notice how some are brighter than others? Those are the newer additions. The older ones have grown dull. There. Got it."

The padlock's hasp slipped from its silvery body with a clatter. Rhys tugged it aside and pushed the door open. The scents of dried herbs welcomed us as we moved out of weather that was doing nothing but growing worse.

I extended a hand and visualized light. A glowing ball formed, floating just above my palm. The interior of the cabin was tidy and well kept. A double bed was pushed against the back wall. Neatly made, it was scattered with many pillows and a hand-sewn quilt.

A leather sofa and chair sat near the woodstove with a pile of kindling and larger pieces stacked nearby. The other side of the structure held a kitchen with a pump handle mounted next to the sink. No refrigerator, which made sense since there didn't seem to be electricity. Trays of dried vegetables and herbs were stacked on one side of the kitchen.

Of course, there wasn't any electricity now, but the place had been off-grid even before the cataclysm. Kerosene lamps were scattered about. Something that might have been a water tank hung above the woodstove.

Joss knelt to build a fire.

I took off my jacket and hung it over a hook near the stove to dry. Rhys and Connor did the same. "Not sure how these survived the transit, but they did." Connor tugged bags out of large pockets in his coat once it was off.

Junk food from the convenience store.

Excellent. I was hungry and reticent to rustle through the various cupboards. Now I was within, the place didn't feel as deserted as it had from outside.

Cleyn returned from a full circuit of the one-room hut. "Witches lived here. Two of them from what I can tell."

It made sense. They often used herbs in their various spells and potions.

"Wonder what happened to them?" I mused.

The crackle of twigs as they burst into flames was followed by Joss saying, "That should go. We'll need more wood to last the night, though."

"Maybe there's a shed," I ventured and walked toward the door.

"I'll come with you." Rhys bounded to my side.

His lack of faith in me rankled. "No need." I bristled and reached for the latch.

He closed his hand over mine. "Yes, there is. Something about this place isn't quite right."

"Should we leave?" Joss tilted his head to one side.

"We should be all right for what's left of tonight," Rhys replied.

"My hawk isn't so sure," Connor said.

When I tried to open the door, Rhys held firm. "We have enough wood for a few hours. Let's eat and dry out."

The splat of drops on the roof suggested it was raining harder than it had been when we sought shelter. I felt off in a subtle way, nothing I could put my finger on exactly.

Probably just tired and reacting to the shit ton of adrenaline that had coursed through me earlier.

Connor dumped the contents of both bags on the kitchen table.

"Let go of me," I told Rhys.

"Sure once you promise you'll stick close. Witches have familiars."

"Pfft. What harm will a black cat do?"

"They cultivate other types. Cats are the least of it. Perhaps they felt safe leaving because they left familiars to keep an eye on their home."

Annoyance growing by the moment, I spun to face him, not caring we had an audience. "Animals have an affinity for me. Or have you forgotten?"

The feel of his magic surrounded my mind. Warm, supportive, worried. I tried slapping up a ward, but I was too late. "Sorry," he murmured as he probed, moving from one part of my mind to another.

Pain jabbed me. I twisted, trying to divest myself of his grip on my shoulders and his intrusion into my thoughts.

"Remain still until I wall this part off."

"Wall what part off?" I squeaked.

Cleyn stood in front of us, wings wrapped around our bodies. The alien feel of his enchantment ran through me, reassuring in an odd way. The right side of my head throbbed.

"What's going on?" Connor asked.

Rhys didn't answer. I felt him cordon off something deep within. The pain retreated as quickly as it had arrived. Irritation receded. I felt myself again, albeit a trashed version.

Cleyn folded his wings. Rhys stepped back regarding me. "That should hold until we leave here. The witches left an entrapment spell. My guess is had you ventured outside, their familiars are waiting in the woodshed."

"It would have been all right," I mumbled. "Animals revere me."

"Not when they're bonded to someone else." Cleyn clacked his beak.

Curiosity invaded my weariness as I considered what might be lying in wait. Or not. "You're overreacting." I tried for dignity.

"You tried to ward yourself earlier," Rhys said gruffly. "Might be a good time to resurrect that effort."

I felt stupid for not diving into a ward as a preemptive strike. Maybe I wasn't firing on all cylinders. Not wanting to dissect my state of mind any further, I made my way to the table and grabbed a chocolate bar and a bag of chips. Cups hung from hooks behind the sink. I filled one with water and sank into a chair intent on regrouping.

Cleyn retreated to the trays of dried herbs and plucked something up with his beak before swallowing it. I hadn't known eagles ate anything besides meat. Made sense he'd be hungry.

Paper crackled as everyone opened packages of junk food. It was one aspect of the previous iteration of life on Earth that could wither with no loss to anyone. Still my flavored Dorito chips tasted good as did the Cadbury dark-chocolate bar.

How long till morning?

A thought intruded. I didn't care for it, but it was important enough not to ignore. I cleared my throat. "Perhaps it wasn't accidental I was drawn to this place?"

"Rather than put a malevolent spin on things," Rhys replied, "it could be something as simple as magic calling to its own."

I drained the remaining water from my cup. "Would dark power have that effect?"

"Some witches wield white magic," he reminded me. "If we ran into trouble, it's like as not built-in protections to guard their home from intrusion."

"Why not hide it behind illusion?" Connor asked.

"Not sure they command that type of magic, or enough to shroud something this big," Cleyn squawked and continued to mow through one of the trays of dried herbs.

Weariness beat a path through me. I glanced at the bed but thought better of disturbing it. Bad enough we were intruding into someone's private space. The tight place in my mind—the one Rhys had worked on—relaxed. I folded my arms on the table, placed my head on top of them, and shut my eyes.

Rhys dropped a hand on my shoulder. "I'll take first watch. Wake you in two hours."

That sure felt familiar. We'd taken turns in the Sedona caves too.

Joss tossed more wood in the stove and curled up on the rug in front of it. Connor mirrored my head-on-arms position on the table. Cleyn tucked a head beneath a wing and stood as far from the fire as he could get. No doubt the hut felt warm to him.

My mind drifted. At least our outer clothing would dry. If the goddess granted us grace, we'd sit the night out without incident.

I raised my mind voice, aiming it at anyone near enough to hear. *"Thank you for allowing us entry. We promise to leave your home undisturbed."*

Part of me felt foolish, but another breathed easier. One of the worst elements of the new normal was no one trusted anyone.

Why should they?

On that cheery note, I drifted into a light, restless sleep.

CHAPTER TEN, RHYS

My heart went out to Alia, but she didn't need my pity. It would only get in the way. Mount Shasta has always been a haven for mages. Perhaps the witches who bided here were only the tip of the iceberg. If that were true, we might have competition for prime locations beneath the mountain.

Anyone who'd been here during the breaking would have survived. If there were a lot of them, the odds of welcome for my small band were questionable. No point getting ahead of things, though.

Tomorrow would be here soon enough.

I layered a calming spell around Alia to ensure she got at least some sleep. Dark circles etched beneath her eyes, and her hands had developed a slight tremor.

The crackle of the fire was soothing. Its light played over the cabin's walls. Everyone was asleep, including Cleyn.

Good opportunity for me to do a bit of sleuthing. I hadn't been outside since we arrived.

I stood, taking care to be as silent as possible, and let myself out the front door patching the warding so it would alert me to any disturbances. The rain had stopped, replaced by a sky shot with millions of points of light. A quick transit of the cottage revealed a wooden outbuilding.

Was this the source of what had drawn Alia?

I started toward the opening but changed my mind and reached with the gentlest touch of seeking magic. Life pinged my way. Perhaps not familiars, but many creatures had taken refuge in the shed.

Mount Shasta might not be quite the wasteland everywhere else had been. I'd assumed since Sedona's vortex hadn't shielded the surrounding area none of the other power spots would either.

A low growl snapped me out of my musings.

"Stand down. No one will harm you." I turned and retraced my steps.

Alia met me before I reached the steps to the front porch. "What are you doing out here?" Her voice was muzzy with sleep.

I wrapped her in my arms. "Why aren't you resting? Not time for your turn to watch yet."

"I sensed you were gone. And then Cleyn alerted me." She snuggled closer. "Why'd you come outside?"

"Reconnaissance."

"Did you find anything?"

I nodded. "There's a primitive shed out back. It might have more firewood, but it's chock-full of animals."

She drew back and looked at me. Her striking face with its defined cheekbones and sculpted chin was illuminated by a half-risen moon. "Whoa. How many witches do you suppose lived here?"

"They're not all familiars," I explained. "Maybe none of them are."

"Then why are they here?"

"Hard to say, except my guess is they were drawn to a spot that felt safe."

She wriggled in my arms. "I want to go say hello."

"Something growled at me."

A smile lightened her features. "Yes, but I was called to this spot earlier. Remember? They might have been drawn to my enchantment."

Anything was possible, and we couldn't afford to thumb our noses at potential allies. I let go and followed her around the side of the cottage.

Alia motioned for me to stay put and walked close to the open door where she sank to her knees and opened her arms. Blue and violet light streamed from her as she cast a welcoming spell.

The first to emerge was a female mountain lion. Probably the source of who'd growled. She padded toward Alia, whiskers twitching. I shrouded my reservations in order to not taint things. Ripples in the air suggested they were talking.

The energy shifted. I tensed, ready to spring into action.

Three kits bounded out of the shed and made a beeline for Alia's lap where they purred up a storm. The mother sidled close, licking her offspring. The scene was so poignant, it tugged at my soul. No matter how badly Earth had been devastated, life found a way of weaving around the wreckage.

"You're beautiful," Alia murmured, stroking soft kitten heads.

What else was in the shed? If my assessment was correct, why hadn't the mountain lion eaten the rodents I'd sensed within?

With a sharp command somewhere between a snarl and a yip, the mother herded her brood into the night. All cats prefer to hunt during the dark hours; keeping the kittens fed had to be a full-time job.

Alia rose and brushed debris off the front of her pants.

I joined her. "What did you talk about?"

"She wanted to reassure herself we'd be moving along."

"Did she mention the witches?"

Alia shook her head. "Mostly, I listened and complimented her family. Wanted to stay on her good side. It must be time for me to take over. Why don't you get some rest."

"I'm okay for a bit more time. Sit with me." I led us around to the front porch.

After I wound an arm around her shoulders, she leaned into me. "Might be my imagination, but we seem to be uncovering more living creatures than we did around Sedona."

"Could be they're venturing out of hiding," I replied.

"But why wouldn't we have sensed them?"

"We've been pretty swamped avoiding this, that, and the other," I reminded her.

She snorted. "Ain't that the truth. Do you think we might end up staying in this area?"

I debated a soothing mix of words but discarded them in favor of, "Hard to say."

"Wheels are turning in that mind of yours. What are your reservations?"

I tightened my grip on her. "Depends what we find closer to the mountain. This area has always housed an active mage community."

"That's a good thing, right?"

"So long as there are enough staples to go around, sure. If people are already squabbling over resources, they might prefer if we moved on."

A sigh burbled from her. "Will we ever have a home again?"

"Not in the way you're used to."

"Ouch. No sugarcoating from you."

I picked my words carefully. "I haven't given up on traveling back in time to see if we can't fix this."

"It's a nice pipe dream, but the odds aren't great."

"The longer this stretches out, the more they improve."

She straightened and ducked from beneath my arm. "You're talking in riddles."

"Not purposefully." I exhaled slowly. "The Sumerians had an endpoint in mind. My guess is, at least so far, it's eluded them. I'm certain they didn't mean to annihilate such a broad swathe of the population. They'd have required some mortals for basic housekeeping."

"Still not following." Alia scrubbed the heels of her hands down her face.

"In a backhanded way, mortals fed into mage power by placing offerings at shrines. Their belief in magic strengthened it. Many of the gods and goddesses had monumental egos. They would compare notes regarding whose shrine received the most gifts."

"How juvenile. It reminds me of kids boasting about how many false friends they have on social media."

It was an apt analogy, and I chuckled. "I'm certain Zeus would salivate at the prospect of a TikTok presence. Why stop at twenty minions when he could gather millions with the stroke of a button?"

"What exactly are you getting at? I'm still having trouble connecting the dots."

"Might be an oversimplification, but by the time we end up trying to move backward in time again, it will have sunk in that their grand plan backfired."

"What would stop them from regrouping and trying something different?"

Alia was on her feet. I joined her. "Hard to say. The higher up in the magical pecking order someone is, the lazier they tend to be. Besides, they wrecked so much, there's really not a plan B out there. Let's get through this next part before we second-guess their current mindset."

A corner of her mouth twisted downward. "Needing everything tacked down and buttoned neatly is an old habit. It's how I survived once my magic manifested. I'm going to return to the shed."

"Mind if I tag along?"

"Don't you want to grab a spot of sleep?" Bits of her energy probed the corners of my mind, a trick I'd taught her.

"No way I'm leaving you out here alone," I growled.

She patted my arm. "Kind of heavy-handed, bud. I'll holler if I run into trouble."

By then, it could be too late...

Where was my doom and gloom coming from? Was it rooted in the fierce protectiveness I harbored for Alia? Or was something real driving it? Perhaps being joined at the hip was over the top, but when we were separated, I ended up reacting to events rather than sticking with plans.

I sank onto my haunches and rested my butt on the bottom step, murmuring, "I'm sure it will be fine. The mother and her kits returned a little bit ago, so they'll be feeding."

She kissed the top of my head. "Thanks for caring."

"How could I not?"

Instead of answering, she walked toward the shed. A shiny spot off to one side dripped Cleyn's energy. Apparently, it was simpler for him than manipulating the door latch.

"Why aren't you with her?" the griffon demanded.

"She asked me to remain here." I didn't mention she'd actually shooed me back inside except I hadn't gone.

"Not a good reason," he hooted and spread his wings. Rather than taking to the air, he used them as foils to move more quickly, tracing Alia's path.

For a time, quiet reigned. I added a small flow of magic to warm myself as the coldest part of the night surrounded me. Positioned between cabin and shed, I dropped markers that would ping if danger intruded.

Was I onto something about the Sumerians? Would they

truly rethink their actions predicated on feedback from the future? Their seers could look both forward and back, so they'd know their plans had sloughed sideways.

Would it make them more determined to try again? Or, having failed, would they pack up their toys and go home? Not that it would matter unless they went to great lengths to reverse the effects of their destructive spell.

For the millionth time, I longed for the library at my guild house. Perhaps the Lemurians had amassed something similar. No way to know until we arrived at the declination beneath the mountain. Some said it had always housed a back door to the lost planet of Mu. I was fairly certain any gateways had slammed shut once Mu sank beneath the ocean's waters.

Still, magic is a funny thing. The Lemurians could have erected a protective bubble around their erstwhile home and might still be living there. Mages have always kept to themselves. My other notion of traveling backward in time and alerting groups of witches, druids, sorcerers, mages, shifters, and others about the danger bearing down on them might not have any impact.

Disaster didn't always make for strange bedfellows. Especially one that had yet to occur.

Rather than being mired in what wouldn't help, I turned my focus to what might. And didn't come up with much because of a phalanx of unknowns. Joss and Connor were still sleeping. Cleyn hadn't returned. Presumably, he was sticking close to Alia.

The wind picked up as dawn neared.

A cave studded with crystals formed behind my closed

lids. I recognized that cave. It sat beneath Mount Shasta. The vision had shown itself to me for a reason. Rather than manipulating it, I withdrew to the edges in hopes it would yield information.

Tall, slender scaled creatures hurried this way and that.

Lemurians.

Humanoid in appearance, they walked on two legs. Arms were graced with talon-tipped fingers. Delicate gray-green scales covered their bodies from head to toe. I've always believed them to be hermaphroditic since breasts and sex organs weren't visible. Their eyes were elongated slits with dark pupils. Two holes sat where a nose should have been. Long, hinged jaws housed shiny, white teeth.

Their language was a high clacking, buzzing sound.

Watching them bustling about was mesmerizing. After a time, it occurred to me no other mages were present. Was it significant? Had the Lemurians chased everyone else away?

I filed the information for future use. We'd proceed with caution. Even more than usual. All quiet from the direction of the shed. Perhaps I could risk—

The peace that had surrounded me blew outward. Slimy black tentacles reached for me. A stench reminiscent of rotten vegetation burned my nostrils. On my feet, I took off for the shed at a dead run.

It wasn't there.

Maybe it was, but I couldn't see it.

The tentacles had followed me, still stretching and trying to latch on with rows of suckers lining their undersides. I blasted one with fire. It hissed and withdrew. I grabbed on to the window it allotted to switch to my third eye.

The shed wavered before me. I dove toward the still-open door and screeched to a halt. If there'd been a dirt floor, it was gone, replaced by a huge hole. Nothing living remained.

Had everyone been sucked into the chasm?

"Alia! Cleyn!"

They didn't answer, but I hadn't expected them to. The place had the feel of a portal to elsewhere. Why hadn't I sensed any of this happening? Had someone planted the Lemurian imagery to distract me? At least the octopus thing wasn't dogging me any longer.

Of course not. It had done its job herding me into what was supposed to be a trap. Absent an overabundance of caution, I'd have fallen into the hole. Its pull was strong, but my skill trumped its enchantment.

"What's going on?" Connor demanded.

He and Joss flanked me. How had they escaped the octopus gauntlet? Perhaps it had disappeared as soon as I was heading in the right direction.

"It's a gateway," Joss said.

I sent a string of power downward. Rather than snapping back and slapping me, something latched onto it. I cut the flow of magic fast before it nabbed me. I'd enter, but I'd do it in my own way.

"Return to the cabin," I told Connor and Joss.

"What are you going to do?" Joss asked.

"Figure out what happened to Alia and Cleyn." My first step was warding, so I went to work building one.

"It feels foul down there," Connor said.

"We need to find another way," Joss seconded.

A grinding noise was followed by movement from below. The chasm was closing over. "There is no other way," I gritted. "Have to do this before the access point vanishes."

Rocks ground against one another. Dirt heaved. No time for anything but to jump. I might be too late, but I had to try. I'd have ordered the men to remain behind, but they were free agents.

The last thing I shouted was, "If you follow me, ward yourselves."

Darkness closed around me. The same nasty smell that had accompanied the octopus thickened. My feet struck something, my shoulder something else.

Was there still an opening?

In desperation, I kindled a light. It illuminated the rapidly shrinking gap but allowed me to aim for the center of its maw. Joss and Connor were above me. Their trust and loyalty warmed me, but I wished they'd remained in the cabin.

I reached for my link with Alia, gratified when it pulsed weakly.

No matter how this turned out, we'd all be in it together.

CHAPTER ELEVEN, ALIA

The shed teemed with life. Mostly rodents, a few birds, two cats, and the mother mountain lion and her kits. Insects bided here as well. Altogether a welcoming spot even with Cleyn clucking over me. When he'd first arrived, the mountain lion had thrown her body between him and her babies.

"He won't hurt them," I promised her. "He's with me."

Despite my reassurances, she sidled out of the shed herding her brood ahead of her. "Tell me again why you're here," I asked Cleyn.

"Something doesn't feel right."

At the risk of kicking the shovel out of my guardian angel's hands, I murmured, "Rhys trusted me."

"Not a matter of trust," he squawked.

Amidst squeals, chirps, and chittering, the shed's residents streamed out the door. Damn it. Had Cleyn spooked all of them?

The griffon head butted my upper arm. "We must leave. Now."

"You scared everyone off. We don't have to go anywhere." I could have strolled outside, but my stubborn streak had been activated.

"Not why they left. They sense the same thing I do."

I faced him, hands on my hips. "And that is what, exactly?"

He moved to my other side and pushed hard. "Leave now!"

"Stop that." I pivoted away from him toward the now empty interior of the shed. I'd be damned if his free-floating fear would infect me.

Pleased with myself for taking a stand, I sat cross-legged on the dirt floor.

"Mistress. Please."

"I am not your mistress. What did you sense?" I repeated my earlier question, smugly certain he was overreacting.

"They're trying again—" His words cut off in a maelstrom of rolling dirt and crashing rocks. Where were they? I heard them but couldn't see anything like a rock avalanche. I tried to stand, but the spot where I'd been seated fell in. I tumbled headlong into darkness, cursing the hubris that had kept me squarely in danger's path.

Ick. The new place stank of death and rot.

Thanks to my stubbornness, Cleyn was right here with me.

What in the fuck was wrong with my head? He'd warned me. Why hadn't I listened? Something large and hard jammed into me. Pain seared my side. I kept on falling. Conserving magic was important—since I'd need a piss pile of it to extricate us from this mess of my own making—but if a boulder swatted me in the head, I'd be no use to anyone.

Reluctantly, I called a light.

We plummeted through a hole that was widening below us. Was there a bottom? Could I activate a jump spell back to the surface? Usually, the simplest fixes work. In between dodging rocks, I ignited a quick-and-dirty transport spell.

I may as well have pissed into the wind for all the good my jump spell did.

"Sorry," I muttered.

Cleyn clacked his beak in clear annoyance. I'm sure he was cursing the day our Sumerian overlords saddled him with me. I considered promising I'd make a concerted effort to be better but couldn't choke out the words.

They weren't true. Given a do-over, I'd have made the same choice. I'll be damned if I'd spend my new life running scared of my own shadow.

"Do you recognize where we are?" May as well find out what Cleyn knew.

"Heading for the common underworld," he squawked.

I ducked to avoid rockfall. "What is that?"

"Where the misfits of all worlds end up."

I choked around my next question but felt compelled to give it airtime. "Is there, erm, a way out?"

"Not normally."

I'd both expected and feared his response. "Means we can't let ourselves reach the bottom," I gritted.

A heart-wrenching squawk set my already raw nerves

even more on edge. A rock must have hit Cleyn. Why hadn't he warded himself?

Something sharp jabbed my shoulder. I pivoted the other direction, smack dab into still more rocks. Alrighty, then. Something sentient had to be running this shit show. I added lumens to my light and examined the walls hunting for something we could cling to.

Everything was in motion, which made identifying a shelf to break our descent difficult. One of Cleyn's wings was partially folded. Crap. I hoped he hadn't broken it.

A promising protrusion caught the corner of my eye. I angled toward it, aiming for a shelf-like flange while shouting, "Over here."

Cleyn had wings. Presumably, it would allow him more latitude maneuvering.

I pushed and pulled the air around me, forcing it into a cushion. The dynamic energy in the tunnel fought me every step of the way. It wanted me at the bottom, a place I'd kill to avoid.

Arms extended, I visualized grasping the edge of the stone shelf.

You can do this.

Great. Cheerleading myself was a diversion, one I did not need. With every shred of magic and consciousness focused on what I hoped would be a lifeline, I swam toward it, pushing my way through what felt like slimy mud.

In a whoosh of wings and magic, the griffon rose up beneath me. "Reach for it," he hooted.

I did. My fingertips grazed rough rock. I clung like a

limpet and jackknifed my body up and onto a platform. It extended back into the wall, something I hadn't expected.

"Room for you," I wheezed.

Cleyn must have figured that out even before my words because he dove past me headfirst, wings folded across his back.

For long moments, the only sound beyond rocks clattering into one another was the harsh rasp of our combined breathing.

"All you did was delay the inevitable." He switched to telepathy, perhaps to conserve power.

"Let's try for a wee bit more optimism," I muttered.

A rough summons pinged off my magical center. Rhys. Goddammit it to hell. Why had he followed me?

Except I knew the reason. He loved me.

A quick scan revealed Joss and Connor too. All three were a considerable distance above us. Revealing our position might be a tactical error, but I'd be damned if I'd let my three companions sink into the common underworld.

"We're here." I reached for Rhys and added a tracking vector.

It tugged at my midsection as he latched onto it. Before I could count to ten, all three men tumbled to a landing on my ledge.

Rhys closed his arms around me; the thud of his heart was loud in my ears.

"Look!" Connor shouted. "There's an opening back here."

Rhys released me abruptly. "Hold up. Do not enter until I get a look at it."

The air around Cleyn sparkled as he leveraged magic, probably to heal his injury. Rhys scooted to where Connor stood next to a stone doorway. It wasn't immediately obvious, but then I'd only been here a scant handful of minutes.

The doorway was about four feet tall and three wide. It glowed as Connor cycled through spells to encourage it to open. Rhys waved him to stand down. The glow changed from blue to white to violet as Rhys probed the fissure that might—or might not—be our ticket to somewhere else.

Amid creaks and groans, the hunk of stone swung inward.

"Did you try a jump spell?" Rhys didn't turn around.

At first, I nodded then realized he couldn't see me. "Yeah. May as well have pissed into the wind." I'd never have admitted it, but I was grateful for his presence. Joss's and Connor's too.

That they'd risked themselves on my account shamed me. If I hadn't been so fucking stubborn, we'd still be topside in the cozy cabin where we'd sheltered for the night.

Finally, Rhys turned and faced us. "We have two choices, and they're not necessarily mutually exclusive. We can join our power and try another jump spell. Or we can see where this tunnel leads. Once we enter, we'll be at its mercy until it spits us out."

"Why wouldn't we be able to retreat?" I asked.

"If you were standing here, you'd feel the pull. It's definitely a one-way corridor."

"Be nice if we knew to where," Joss muttered.

I sidled around him and Connor to where Rhys was and

tested the opening. Enchantment was snatched out of my hands with remarkable speed. "Whoa. See what you mean."

My heartrate escalated again, thumping against my ribcage. We needed a test case. Since this was my fault, it had to be me.

"I'll go," I said. "We'll keep a line of communication open, so I can let you know if it's safe."

"Not sure I even fit in there." Cleyn waddled next to me and peered into the hole.

"It widens and gets taller on the other side," Rhys told him.

Erg. They were ignoring me. No reaction at all to my "I'll go," declaration. Why in the fuck didn't anyone take me seriously? Fueled by anger, my fear retreated to the sidelines.

"Wait until I say it's safe," I shouted and leapt through the opening.

Something like a tractor beam straight out of *Star Trek* grabbed me, propelling me forward at a breathtaking pace. Rhys's shouts and Cleyn's outraged squawks followed me.

Rhys's distinctive energy latched onto my magical center. I lunged ahead, testing the passageway for alien magic. In a too-little-too-late move, I warded myself. My speed slowed incrementally.

The dirt corridor twisted left, right, and then left again. It climbed and sank. One of my worries had been it was another route to the common underground. Unless it rose up to meet my channel, that option appeared increasingly unlikely.

I'd expected Rhys and Cleyn to dive in after me.

Why hadn't they?

"Alia!" Rhys shouted.

"Still here," I called back, followed by, *"Seems okay."*

Cursing was followed by, *"Trying to pry the entry open."*

Mmph. Explained why I was alone in here. An icy chill tracked down my spine. Had I walked into a trap? One set precisely for me, tuned to my specific energy signature? I unwound some of the power I'd been directing in front and checked in a full arc around me. If anyone was here, they were well concealed.

If. Bullshit. Someone's paws had to be all over this. The vector dragging me forward was fueled by magic. I slapped a palm to my forehead.

"Brilliant, Sherlock," I muttered and set about unraveling just whose magic had me in its grasp.

I'm not very good at any of this, so it took me longer than it would have taken Rhys. While I poked and prodded, my trajectory slowed perceptibly until I was moving forward under my own power rather than being dragged.

The tunnel opened into a circular enclosure studded with crystals. A tall, sylphlike creature took shape in front of me. I'm not used to looking up—at anyone—but this... apparition must have topped seven feet. It was garbed in a cream-colored robe that fell to ankle level. Feet sporting long, reptilian toes and bright red talons stuck out beneath. Wispy fair hair poked out at all angles. White eyes with milky pupils regarded me as if I were an intriguing specimen.

The creature's hands were similar to its feet except the talons were longer.

I resisted an inane desire to fall to my knees, but I'd be damned if I'd bow to anyone.

"Why do you trespass?" The creature's voice was multi-tonal and held a buzzing quality. I couldn't tell if its owner was male or female. Perhaps male judging from its height. The language wasn't English, but I understood the meaning well enough.

"Apologies. Wasn't aware that I was."

"Those who trespass on our lands are punished." The thing tilted its head on a stalk of a neck. Faint scales covered its skin.

I nodded. "Again. Apologies. Ever since the world broke, rules haven't been at the top of my playlist."

"You speak in riddles."

Oops. "What I meant was none of the old rules seem to apply any longer."

"They do here."

Rules, eh. It wants rules. I took a step closer and held out a hand. "My name is Alia. Pleased to meet you."

The thing sighed audibly. "You are either very young or very stupid. Never, never offer up your name to a stranger."

Oh, yeah. That little ripple. I dropped my hand to my side and considered asking for clemency and the release of all of us in return for a promise we'd hightail it out of here.

"I have been considering just that." The buzzy quality increased.

I cringed. Of course it could read my thoughts.

"Aye, I can indeed."

Okay. Verification is always nice. My breathing had escalated. I felt trapped, but I stood my ground. "Who are you?"

Its alien visage radiated disbelief. A knifelike sensation probed the side of my head. "You truly do not know."

"If I did, I wouldn't have asked."

"I am a Lemurian. This is my home."

"But I thought you lived under Mount Shasta."

"Boundaries throughout this region are fluid."

"Do you control the common underworld?"

The thing's arm shot out. A thin beam of white light hurt as it jabbed me. "Heresy. Watch your mouth."

I held up both hands. "Sorry. Logical error on my part. Before I found this passageway, I was heading for the underworld, or my griffon thought we were."

"Aye. He is one of the reasons you still draw breath."

It was a long shot. "Do you know C..., er him?" I nearly blurted out his name, but caught myself.

"Aye, in another world and another time."

I tried a different tack. "We are here because we were hoping to shelter beneath your mountain. Nowhere is safe anymore."

"Nor will it ever be again." The Lemurian's face crinkled in what might have been sadness or dismay.

I waited for him—or her—to say more. Minutes ticked past. Was it going to allow me to leave? Where was everyone else?

"Um, if I keep going"—I waved a hand in the direction I'd been moving before the tractor beam spit me out—"will it lead to the surface?"

Milky eyes zeroed in on me as if the thing had forgotten I was standing in front of him. "I control these tunnels."

"Will you let me out of here? And my associates as

well?"

"Gutsy for someone with little leverage and fewer choices."

I swallowed a sharp retort. "If you have plans for me, I'd appreciate knowing about them."

"Your people have requested your return."

There it was. How could the Lemurians possibly have joined forces with Sumerians?

"They are not *my people*. I never even knew about them until they blew up the world."

The Lemurian stared so hard I expected a laser to chop through me. "Your words hold the ring of truth, yet how could that be?"

I settled my hands on my hips. If the creature was going to kill me, I'd be dead. "They created me, held me in stasis for centuries, and only called on my essence once their plans to lay waste to Earth ripened."

"Interesting. They did not entrain your ability?"

I shook my head.

"Perhaps you would do well to return to the fold, youngster."

Breath hissed from between my teeth. "You may as well kill me now. I'd rather be dead than join them."

Through all this, the Lemurian spoke in its language, punctuated by clicks and clacks, but I understood its meaning.

"I see." It raised a hand, talons extended. Power surged around me. "Your friends will be here soon."

Soon was an understatement. Cleyn, Rhys, Connor, and Joss literally blew into the room. The griffon surged toward the Lemurian, wings spread for balance. To my surprise, the Lemurian knelt so they were at eye level and stroked talons over Cleyn's wing feathers.

The griffon made cooing noises. The Lemurian clicked and clacked back.

Rhys grabbed me from behind, holding on for dear life. "Do. Not. Ever—"

I twisted in his arms. "This is my mess. I was trying to clean it up."

He laced a hand into my tangled hair. "Lemurians control everything in this region. Once you jumped through the opening, the stone rolled back into place, blocking the tunnel. I tried everything, everything I tell you, and couldn't get it to budge. Cleyn tried too."

I glanced over a shoulder. Griffon and Lemurian were still deep in conversation. While they were occupied, I placed my mouth near Rhys's ear. "Apparently, the Sumerians have put out the word that they want me returned."

Rhys's mouth twisted into a frown. "Figured it had to be something like that since this had your name all over it."

Connor and Joss sidled close, dusting dirt off their clothing. "Will it let us leave?" Connor asked.

Rhys didn't answer. He let go of me and walked toward Cleyn and the Lemurian. When he got close, he bowed low. "Greetings, Elder."

The Lemurian rose to his full height. "Greetings, sorcerer."

"We seek asylum," Rhys went on. "Even a night or two would help as we determine what to do next."

The Lemurian cocked his head to one side on his stalk of a neck. "Why here?"

"There used to be portals to the Old Country. I would visit my guild house to seek answers in its library."

"Can you not teleport?"

"Aye, but the channels have been poisoned by evil."

"We did not know. But then, we wouldn't, since we have our own portal system as you noted."

I walked between Rhys and Cleyn, waiting for a reply to Rhys's query.

The Lemurian's attention settled on each of us briefly before he said, "I must consult with others. You shall remain here until I return."

"We would prefer to wait above ground," Cleyn said.

"Fine." The Lemurian snapped its jaws. "You will return to your starting point where you will wait for me."

The cavern shattered in a flash of greenish light. When it cleared, we were back in the shed. I started for the door.

Pain seared my upper arm as Cleyn grabbed me with his beak. "He said wait here."

"Ouch. Let go."

"Only once you promise to stay put. For once."

Grumbling under my breath, I sank to a crouch. "Any idea how long he'll be?" I asked.

"No, but we will remain for as long as it takes."

Before I could ask why, Rhys cut in with, "How do you know the Lemurian?"

"I'd like to know, too," Joss said.

"'Twill be a good way to pass the time," Cleyn replied. "Millennia ago, my family and clan were still alive..."

CHAPTER TWELVE, RHYS

Fury vied with annoyance and sheer terror when the stone blocking the passage ground into place blocking access. That it happened right after Alia bolted through meant this had to be a trap, one designed uniquely for her.

Perhaps it explained her stubborn insistence that placed her squarely in harm's way. After one miscalculation had landed her plummeting toward Hell, I'd have thought she'd be more careful.

Whoever was orchestrating this was probably planting subliminal suggestions. Alia was headstrong, willful, but she was far from stupid. And she'd never drag the rest of us into danger unless it couldn't be helped.

None of my musings made me feel a whit better.

"What are we going to do?" Connor left off battering the large, rectangular stone with shifter magic.

"Move over." My tone was gruff. I was mostly certain

nothing I could do would alter the status quo, but I tried my damnedest anyway. After cycling through each of the four elements, I began working on combinations.

The griffon was uncharacteristically silent.

Despite the chill of our underground perch, sweat beaded my face. I swiped the back of a hand across my forehead to keep it from rolling into my eyes.

"Can we help?" Joss asked.

"Don't see how," I muttered and withdrew the power I'd been battering the rock with. Running my ability down to fumes wouldn't help anyone.

My breath came fast; I rocked back on my heels regarding the intransigent piece of granite and urging it to communicate with me.

"It's Lemurians," Cleyn said.

I stared at the griffon. "How? We're a couple of miles from Mount Shasta."

"Doesn't matter. This is their territory. I feel their power. If you'd slow down long enough to pay attention, you would too."

Ouch. That stung. Still, he was right. Absorbed by my single-minded effort to reach Alia, rational thought had all but deserted me. I gathered my skill close, intent on a five-minute break before I tried anything else, like assessing ambient energy signatures.

"What the fuck," Joss cried just before the stone slammed against its stops and a hurricane-force gale dragged us through the opening and along the corridor. Cleyn first then Joss then Connor then me.

My first impulse was to fight against the power that had

us in thrall except it was bringing us closer to Alia. I felt her essence pulsing brighter as we were dragged forward.

Connor's hawk formed behind him, a sure sign the shifter was nervous. Hard to fault him. For all I knew, this was a one-way street to shackles and a cell it would be tough to break out of.

The tunnel opened into a rounded cave perhaps fifty feet across. Alia's mage light illuminated both it and her companion, a Lemurian. Score points for the griffon. He'd known.

I might have if I'd taken the time to run an assessment. Being blinded by my love for Alia wasn't helping any of us. To my surprise, Cleyn made a beeline for the Lemurian, who knelt so they were at eye level. The two touched and made cooing noises.

I wrapped my arms around Alia from behind, thankful beyond words she was whole. "Do. Not. Ever—"

"This is my mess. I was trying to clean it up."

She turned in my arms; I threaded fingers into her tangled hair. "Lemurians control everything in this region. Once you jumped through the opening, the stone rolled back into place, blocking the tunnel. I tried everything, everything I tell you, and couldn't get it to budge. Cleyn tried too."

Alia spoke softly right next to my ear. "Apparently, the Sumerians have put out the word they want me returned."

No wonder I hadn't made any headway with the stone. "Figured it had to be something like that since this had your name all over it."

Connor and Joss walked to where we stood dusting dirt off hands and clothing. "Will it let us leave?" Connor asked.

Rather than answer, I strode toward Cleyn and the Lemurian and bowed low. "Greetings, Elder."

The Lemurian folded upright creakily. "Greetings, sorcerer."

"We seek asylum," I continued. "Even a night or two would help as we determine what to do next."

The Lemurian regarded me as if I were a not-very-interesting specimen. "Why here?"

"There used to be portals to the Old Country. I would visit my guild house to seek answers in its library."

"Can you not teleport?"

"Aye, but the channels have been poisoned by evil."

"We did not know. But then, we wouldn't, since we have our own portal system."

Alia moved until she stood between Cleyn and me. The Lemurian sniffed audibly before he said, "I must consult with others. You shall remain here until I return."

"We would prefer to wait above ground," Cleyn said.

The Lemurian snapped its jaws. "You will return to your starting point where you will wait for me."

He wasn't kidding. The cavern disintegrated, accompanied by flashes of green light. Five seconds later, we were back in the empty shed. Alia started for the door and yelped when Cleyn grabbed her biceps with his sharp beak.

"He said wait here," the griffon said sternly.

"Ouch. Let go." Alia twisted this way and that.

"Only once you promise to stay put. For once."

Alia folded into a crouch. Cleyn released her partway down. "Any idea how long he'll be?" she asked.

"No, but we will remain for as long as it takes."

The griffon was being hard on Alia, but following orders wasn't her forte. I batted back a desire to defend her and switched subjects by asking Cleyn how he knew the Lemurian.

"I'd like to know too," Joss said.

"'Twill be a good way to pass the time," Cleyn replied. "Millennia ago, my family and clan were still alive. All the elder mages of the world considered ourselves kinsmen. We visited one another amongst different locales both on and off Earth, experimented with spells and magecraft, and enjoyed one another's company. In those days, Mu was still a continent, and we passed many an idyllic month there. The Lemurians were always pleasant hosts."

"Um, wait a moment," Alia said.

The griffon focused lidless avian eyes on her and batted a wing her way.

"I thought the Sumerians created you when they created me."

Cleyn shook his feathered head. "Nay. They merely tapped me to be the one tasked with your safety."

"Wonder how I got that wrong," she mumbled, followed by, "Go on."

"A cataclysm upended Mu. It took its sweet time sinking, though. Could have taken a hundred years from the beginning to when the top of the tallest mountain range sank beneath the sea. During that time, the Lemurians deployed scouts to search for a new home. They tested several locations and finally decided the innate energy surrounding Mount Shata was as close a match for their enchantment as they were likely to find."

The griffon paused for a couple of beak clacks before continuing. "Akbar and I met when he was scouring the Greek Islands in search of a new home."

"That's his name?" I broke in.

Cleyn nodded. "Except it's not a him, or a her. They're actually both."

I'd known that.

"How do they have children? Or do they?" Joss asked.

"They're hermaphroditic," I replied. "While I'm unsure of the mechanics, they inseminate themselves, but they produce very few children."

"Is there some deciding factor like a lottery?" Connor cut in.

I shrugged.

"No one knows," Cleyn told him. "They have always been closemouthed about what they consider personal business. Back to Akbar, we always got on well. Our magic meshed seamlessly. He is one of very few outside my clan I consider a friend."

Alia pushed upright and walked to the griffon. "First off, I'm so sorry I didn't listen when you told me to leave the shed. I have no idea what got into me."

"I do," I said sourly. "Even then, you were being manipulated."

"But how? I was warded. Mostly."

"Stronger magic than yours exists." Cleyn shook a talon at her.

Alia's pale cheeks developed a rosy hue. She looked away. "I deserved that."

"No one deserves any of this," Connor said.

"But here we are," Joss murmured.

Alia flapped a hand our way. "I wasn't finished," she told the griffon. "The second thing I wanted to say was I'm happy you've been reunited with Akbar. At one point he said you were the reason I was still alive."

"What I suspect happened," Cleyn went on, "is the Sumerians have made it known they want either you, or you and me, returned. There may well be a generous reward."

"Right as usual." The clicks and clacks of the Lemurian tongue announced Akbar before I could see him.

Rather than stepping through a portal, he took his sweet time becoming corporeal. Was it a sign his power was waning? Or that of his people? I shuttered my thoughts as fast as I could. I'd requested a boon. Like as not, he'd view any disparaging assessment of his power as grounds to give us the boot posthaste.

Alia restrained herself until the Lemurian was fully visible before standing toe-to-toe with him. Head tilted back to make eye contact, she announced. "No matter what you've decided, I will die before I allow you to forcibly return me to the Sumerians. They ignored my existence until they blew up the world. And then they assumed I'd be their lackey."

Spots of color formed on her cheeks. "At first, they were shocked when I pushed back, and then they were furious. They've been setting traps for me ever since. For Cleyn too. Pfft. As if we don't have enough problems."

I readied defensive magic as surreptitiously as possible in case the Lemurian took exception to Alia's forthright manner. It was scarcely an even match—unless my guess about his waning ability had been spot on.

The corners of Akbar's long, thin mouth twitched before he tossed back his head and howled laughter. When he was done, he blurted, "They only think they want you returned. You'd be more trouble than you're worth to them."

"That's just it," Alia plowed on. "I'm worth nothing to them. At whatever point someone had the bright idea of creating me, I was supposed to be some sort of envoy between past and present. Except, they wiped out so much of humanity, my position on the game board became moot."

Akbar cleared his throat. It sounded like a muffled buzzsaw. "The consensus amongst us is to let things be. You cannot remain here for long, yet a few days would be acceptable—so long as you do not make any trouble. Many have sought shelter beneath our mountain. Maintaining peace is critical. The energy currents linking Mount Shasta to other places are sensitive to disturbances."

His flattened nostrils flared as he sucked in a breath. "'Tis little known, but violent disagreements were what caused the downfall of Mu. We would avoid another such disaster."

I worked to maintain an even expression. I'd always assumed Mu had fallen secondary to natural causes. "Were the perpetrators ever brought to justice?" I asked.

"And then some." The Lemurian made a sour face.

Visions of drawing and quartering or keelhauling rolled across my mind, followed by asps feeding on tender flesh as they injected lethal toxins. Had I come up with those things? Or was Akbar funneling them to me.

His statements must have sunk in because Alia lowered her gaze and murmured, "Thank you very much. All of us are tired. We could use a few days' respite."

Akbar shook a tapering index finger her way. "It cannot be more than that. So long as we are clear. You will bide one more night in the witches' hut. Once the morn arrives, come to the opening at the base of the mountain. I shall instruct it to allow you entry."

Before I could tack down the precise location of the opening he was referring to, he was gone.

"Not quite what I'd hoped for," I murmured.

"Better than nothing," Connor said.

Alia slid the rolling door to the hut open. A gaggle of creatures dashed inside, including the mother mountain lion and her kits. This was clearly their home. Other routes leading within probably existed, but they'd been leery of expended magic.

Alia walked outside; the rest of us trailed after her. Light was leaching from the day. We'd burned through hours underground.

Cleyn spread his wings. I didn't ask where he was going. We were near enough to his Lemurian friends, he should be safe.

"I'm going to hunt for greens for a stew," Joss announced.

"I'll help," Connor said. "We'll lose the light soon, and your task will go quicker with two."

"Feel like a walk before we go into the hut?" I asked Alia and offered a hand.

She nodded and laced her fingers with mine. I set out

along the road leading to the cabin. For a time, we walked in silence.

"Will we ever find a place where we can stop running?" she asked.

"We're not exactly running," I reminded her.

"Yeah, we are. Sedona didn't work out. We lost the shifter sisters and Nola the witch. Every spot we try to stop feels...unfriendly."

We reached a T-junction in the road. To the west, the sky was turning blue and violet with the sunset. At least some small pieces hadn't changed. I stopped walking and wrapped my arms around her.

"We could have had a worse outcome."

She shivered against me. "I'm whining, but I've never not had a home."

I stroked her hair and started to tell her this was temporary, but I sat on my words. They weren't true. I also didn't say everything would be okay. We were living on the ragged edge and dependent on many elements outside our direct control.

"I know all that," she mumbled. "Are you really planning another trip to your guild house?"

"Yes. We didn't get enough time there before."

She tilted her head and looked at me. "Didn't you mention the Lemurians might have source materials?"

"Assuming they salvaged their books and scrolls before Mu sank, then they do, indeed."

"Why not start there?"

"Because they might not welcome me."

"Doesn't hurt to ask. Did they have seers?"

I nodded.

"Would they be willing to talk with us?"

I had no idea, but it was one more avenue to explore. "Cleyn has an in with them."

"Perfect. We'll ask him to run point."

The swoosh of wings overhead drew my gaze upward. Perhaps the griffon had sensed us talking about him because he was winging toward the cabin. Something dangled from his beak and both front talons.

"Looks like he hunted for all of us." I pointed in his direction.

"We should head back," Alia murmured. "I used to love nighttime—until I found out about vampires and werewolves."

"Oh come on." I tried for a bantering tone. "Surely, you knew about them before."

"Yeah, but back then I didn't think they were real. At least it's been a while since we've seen a Watcher." She made a face and laughed hollowly.

We retraced our steps. Nearby trees whispered in a gentle breeze, boughs sighing as they brushed against each other.

Alia reached for my hand again. "Thanks for sticking by me in spite of the stupid shit I pull."

I grasped her chilly fingers. "Some of it is scarcely your fault."

"You're being kind. I've always had tunnel vision when I want something."

"We'll never know why you insisted on holing up in the shed and then bolting down the tunnel. My money's on

Lemurians being behind it. Don't waste time replaying what's already happened. Work on your magic. We need you at the top of your game."

"Ever practical." She leaned into me.

Cleyn met us in the yard. "Rabbits are on the porch. Going back for a few more for myself."

He'd no sooner spread his wings and left when Joss and Connor came into view. They'd turned Connor's jacket into a basket filled with greens. The rich smells of loam and freshly uprooted vegetation tickled my nostrils.

Connor cupped a hand around his mouth and yelled, "Thank you," in Cleyn's general direction before trooping up the steps and into the hut.

Alia and I followed them to the front porch. I snatched up three fat rabbits. "Be back as soon as I've cleaned and gutted them," I said.

"Bet the entrails would be a hit in the shed." Alia smiled and slipped through the open door.

I slid the small dirk I always carry from its sheathe and made my way back to the shed. Once within, I kindled a light, keeping it low, and went to work. I've been in positions like this before, ones where I lived from moment to moment. Something had always intervened.

This time, the *something* was us. What we did—or didn't do—would make all the difference. Not a whole lot of latitude to choose wrong.

How firm was Akbar's timeline? Was his method of counting days the same as ours? Maybe if we made ourselves both invisible and useful, he'd relent and allow us to remain longer.

We needed allies. So far, they'd been few and far between. He'd alluded to many mages seeking asylum beneath the mountain. Had all of them started their tenure on probation?

I tossed the last bits of innards into the darkness and was rewarded by a rich purr. After dousing my light, I walked out the door, sliding it mostly shut behind me. We'd see what tomorrow brought.

For tonight, I'd follow my own advice and live in the moment. The homey smells of cooking wafted my way as I covered the short distance to the hut. Before I went inside, I checked for Cleyn, gratified to feel the griffon moving closer.

I waited until he touched down before I motioned him inside. Satisfied my little brood was safe, I followed him and sealed the doorway with magic.

CHAPTER THIRTEEN, ALIA

The rabbit stew had been delectable with wild onions, watercress, anise, and a couple of other items I wasn't familiar with. Such a stroke of luck one of us enjoyed cooking. Enough remained in the pot to take care of breakfast. Connor and Joss had sacked out in front of the woodstove. Now that I was familiar with the lay of the land, I'd hauled in more wood while dinner was cooking. Cleyn hunkered over the remains of his rabbits, cleaning his feathers.

Rhys and I lay on the bed. I hadn't wanted to disturb it the previous night, but some sixth sense told me the witches wouldn't return for a long while—if ever. It was late, past midnight judging from the juxtaposition of stars and moon barely visible through the dirty window. I should sleep, but worry dogged me.

Worry about things I had no control over. My hamster-wheel thoughts led to the same place over and over. I was a magnet for trouble. The group would be better off if I went off on my own, duked it out with the Sumerians, and let the chips fall where they would.

What in the hell was wrong with me? Why did I have one foot out the door? It wasn't like me. Even though I'd had painfully few friends in my short life, I was always loyal. I shut my eyes. They felt hot, gritty. Was Rhys onto something when he'd suspected my thoughts weren't entirely my own?

A creepy, crawling sensation worked its way down my spine leaving a cold sweat in its wake. Had the Sumerians inserted some kind of remote access programming into my makeup? I squeezed my eyes shut tighter and chided myself for being ridiculous, a product of too many science fiction novels.

It had never occurred to them they'd need to control me. The root of their current snit was I hadn't turned out to be the docile minion they'd anticipated. I moved nearer Rhys, careful not to waken him, and cleared my mind. I was part of this team, goddammit. Who knew what the morrow would bring, but I'd be better prepared if I wasn't running on fumes.

I wove a calming spell not expecting much. Results were far from instant, but when I opened my eyes, daylight spilled through the window. Cleyn's head was under his wing. Other than that, no one had stirred from their positions the night before.

I didn't feel as crappy as I'd thought I would.

"Morning." Rhys's voice was scratchy from sleep.

I wanted to snuggle close and shut out the world, but it wasn't possible.

He chuckled softly. "We'll find time together at some point."

"You're in my head again."

A lopsided grin split his striking face. "What else is new?"

Joss groaned. "Ugh. You're talking. Must be time to get rolling."

After a couple of muted beak clacks, Cleyn stretched his neck and waddled toward the door.

"Hang on," Rhys told him. "I sealed us inside." A beam of white light flowed from him to the cabin's door. It popped open.

"Don't go far," I called after Cleyn. He didn't answer, but I heard the scratch of talons on wood as he hopped down the stairs.

It didn't take long for the lot of us to set ourselves to rights. By the time I returned from a handy outhouse, Joss had dished up the remainder of last night's dinner.

"Do you know where Akbar meant for us to enter their stronghold?" Connor asked Rhys between bites.

"Not exactly, but we should be able to sense the proper spot when we get closer."

"I wonder what happened to the witches who used to live here," I mused as I scraped the last of the food out of my bowl.

"Probably part of the collection of mages living under Mount Shasta," Rhys replied.

"But why there when they have a house so close?"

"What made you think about them?" Joss arched a russet brow.

"Pretty sure I dreamed about them." I set my fork down. "If I'm correct, two women lived here. Back before the mortals were wiped out, they did a fair trade in spells, herbs, and potions."

Rhys scraped his chair against the floorboards as he got up. Gathering dishes, he carried them to the sink and pumped water into it. Joss stood and grabbed a dishtowel, drying bowls and utensils once Rhys finished with them.

I flattened my palms against the table's uneven surface and got to my feet. After my rough go before falling asleep, I'd done a credible job remaining in the present. Curiosity about what we'd find underneath the magical mountain eclipsed worries about what we'd do once our time here was up. I tidied the bed just in case the witches returned.

Maybe I'd get used to being a vagabond.

No maybe about it since it was the only game in town.

While the men finished the dishes, I wandered outside. A weak sun suggested it was around ten. The day wasn't overly cold, and there wasn't any wind. The swoosh of wings told me Cleyn was returning. He skidded to a landing a few feet away. I'd figured he'd gone hunting, but nothing dangled from his beak or claws.

"Where'd you go?" I asked.

"To look at the mountain."

I waited, but he didn't add anything, so I added, "Find anything?"

He nodded. "I spoke with Akbar and two of his kinsmen. They were wondering why we hadn't yet arrived."

"What'd you tell them?"

"That we'd be along presently."

Rhys, Joss, and Connor emerged. Rhys shut the door and muttered an incantation designed to keep mortals out. We hadn't had much when we arrived. Joss and Connor carried bags with the remains of the junk food they'd gathered from earlier stops.

"Cleyn's already been to the mountain," I told the men.

"What'd you find out?" Rhys asked.

"Only that they expected us earlier. We should leave."

Rhys frowned but thought better of saying anything beyond, "Lead out since you know where the entry point is."

"Head northwest." The griffon extended a wing. "I will meet you in a large clearing next to the base of the mountain."

I sent warm thoughts to the mountain lion and her cubs before starting out at a brisk trot. Rhys led us along the same road we'd trod the night before. Other cabins dotted the roadway, growing more numerous as we neared the remains of town.

By now, I'd grown used to the collection of abandoned vehicles lining nearly every street. Something else caught my attention, though. "Why aren't all the buildings falling in?" I asked.

"I was wondering the same," Joss murmured.

"The mountain's energy must have conferred a level of protection," Rhys replied. "Might bode well for locating mortals who escaped the cataclysm."

I didn't see what good they could do but stopped myself. If Earth was going to recover, it would need a critical mass of committed workers.

We traipsed through the deserted town. I sent rays of

seeking enchantment this way and that, receiving an occasional ping in return. Mostly animals, but a few people as well. Rhys was onto something with his theory about protective energy.

The road turned uphill. We passed a sign saying the turnoff to the ski area was in four miles. We could have employed a jump spell or borrowed one of the abandoned vehicles.

"We could have driven," I said.

"We could have," Rhys agreed without adding anything else.

A rutted track led off the road. We started along it.

"Best to not comingle trappings of modern times with ancient magic," Rhys said long after my comment about driving. So long, it took a little while for me to connect the two.

He stopped and turned to face us. "Remember, we are guests here. No matter what anyone says, don't argue or talk back."

"That might be...difficult," I admitted. "Depending on context."

"Once they figure out you and Cleyn are an elemental part of why they're holed up beneath Mount Shasta, comments could turn ugly," Rhys explained, followed by, "forewarned is forearmed."

After that sobering warning, we covered the next couple of miles in silence. I felt prickles and a hot-and-cold sensation the farther we went, no doubt a by-product of the mountain's strong magic. The griffon circled overhead. He'd materialized about the time we left the highway. When he wasn't flying figure eights, he led us in the same direction as the cattle track we were following.

We crested a steep rise. At the bottom, a small group of Lemurians stared in our direction. Cleyn fluttered to the ground next to them. One detached from the others and joined the griffon. Had to be Akbar. At least from this distance, the Lemurians all looked quite similar with their long, lanky bodies, wispy hair, and milky eyes. Granted, their robes were different colors, but it seemed to be the only distinction.

"Half the day is gone," Akbar said by way of greeting when we were a few feet away.

Rhys bowed low. When he straightened, he replied, "Apologies, Elder. I did not realize you wanted us here earlier."

Akbar sniffed audibly, flattened nostrils flaring. "Your memory is poor, mage. You requested asylum. Least you could have done was be on time."

I opened my mouth to protest we hadn't been assigned a time but shut it fast. Getting along was the name of today's game. Contradicting our primary host would buy me less than nothing.

"Apologies." Rhys bowed again.

The Lemurians clicked and clacked at one another. I made a note to ask Cleyn if he understood their language. My bet was he did.

"Once you are within," Akbar said, "you may not leave until one of us releases you."

If I'd had hackles, they'd have shot up the length of my back. Being imprisoned isn't high on my list.

"*Ssht,*" rustled through my mind, courtesy of Rhys. He knows me way too well.

"Follow us," Akbar continued. "Interaction with others is not allowed unless we give you leave."

That did it. "If we can't say anything to anyone," I piped up, "why warn us we have to get along?"

"You will see," one of the other Lemurians replied and strode toward what appeared to be an impenetrable wall at the base of the mountain. The energy I'd noticed a while back pulsed more strongly. Not exactly welcoming, it held shades of warning. The hot-and-cold intensified. The prickles grew painful.

Did everyone feel the same thing as me? I wanted to ask but didn't.

The lichen-covered rock wall swung inward on unseen hinges. Cleyn was with the group of Lemurians. Rhys had moved to my side and taken my hand. Connor and Joss were behind us.

"*Have you ever been inside?*" I asked Rhys in what I hoped was shielded mind speech.

Rather than answering, he said, "*We'll talk later.*"

The sound of stones grating together rasped against my ears as the gateway shut behind us. Was it the only one? Concern about finding it again loomed large, so I built a rough map in my head as we walked.

Darkness yielded to shadowed light as rush lanterns flickered to life. We were in a circular chamber studded with crystals that reflected the light at crazy angles. The effect was beautiful in a mesmerizing way. I would have stopped to examine the stones more closely if Rhys hadn't had my hand in a death grip.

The chamber opened into a gradually down sloping tunnel with rounded sides. Doors opened on both sides; we walked past several sets. The hum of voices and the feel of expended magic—burnt and laced with ozone—followed us. After a time, the tunnel took a hard right turn and began to climb. Eventually, it opened into a common room.

More than twenty mages glanced our way, but no one greeted us. A quick scan revealed shifters, sorcerers, witches, and some oddball magics I'd never run across before. Big surprise. My tenure in the magical world was short by anyone's standards.

"Thought we were done with newcomers," a shifter grumbled.

"We were," Akbar clacked. "Meet Cleyn, Rhys, Alia, Connor, and Joss. They will be bound to our rules regarding silence until I release them."

Sharp probing turned my skull into a throbbing, painful nightmare. Hissing with pain, I warded myself.

"What of food?" Cleyn squawked. "If we cannot leave, we cannot hunt."

"Water and provisions will be made available," Akbar told his friend.

"Where?" the griffon pressed. "I do not smell anything edible."

"This was a bad idea," another of the Lemurians clacked.

"I will see to their needs." A short squat woman wearing black witch's robes padded forward. "They stayed in my cabin and left it as they found it."

How in the hell did she know? Was she linked to her home in some arcane way? Seemed plausible.

Grateful I'd had the presence of mind to make the bed, I nodded thanks her way. Too late I remembered the no communication rule. Since I couldn't withdraw my nod, I laced my fingers behind my back and looked away. How were we going to share space with all these people and avoid talking with them?

"Now that you have met others in similar circumstances, come with us." The Lemurian contingent exited the chamber. We trailed after them.

Half an hour later after circuitous ups and downs that left me guessing about our actual location, we ended up in another cave not unlike the one with the other magic-wielders.

Muted power flared from Rhys as he explored our appointed place. The Lemurians turned as a unit, intent on leaving. Did they operate from a type of hive mind?

"If you could, hold up a moment, please." Rhys walked toward Akbar.

"Do not make me sorry I offered you this boon, mage," the Lemurian growled sounding like Cleyn when he was in lion mode.

"I'll do my best." Rhys's tone was mild. "The primary reason we requested a brief stay here was to access the portal system."

"'Tis why we brought you here," another Lemurian clacked. "Can you not feel its pull?"

Rhys shook his head. "No, but if there is one nearby, I

will find it. Do I have your leave to utilize your portal system?"

After a pause that was a shade too long for my taste, Akbar barked, "Aye," and hurried from the cave.

"That was odd," Connor said.

"Yeah, why not leave us with the others?" Joss chimed in.

"They worry about the integrity of their kingdom," Cleyn squawked. "Let's look around."

I didn't see how adding us to the group we'd met would spawn an insurrection, but what did I know.

The griffon glided forward with his awkward gait and almost collided with the witch we'd met in the other cavern. She bustled through the door and dumped a generous armload of raw meat and greens on a square of canvas in the center of the room. Good provisions for the griffon; marginal for the rest of us.

Joss and Connor still had their bags of junk food. Maybe we wouldn't be here long enough to starve. I held no illusions about being able to find our way back to our entry point.

The witch was gone as quickly as she'd arrived.

Cleyn shuffled into the corridor. We joined him. Something similar to a flare materialized next to him and plopped to the ground. "So we can find our way back," he explained.

No longer constrained by the Lemurians' presence, power flowed from Rhys as he searched for the gateways that were supposed to be nearby. "This way," he said tersely.

"Um, they only gave you permission," Joss pointed out.

"They didn't say only me," Rhys muttered.

"That's splitting hairs," I spoke up. "You asked if you

could use their gateways, and they said *yes*. I'm not seeing where it gives the rest of us..."

He shot a stern look my way. "I am not leaving you here. Any of you."

A bugling hoot from Cleyn brought us at a run. He stood in front of an iridescent panel that flowed from as far up as I could see before being absorbed by the dirt floor. Colors ebbed and flowed. The panel was about three feet wide. I tilted my head to hear its song. Almost as if it knew it had my attention, notes soared, filling my chest with poignant emotion.

"It seems to know us," I murmured.

Rhys clamped a hand around my upper arm hard enough to hurt. "Do not allow it entry."

"Good to know," Connor mumbled. The specter of his hawk formed behind him, wings fluttering.

"We need to leave now," Cleyn hooted. "We will meet on the Isle of Skye, the southwestern beaches."

Faint scratching suggested our hosts were approaching. The griffon jumped through the panel, wings tucked against his broad back. Rhys moved his hand down until he clasped mine. "Hang onto one another," he instructed Joss and Connor. "I've just sent you an image of our destination."

"Got it," Joss said tersely. He and Connor followed Cleyn.

"This wasn't part of the agreement," floated from behind us just before Rhys pulled me through. Great. We'd pissed off our hosts. Would they bar the gates so we couldn't return?

Worse, could they sabotage their own portal system, so

we ended up on some barren borderworld. "Told you they wouldn't like it," I mumbled.

"Too late," Rhys said. "I tossed the dice and may have won. We'll know in the next couple of minutes."

"Know what?" Tension wrapped around the base of my spine like a cobra.

The familiar feel of Rhys's power surrounded me. I clung to the same image he'd sent Joss and Connor trying to boost our odds of success. The portal's song first quieted and then sour notes interspersed. A discordant symphony stating louder than words we were no longer welcome.

The darkness around us developed lighter edges.

"Won't be long now," Rhys said.

I pushed toward the beach blazoned across my mind. Pushed and hoped and prayed, although I wasn't the praying type.

With no warning, we punched through a barrier and tumbled downward. I lost Rhys's hand and drew air currents into a basket to cushion my fall. Wherever we were, it was daylight, which helped. An island took shape beneath me.

Was it the right one?

Wet sand studded with rocks rose up and met me. Luckily, I didn't land on any of the sharp boulders. They'd surely have broken something. Before I had a chance to roll to my feet, Rhys ran toward me.

"Come on," he yelled. "Cleyn's in trouble."

Motion caught the corners of my eyes. Joss and Connor were bolting toward something. Upright, I followed Rhys taking care not to twist an ankle on ice-slick rocks. I heard bellowing. What in the hell was Cleyn fighting? We cleared a boulder field that had obstructed my vision.

The griffon stood in the midst of a writhing mass of tentacles, hissing and roaring. What in the fuck was it? Dark gray and studded with barnacles or limpets it looked like a cross between an octopus and artists' renditions of the Loch Ness monster. Eyes bulged all around its obscene head, red with inky pupils.

Connor had shifted and was flying this way and that, pecking at the monster. Rhys shot bolts of power into the creature's head. I waded into the fray, slashing at the thing with a sword that had materialized in one hand. For every tentacle I chopped through, another grew to take its place.

Christ, was this a *fuck you* from the Lemurians? I didn't see how it could be, yet I wouldn't put it past them.

"Alia!" Joss screeched.

I pivoted, twisted, but didn't see the tentacle that wound around my waist until it was too late. The thing lifted me high in the air. If I sliced through it, I'd fall.

The tentacle squeezed tighter, cutting off breath. Trapped between falling and suffocating, I began hacking at the tentacle with the sword, but the angle was awkward.

My lungs burned from lack of air. My vision hazed over with a grayish light. I stabbed over and over, desperate to be free. Rhys and Joss called to me, yelled what might have been instructions or encouragement, but my ears weren't working well.

Fumes from spilled monster blood made me even more lightheaded. Giving up on the sword, I focused a bolus of destructive power and sent it spiraling into the thing's massive head. The combination of limited oxygen and toxic gases was horrible. Plus, the thing stank of rot over and above its noxious blood.

If I died so Cleyn and the others could live, so be it. Digging deep, I sent one more blast of destruction into the monster's hideous rounded head before everything turned black.

CHAPTER FOURTEEN, RHYS

I hadn't thought the Lemurians would put up a fight to hold us beneath Mount Shasta. Still, I'd hoped to remain on good enough terms with them to return courtesy of their portal system. If they were furious about what I'd frame as an honest misunderstanding about just who would be utilizing their gateway, not much I could do about it.

I've always been of the school it's better to ask forgiveness than permission. Had I mentioned all of us would go along for the ride, Akbar might have said no. In that case, I'd have been clearly in the wrong. The way things stood, I was hoping for sufficient gray area to bail us out.

They left us alone in the transit channel. If they'd chosen, they could have intervened. After all, we were squarely on their turf.

The journey had been smooth until the tail end when

we'd been chucked into chilly marine air. Even that hadn't posed a problem. Not until we landed on a barren spit of land, and Cleyn's bellowing alerted me to his predicament.

I reached with magic to determine what we faced and reeled it in quickly.

Where in the hell did a kraken come from? They'd plied the Irish Sea centuries ago, but I'd assumed they'd either died out or moved off world or retreated to the ocean bottom.

Perhaps the others had, but the one battling the griffon was plenty real. Judging from his size, he was one of their elders. The absence of mortals with their stun guns and boats might have encouraged him to scout out one of his kinsmen's old haunts.

Hard to say about these things. Ancient beyond measure, krakens were mostly brawn. The ones I'd met had been quite thick-headed. I hated to harm him, but losing Cleyn was unthinkable, so I hurled bolt after bolt of destructive enchantment at his thick, scaled hide.

Connor had shifted. His hawk dive-bombed, pecked, withdrew, and did it again. He tried for spots that might make a difference, but the kraken's hide was like untanned leather. Joss threw rocks, aiming for eyes. He managed to take out two of them, but many remained.

Cleyn shrieked, hissed, and buried his beak in the creature. A tentacle was wrapped around the griffon's midsection where he concentrated his efforts to free himself.

Alia looked like an eldritch goddess. Light streamed from her as she went into full attack mode. Joss saw the kraken make a move before I did. With unbelievable speed, another tentacle trapped Alia.

I made my way toward her, leaping over unpredictable tentacles. They lashed this way and that with no apparent pattern. All the while, I kept up my barrage of destruction, aiming for his head and remaining eyes. If it couldn't see, we'd have effectively crippled it.

Krakens are almost impossible to kill, particularly the elders, since their hides grew thicker with each passing year.

Alia went from upright and chucking magic to slumped over. Had the tentacle choked the life out of her? "Hang on," I screeched and grabbed the nearest tentacle, intent on scaling it to gain proximity to her position close to the kraken's body.

Meanwhile, I tried something else.

"We are not your enemy," I called in old Gaelic, a language I was certain it understood.

In the momentary pause, when its attention shifted to me, Cleyn wriggled free. Wings spread, he pumped furiously to establish space between him and the kraken.

"Alia. Wake up." I jabbed her mind along with my words. She didn't stir.

Using magic to balance me, I climbed the tentacle I'd taken possession of with one hand extended to snatch the sword from Alia's hand. Despite her desperate condition, she hadn't let it go.

One of Joss's stones flew past, nearly clipping my shoulder.

Connor's wings brushed against me as he closed for another attack. The griffon moved in from the other side and grabbed the tentacle upstream from Alia with his sharp front talons. Once he had a good grip, he ripped and tore, intent on separating the appendage from the kraken's body.

I was close to the sword. Almost there. Alia's fingers opened. Before the weapon clattered to the beach, I lunged and snatched it. The blade cut into me, but my blood would marry with the sword's magic.

The kraken's roaring nearly deafened me. Repositioning my hand around the hilt, I hacked at the tentacle holding Alia prisoner. Between Cleyn ripping reptilian flesh and me slicing as near Alia as I dared, the kraken must have decided he was engaged in a losing battle.

With no warning, the tentacle slithered from its attachment point. Still wrapped around Alia, the whole thing plummeted toward wet sand. Cleyn was quicker than me. He dove beneath her and cushioned her fall with outstretched wings.

I leapt to the ground, sword still in one hand. Dropping it, I rushed to Alia and tugged the ruined tentacle away from her body. It wasn't easy. Joss helped. Connor too, back in his human form.

As soon as I arrived, Cleyn slithered out from beneath Alia and raced along the beach after the departing monster who was heading for the sea. He must have decided we weren't worth the trouble.

Or he was looking for reinforcements.

I couldn't worry about any of that. Finally extricated, Alia slumped against my chest where I held her close. Life still beat strongly within her. Why wasn't she coming around?

Cleyn skidded close. "He's gone. What's wrong with her?"

"Not sure. Come close, everyone. I'm jumping us to my guild house. It's not far."

"Maybe they'll have robes or something," Connor said through chattering teeth.

Of course, he'd be cold. His clothing must be in tatters from shifting. I launched my jump spell. The stone walls of the medieval manor house my guild had claimed for its own rose around us.

Footsteps clattered against scarred wooden floors. Of course, my guild brothers would have felt us arrive.

Micah led the group, iridescent light blazing around him. "For the love of the goddess," he sputtered. "You nearly gave us heart attacks." Tall and thin, coal-black hair framed a bony face with a squared-off chin and a beak of a nose. Green eyes blazed with indignation.

"You're the source of this madness," Brice pronounced.

"Aye," Darius seconded. "How dare you show your face within these walls." Russet hair streamed down his back; green eyes glared at me.

I walked toward them, Alia still clasped against me. "Shove it, Darius. I need a healer. We had a run in with a kraken on the beach, and—"

"But they left eons ago," Micah protested.

"Not this one," Cleyn squawked.

Perhaps the others hadn't noticed the griffon because a collective sharp intake of breath filled the hallway.

"We'll tell you everything later," I said and started for

where the infirmary used to be. I was prepared to mow down anyone who stood in my way, but no one did.

Someone must have communicated with Thos and Morris, twins who'd been our healers since the middle of the 1500s because the door to their domain stood open.

"What happened?" Thos asked as I laid Alia on a raised dais.

"Kraken tried to squeeze the life out of her."

"Step back, Rhys. Give us space," Morris instructed.

I didn't want to leave her side, but I retreated a pace or two. Meanwhile, Joss, Connor, and Cleyn joined us.

Morris's russet brows crawled up his forehead, but he didn't question why a griffon was with me. Identical to his twin, bright hair streamed down his back. He wore blue robes that matched his eyes. An onyx amulet hung around his neck. It hummed with suppressed magic. Thos wore an identical amulet but crafted from a fire opal. I'd always suspected the stones complemented one another's energy. The twins were slender and on the shortish side. Both wore leather sandals.

Connor was still shivering.

Micah must have noticed because he entered the infirmary with a woolen robe slung across one arm. "Return it when you can," he said gruffly and handed it to Connor.

"Thank you. Didn't have time to disrobe before I shifted." He slid his arms into the robe and tied the sash.

Micah's eyes narrowed as he assessed Connor's magic. Connor flinched but didn't protest.

Thos and Morris had begun a low chant. Beams of light crisscrossed Alia's body forming a protective canopy.

It took all my self-control not to pepper them with questions.

Cleyn made his way to the raised platform cradling Alia. "I am her protector, and I failed her," he hooted.

Thos glanced up, blue eyes widening before he returned his attention to Alia.

"Do you know what they're doing?" Joss spoke low, mouth near my ear.

"Not exactly, but I trust them."

"Good enough for me," the druid said.

Time dribbled by. People came and went, but my attention was glued to Alia and the rise and fall of her chest. Her color, which had been ashen, seemed better. Cleyn positioned himself at the foot of her pallet. With his wings spread, they reached both sides of the infirmary. Joss and Connor flanked me.

The canopy above Alia folded in on itself. Thos gripped one of her hands. She squeezed back. He straightened and faced me. "We have called her back from where she wandered. She will recover once she has rested."

Morris tucked a pillow beneath Alia's head. Next, he lifted her neck so she could drink from a crystal beaker. After mumbling, "Thank you," she fell back, and her head lolled to one side.

I started forward, but Thos extended a hand. "Leave her to rest for the next few hours, Rhys. We will watch over her."

"Come with us," Micah said. "We would hear everything that has transpired since last you were here." Although it was couched as a request, it was more than that. He was correct that I owed my brethren an explanation.

"All right. Can Joss and Connor accompany me?"

After a pause, Micah nodded tersely. We didn't usually allow anyone outside our guild to take part in group discussions.

"I will remain with Alia," Cleyn squawked.

It made leaving her side a bit easier. The griffon would alert me to any changes for the worse. Despite Thos's warning, I moved close to Alia, took her hand, and kissed her forehead.

"Rest, darling. I won't be far away."

Her eyelids fluttered, but it might have been my imagination.

"Any time today." Micah's dry tone got me moving into the corridor toward our primary meeting room. Joss and Connor fell in behind me.

A few twists and turns and we entered a high-ceilinged room with a fire blazing in the hearth at the far end. Stone walls were studded with thick wooden beams. Candelabra hung from several spots in the high ceiling blazing brightly. A long table capable of seating thirty ran the length of the room. Chairs were scattered this way and that. Someone had called for refreshments because platters of bread and cheese had been laid out alongside bottles of mead. Guild members filtered in. I greeted each of them and introduced Connor and Joss.

Once everyone was accounted for, they retreated to seats lining the walls.

Micah dragged me to the head of the table. "Let's hear it."

I elbowed him. "What happened to manners?"

"Pfft." He flapped a hand; a bottle of mead took flight drifting toward him. He snatched it, pulled the cork, and took a long swig. "Since you showed up in the library after time traveling—"

The room erupted in questions. Clearly, Micah hadn't bothered to tell anyone about my previous visit. "It hasn't been that long," he sputtered. "A couple of years ago, which is nothing by how we measure the passage of time."

I waved the room to silence. "By now all of you are familiar with the cataclysmic event that struck Earth. I was in the midst of it when it happened. Since then, we've been one step ahead of the Sumerians working out a strategy to alter the pattern that wrecked the world. We've also dealt with vamps and werewolves."

"What do the Sumerians have to do with any of this?" someone called.

"Wait until I'm done before you ask questions," I bellowed. "One of the challenges we face is teleport channels that are riddled with evil. To overcome that problem, I taught myself the rudiments of time travel and visited the guild house a few weeks back in my time but a couple of years back in yours. Alia and I weren't here long, but we picked up some important information from the library."

"Don't forget the griffon," Micah muttered.

"Let me start at the beginning," I said and recapped our flight from my retreat center in the Sierra Madre mountains in Mexico. In the interest of time, I glossed over much of our journey.

"Mostly, I've been grasping at straws," I went on. "My

last idea was to seek asylum with the Lemurians. It might have worked out better if they weren't so set on protecting their territory. They agreed to lend their travel portals—to me. I brought my small group along, which might have led to the kraken greeting party on a beach not far from here."

"Unlikely," someone muttered.

"Aye," another said. "Krakens are only loyal to their own."

"Are you certain it was a kraken?" Darius asked. "We haven't seen one in centuries."

"Quite sure," I said dryly. "Tough to mistake them for something else."

"What happened to it?" Micah asked.

"We chased it into the sea, minus a couple of tentacles."

"I'm missing the Sumerian connection," someone called from the back of the room.

"We believe they're behind breaking the world. Alia was their creation. They moved her essence into a mortal vessel twenty years ago, but once she was born, they neglected to educate her regarding her role in what was to come."

"Are you certain of that?" Darious's gaze bored into me.

"Quite. She's the most ambivalent magic wielder I've ever come across. She signed up for my sorcery retreat to discover a way to bury her power."

A collective hiss ruffled through the room. Magic was a point of pride in our guild. For anyone to eschew it ran counter to wisdom.

I forged ahead. "The griffon was assigned as her guardian. She didn't accept him for quite some time, either. Until he was injured, and the bond motivated her to save him. We believe the Sumerians didn't intend to wipe out as much as they did, but powerful spells are tough to contain. Alia was supposed to be some sort of cultural mediator between her makers and what was left of humanity."

"Mmph. That job went the way of the Dodo bird," someone mumbled.

"It did, indeed. But Alia has been opposed to the entire concept since she found out about it. Sumerians have approached her more than once. She's told them to fuck off."

"How is she still alive?" Micah's tone was laced with incredulity.

"Because her magic rivals theirs. She's a fierce adversary, and they haven't tried very hard to rid themselves of her."

"They have tried," Connor spoke up. "She's beat them every time."

Every eye in the place focused on the shifter. He raised both hands, palms outward. "Sorry. Forgot myself."

"Not much more to tell," I said. "We won't be here for more than a day or two. Three at the most."

"What if the Lemurians have closed their portals to you?" Micah asked.

"I'll cross that bridge when I reach it."

"How did you learn to time travel?" Darius asked. "'Tisn't one of our usual skills."

"By accident at first. A vortex swept me out of Sedona. When it dropped me, I was fifty years in the future. Had to scramble to find a way back."

"Did you say vampires are in the New World?" someone called.

I nodded.

"How?" someone else sputtered. "They hate water."

"Eh, just be grateful there are a few less for us to stumble over," Micah told him.

"Alia is awake. You should come." Cleyn's voice lit a fire under me.

I grabbed a nearby bottle of mead. "If you'll excuse me, Alia regained consciousness."

"But we have questions," Darius protested. "Surely, she can wait for a few minutes."

"She could, but I don't want to. We'll address loose ends after dinner."

I didn't hang around to argue. My offer had been take it or leave it, not talk me out of it. Connor and Joss were standing next to the door. They followed me into the hall.

"Reminds me of Druid gatherings," Joss said.

"Yeah. Shifter ones too," Connor added.

I led the way from the meeting hall to the infirmary at close to a dead run, slowing as I slid through the door. Alia was propped on pillows with Cleyn next to her. The griffon had a protective wing placed over her torso.

Before approaching Alia, I bowed to Morris and Thos. "Thank you, brothers."

Thos inclined his head. "Many thanks for an intriguing case."

Connor and Joss huddled near Alia. I set the mead on the floor, knelt between them on the opposite side from Cleyn, and took her hand. "Thank all the gods you're okay."

"Makes two of us." Her smile lit my world.

"Indeed." The griffon clacked his beak. "Wait until you hear what happened."

She squeezed my hand. "Such an odd twilight place after the kraken wrapped me in his tentacle. I could hear and see, but it was like a veil separated me from the world. He has brothers and sisters. Lots of them. They were watching everything. They wanted me."

My heart thudded against my ribcage. "For what?"

"My magic. It fascinated them." She trained eyes that glowed green in the muted light of the infirmary on me. "But the worst part was after a time, I would have happily joined them. They promised me...many things. Riches galore. A palace beneath the waves. It was all true seeing. Until I decided I had to fight back. Then the thing tried to kill me."

"That was why it took us so long," Morris spoke up. "We had to cleanse her mind of their taint."

"Did they know about you before?" I asked.

Alia nodded. "Not sure how, but they did. It's like I was part of some urban legend."

The hand not holding hers balled into a fist. The Sumerians had a long reach. What myths were they propagating about Alia? For what purpose?

I held my tongue. She needed peace to recover, something available in spades at my guild house.

Her gaze shifted to Morris and Thos. "Is it all right if I get up now?"

"Of course," Thos said. "It has been a privilege to take part in your healing."

I helped her to her feet. At first, she swayed before balancing on her own.

"Where will you take her?" Morris asked.

"To my suite of rooms."

"Excellent. We shall check on her later," Thos said, followed by, "Don't forget your mead." He handed the bottle to Connor.

As we walked the familiar halls of my guild house with Joss, Connor, and the griffon, my mind was working overtime. The Sumerians were far from stupid. If they couldn't corral Alia directly, there were a thousand ways they could take her off the board. Burying her in a kraken pod would work handily.

"Here we are," I said and barked a word to release the spell I'd set around my door eons ago. It creaked open. I led everyone into my sitting room. Beyond it was a small kitchen, a bedroom, and a washroom.

"Make yourselves at home," I told everyone. "I'll work on getting something sent up from the kitchen."

"I'll break out the mead," Connor said and walked into the kitchen, probably on a hunt for mugs.

Once Alia was settled in a leather easy chair, I brushed my lips over hers before hustling into the corridor intent on locating healing broth, more bread, and cheese.

We'd escaped disaster once again, but I had an eerie feeling our luck wouldn't last forever. The thought no sooner surfaced than I pushed it aside. Believing in positive outcomes was key. We could do this. If I'd had any doubts about Alia being a lynchpin, they disappeared.

She sat at the center of the current maelstrom. Perhaps I'd find clues within our voluminous library. As with any search, asking the right questions was critical, and I was homing in on them.

Keeping her close and safe was instrumental, except

she'd never agree to sit back and watch while the rest of us fought. Whether I liked it or not, she had a role to play. If I could tease out what it was, I'd rest easier.

One step at a time. For now, all was well. I'd deal with tomorrow when it happened.

The kitchen's swinging doors opened without me pushing them. Parts of this building were sentient. Because I'd visualized food items, they materialized on a long ledge in front of me. After wrapping them in a spell, I sent them back to my rooms.

Probably could have skipped the walk to the kitchen, but it had helped bleed the tension out of me. With a somewhat lighter heart, I made my way back to Alia and the others. Cleyn would probably want to hunt.

Or not.

I had a feeling he'd stick to Alia like fly paper until he was convinced she was fully recovered. After all, she'd waded into the kraken fray to save him.

And done it without a second thought.

Pride for her courage filled me. Perhaps someday we'd be able to enjoy one another's company without being constantly on edge waiting for the next shoe to drop.

Someday.

Clearing my mind of everything except mapping out our next steps, I stepped through the door that was still propped open. The others, Alia included, stood around a table where the food had landed.

She flashed a warm smile my way. It melted me down to my toes. To cover my emotional reaction, I grabbed a plate and a mug and got in line to serve myself.

"You okay?" I asked Cleyn.

The griffon clacked his beak. "I shall hunt later."

"I'll keep an eye on things if you want to go now."

The air around him shimmered. In a flash of feathers and magic, he was gone.

CHAPTER FIFTEEN, ALIA

Once I stopped struggling in the kraken's grasp, I realized they were beautiful. A long and august history as kings and queens of the seas filled my mind. They wanted me to join them. Cleyn had been incidental. Wrong place, wrong time. All I had to do was agree to become part of the pod, and they'd release him and the rest of my companions.

The thought was enticing. I came within a hairsbreadth of capitulating before I came to my senses. No one manipulated me.

No one.

A sword snapped into place, the hilt plopping into my outstretched hand. Before I could marvel at how the proper weapon managed to show up when I needed it, the tentacle wrapped around my midsection squeezed tighter.

The thing recognized I'd rejected it. How badly could it have wanted me if plan B was crushing the life out of me?

Frantic to escape, I hacked at the tentacle. Black blood oozed. Where it touched me, it burned. It also stank of death and rot, reminding me more of vampires than anything that lived in the sea.

"Why are you doing this?" I shrieked, except it came out as a burbling gasp.

The thing didn't reply. I'd gotten my answer earlier with lush imagery of underwater crystalline palaces.

Had any of it been real?

Strength was deserting me along with oxygen. I saw the others out of the corners of my eyes. Everyone was fighting to free both Cleyn and me. The griffon had bitten halfway through the tentacle surrounding him. Connor divebombed the thing's head. Rhys was moving toward me.

I clung to consciousness with all the desperation of a drowning woman, but between fumes from the thing's blood and an almost total lack of air, it was a losing battle. My heart beat too fast; breath seared my throat. I couldn't see or hear properly.

Through it all, I hung onto my weapon, but I'd stopped carving the tentacle cutting off my air. Probably should have used magic. Or tried. Yeah. A day late and a dollar short...

Everything went black.

When I came to, I was lying on a pallet in an unfamiliar room. Two mages bent over me chanting. A canopy constructed of light beams cradled me. Despite not knowing where I was, I felt safe, warm.

"I'm all right," I protested muzzily and tried to sit.

"Not yet, you're not," one of the mages said in Gaelic. I

realized then they were identical, or maybe I was seeing double.

I closed my eyes, opened them, and tried again to focus. Unless something was wrong with my vision, the mages were spitting images of each other. "Where is Rhys?" I blurted, grateful my voice sounded stronger.

"He is fine. He brought you to us. Right now, he is with our council explaining what transpired."

"Quiet. We're nearly done," the other mage instructed.

Questions bounced from one side of my brain to the other, but I held on to them. These men were helping me. It would be worse than rude to make their job harder.

"*I am here,*" Cleyn said into my mind and moved to a place where I could see him.

Relief surged, driving me perilously close to tears. "*Thank all the gods you're unharmed.*"

"Silence includes telepathy," one of the mages said sharply.

After a few moments, the light canopy dissipated. Cleyn draped a wing over me. "What was wrong?" I asked the mages.

"In a nutshell," one said, "your mind was poisoned by the kraken. In his attempt to coopt you to his pod, he left trace elements that had to be eradicated."

"So they wouldn't have long-lasting ill effects," the other mage added. "By the way, I am Thos. My brother"—he gestured at his twin—"is Morris."

"Thank you." I tried for a smile.

Rhys, Connor, and Joss skidded into the room. Rhys

bowed to the two mages and thanked them before kneeling by my side, his relief palpable.

"Thank all the gods you're okay."

"Makes two of us." I tried to lighten the mood.

Cleyn clacked his beak. "Wait until you hear what happened."

I clung to Rhys's hand. "Such an odd twilight place after the kraken wrapped me in his tentacle. I could hear and see, but it was like a veil separated me from the world. He has brothers and sisters. Lots of them. They were watching everything. They wanted me."

"For what?"

"My magic. It fascinated them. But the worst part was after a time, I would have happily joined them. They promised me...many things. Riches galore. A palace beneath the waves. It was all true seeing. Until I decided I had to fight back. Then the thing tried to kill me."

"That was why it took us so long," Morris said. "We had to cleanse her mind of their taint."

"Did they know about you before?" Rhys asked.

I nodded. "Not sure how, but they did. It's like I was part of some urban legend."

I looked from Morris to Thos. "Is it all right if I get up now?"

"Of course," Thos said. "It has been a privilege to take part in your healing."

Rhys helped me up. At first, balance was a challenge, but my dizziness passed quickly.

"Where will you take her?" Morris asked.

"To my suite of rooms."

"Excellent. We shall check on her later," Thos said.

After a short walk, we entered a cozy apartment. It reminded me of Rhys, spartan yet not lacking in anything essential. I lowered myself into a leather easy chair. After a brief kiss that left me wishing we were alone, he took off in search of food.

"One more interesting adventure," Connor commented as he set a bottle of some sort of spirits on a coffee table along with several mugs. "Feel like a shot of mead?"

I hesitated. My stomach was empty, and I'd been through a magical healing. Food was on the way, though, and liquor might soothe some of my raw places. The experience had left me more shaken than I was willing to admit. Everyone else was holding up. The least I could do was present a brave face.

What I really wanted was hole up somewhere safe—if such a spot existed—and not surface until I felt stronger. Yeah, like that was going to happen.

"It will be all right," Cleyn said.

"I know."

"None of that, you two." Joss wagged a finger in our direction. "If you have something to say, it's for us all."

The door popped open. Trays and a pot floated through and settled on a side table, or maybe it was a buffet since it had drawers. Connor made another trip to the kitchen and returned with plates and silverware.

Rhys walked through the door, pushing it shut behind him. I'd gotten up and was dishing food onto a plate and pouring broth into a cup. I smiled, hoping it looked jauntier than I felt.

Rhys smiled back. "You okay?" he asked Cleyn.

The griffon clacked his beak. "I shall hunt later."

"I'll keep an eye on things if you want to go now."

The griffon must have been hungry after his battle with the kraken because he vanished in a flurry of feathers and magic.

"Will he be all right?" Joss asked.

"He should be. The power keeping this guild house afloat casts a wide net," Rhys replied.

"I'd like *will* rather than *should*," Joss murmured.

"If I was worried, I wouldn't have let him leave," Rhys retorted.

I was back in my leather chair with a plate on my lap and the cup of broth on a table in front of me. I tried to suppress it, but a snort of laughter escaped.

"What's so funny?" Rhys arched a fair brow and sat on the floor across from me, sharing the same table.

"The idea of you—or anyone—controlling Cleyn," I managed between snickers. "Since he dumped the Sumerians, I'm pretty sure he'll never let anyone have agency over him again."

Rhys grinned. "Good point."

Connor dropped a generous mug of mead between us. It reminded me I hadn't actually gotten any when he'd offered it before.

"You guys good sharing?" Connor asked.

We both nodded. For a time, we ate and drank in a companionable silence. Our last meal had been breakfast at the witches' hut. That might have occurred days ago. We'd never returned to the food left for us in our quarters beneath Mount Shasta.

Rhys nudged the mug my way. "How about if you kill it."

I obligingly tipped it to my mouth and swallowed the last few drops.

A light tap on the door was followed by Morris and Thos. "We're here to check on our patient," Morris said. Or perhaps it was Thos. Telling them apart was almost impossible.

They flanked me, poking and prodding and flooding me with soothing magic.

"Excellent." Thos straightened. "You'll have no further need of our services."

"Next time, ward yourself." Morris waggled a finger my way before the two of them faded from the room.

"How do you tell them apart?" Joss asked.

"Sometimes I can't," Rhys admitted. "They have amulets. Morris's is onyx. Thos's is an opal. But sometimes they're buried inside their robes and aren't visible. I'm going to the library to do some research. Does anyone want to come along?"

It was the only room in the guild house I was familiar with from my last sojourn here. "I'll go," I said.

"Us too," Connor replied.

"Great. We'll make far more headway with four than two." Rhys began ferrying dishes to the kitchen.

I wondered how Joss and Connor would do with scrolls that were in other languages, but I'd figured them out. Perhaps they could as well.

"What are we researching?" Connor asked as we walked out of Rhys's rooms.

"Several things," Rhys replied. "Sumerians. Alia. Time travel. Also if there's any written prophecy concerning the cataclysm."

"What about the prophecy Micah alluded to last time we were here?" I asked.

Rhys made a face. "The one about disaster following close on the heels of my setting foot in the guild house?"

I nodded. "Yeah. That one." I hesitated before adding. "If you and I were destined to meet, you're in this up to your eyeballs."

"Good point," he murmured and guided us along branching corridors.

"How do you keep the layout of this place straight?" Joss asked.

"Not easily," Rhys joked. "Things move around from time to time, which adds to the challenge. Oops. Let's backtrack. We should have turned left at that last junction."

After perhaps a quarter hour, we entered a familiar corridor. The doors to the library opened as we drew near.

Connor whistled long and low. "Whoa. Look at all those source materials."

Books and scrolls plopped onto the table I'd sat at last time I was here.

"We can each take a topic," Rhys suggested and gestured at four piles. "This one is Sumerians. This one, time travel. This one, Alia. And that one is the cataclysm."

Researching myself felt weird, so I selected the Sumerian

stack and picked the nearest chair. Considering I'd been through a magical healing, I felt decent. Clear-headed and ready to take on damn near anything. I opened the scroll on top of the heap and began skimming. The more I could discover about my kin, the better equipped I'd be to eventually meet with them.

I stopped myself. Was I still hanging on to that delusion? They had less than no interest in talking with me. I was a tool, a construct. Nothing more, nothing less. Nope. If they were ever going to sit down with me, I'd need bait. With that in mind, I kept reading.

Neither Joss nor Connor were complaining about not being able to read their respective piles, so either they'd drawn tomes in English, or I'd underestimated their linguistic ability.

"Plenty of warning about what happened," Connor said after about half an hour.

Rhys nodded. "Aye, I've known for ages. It was one of the reasons I developed the sorcery retreats. What was less clear was when."

"So you assumed you had more time?" Connor arched a dark brow.

"Hoped rather than assumed," Rhys said. "Look for clues addressing antidotes."

"Got it." Connor returned to a dog-eared leather-bound volume open to about the halfway point.

"Are you certain you gave me the proper stack?" Joss asked. "Because there's nothing about Alia in here."

"That's odd." Rhys left his chair and went to stand behind Joss. "Usually, the library is spot-on when I make requests." He spoke a few words in Gaelic, but no other volumes fell from the shelves.

"Didn't you find information about me at the Sedona vortex?" I asked.

Rhys nodded. "Hate to have to go all the way back there."

"How's time travel coming?" Connor asked Rhys.

He shrugged. "I looked it up last time we were here. Not finding much else, but I'm not done searching."

"What are you hoping to find?" I glanced up from a particularly long-winded portion glorifying my kinsmen.

"Something simpler and foolproof." Rhys cracked a crooked grin.

"Good luck with that," Joss joked.

"Is our plan still to retreat in time to before the mess and try to reason with the Sumerians?" Connor asked.

"Unless one of us comes up with something better."

"Why not toss it out for discussion with your guild brothers?" Connor suggested.

"That's a really good idea," Joss chimed in. "More minds might settle on something we're missing."

"It is a good idea," I said. "At this point, they have a stake in outcomes too, since they're living with the consequences."

"Indeed we are." Micah's voice drifted in from the hallway. Moments later, he stood in the doorway. "Dinner is in half an hour. You might want to clean up a bit, first."

He was kind not to chide us for not straightening up before we sullied his library. My clothing was splattered with kraken blood. It still stank. I'm sure I didn't smell much better.

"I have laid out robes for you"—he glanced at me—"and you." He nodded at Joss. "They're in Rhys's quarters."

"Thank you," I said. "You're most kind."

"Do you mind if we leave these out until tomorrow?" Rhys swung an arm to encompass our worktable.

"In this one instance, it will be allowed," Micah said. "Dinner is in twenty-five minutes. Best get moving." He turned on his heel. The slap of his leather-soled sandals on the wooden floor indicated he was moving quickly.

I stood. So did Rhys, Joss, and Connor. We hustled out of the library.

"What happens if you're late for dinner?" Connor asked.

Rhys laughed. "You don't get to eat."

"You're joking," I muttered.

"I am not. We have few rules, but punctuality is one of them."

The trip back to Rhys's apartment seemed faster than the outbound leg. Cleyn greeted us when Rhys opened the door. The griffon hunkered in a corner over a freshly killed something-or-other. I decided not to look too closely.

"Do you want to come to dinner with us?" I asked him. "I know you already ate, but—"

"I was already told I am expected." Cleyn's tone held an odd formality.

I wondered why but couldn't take the time to ask him. In the three minutes I allotted myself for a shower under gloriously hot water, I fretted about all the things I didn't know about mages and magic.

The healer was right. I should have warded my mind against the kraken. It never occurred to me. I also should have picked magic as my first line of defense. Hadn't done that, either.

My only excuse was frantic worry about Cleyn, but in the end I'd turned into one more victim to rescue.

Lecturing myself about doing better next time—because there would, unfortunately, be a slew of next times—I towel dried my hair, finger combed it, and slipped my arms into a velvety soft cream-colored robe with a teal sash.

Rhys wrapped me in his arms. "You're gorgeous."

"You always say that to half-naked women."

"You're covered."

I glanced around his body. "What happened to my clothes?"

"I sent everyone's, including mine, to be laundered. They should be done by the time dinner is over." He released me and said, "This will go against the grain, but wait until you're addressed to offer opinions."

"Pfft. No women, huh?"

He nodded. "Don't take it personally."

My prickly side took a hike. "I won't. I'm just grateful as hell for something clean against my skin and another hot meal."

Connor and Joss and Cleyn joined us.

The familiar feel of Rhys's magic crafted a mini jump spell that spit us out in front of carved double doors. The smells of meat, bread, and spices made my mouth water.

"Right on time." Micah smiled as he gestured us inside.

Cleyn waddled to a nearby wall.

"*Uh-uh.* This way." Darius walked to the griffon.

"Having you in our midst is an honor. We have a spot for you at the head of the room."

Cleyn fluffed his feathers. His lion's tail plumed as strolled in the indicated direction. After all the losses he'd sustained on my account, I was happy for him.

I opened my mouth to ask where Darius wanted the rest of us but remembered Rhys's warning.

"All of you, follow me." Darius led the way to a raised dais at the front of the large room. Most of the seats were occupied. I'd had no idea Rhys's guild was this large. Perhaps fifty mages were scattered through the room.

Once we were seated, a gong sounded. The mages began to chant. Rhys joined in. Rather like grace, but far more poignant. It reminded me of Gregorian melodies or solfeggio. The iron band of tension that had gripped me since we'd fled from the Lemurian's stronghold began to loosen.

Tomorrow was an unknown; I settled in to make the most of tonight.

CHAPTER SIXTEEN, RHYS

When the pre-dinner prayers began, it struck a chord deep within me. I was home, a place as familiar as my own name. And then I reminded myself there was no longer any such thing. I had a task: righting the cataclysm. If it eventually led me back to my guild house, so be it.

There would only be a place for me here if they bent longstanding rules and allowed Alia to join me. She and I didn't talk about the future, but we'd have one if it took everything in me to forge a path.

Devotions wound down. We rose table by table and helped ourselves at a buffet running the length of the kitchen side of the room. Because we sat at the head table, we were first. I had no idea how the guild were replenishing supplies, so I was sparing with what I put on my plate. Joss, Connor, and Alia noticed and followed suit without me sending muted telepathic messages.

We'd just had a snack in my rooms, after all.

Tonight's meal consisted of roast venison, potatoes, wild greens, and fresh bread with butter. Unless we'd taken to growing grain, the latter was a luxury. Did goats and cattle still roam the Highlands? The butter must have come from somewhere.

I'd have asked, but the guild never mixed conversation with eating. Clean up had always been a rotating task. Once it was completed and the brethren responsible back in their seats, Micah stood.

"Tonight, we host guests. They come to us in dark times." He stepped back and tapped my shoulder.

I understood what it meant, but the gesture surprised me. I got to my feet. "Thank you for the warm welcome. We have been through much, and it means a lot, particularly in light of the prophecy linking me to the dark times Micah alluded to.

"I have already shared much of our travails. Since we are here, I would ask a boon of the guild." My tone was formal; my words in Gaelic.

"What could you possibly want after wrecking the world," someone muttered from the back of the room.

Cleyn growled low and moved to my side.

"Enough," Micah thundered. "Rhys is one of our founding members. You will treat him with respect."

"When we were in the library this afternoon," I went on, "Connor had the idea to ask all of you to consider possible solutions to address our current dilemma. The best one we've come up with is traveling backward in time to before the cataclysm. From there, we would hunt for the

Sumerians, and—"

"And what?" someone boomed. "Sweet talk them out of their plans?"

"Why are you even so certain it's them?" another brother asked.

Because of the muted lighting in the room, I couldn't identify either speaker.

Alia raised her hand.

"Stand and address the guild," Micah instructed.

"We aren't certain," Alia said, once she'd pushed to her feet. "Most of our assumptions rose from conjecture and the research Rhys has done. What we know is I—or my essence—was created long ago. I was held in stasis until the Sumerians decided it was time for my role to unfold. At that point, I was born of a mortal woman. No one told me anything. I didn't discover I held magical ability until I was fifteen. When it manifested, I wanted it to go away."

"I was assigned as her protector," Cleyn squawked. "Our masters notified me it was time to jump into action after the world broke."

The murmur of side conversations rose in a whispering susurrus.

"You may sit," Micah told Alia.

She wiped a surprised look off her face and complied. Perhaps she'd had more to add.

Darius stood. "Seems to me events might be synchronous rather than contributory."

"What do you mean?" Micah asked him.

"From what Rhys told us earlier, Alia wouldn't have a role to play under the current circumstances. She was held in abeyance as some sort of cultural ambassador. Given the almost total lack of mortals, her skills weren't required."

"What skills?" Alia blurted. Clapping a hand over her mouth, she said, "Sorry."

"Another salient point," Darious went on. "No one took the time to train her despite having years after her birth to do so. Did they ever approach you?" The question was directed at Alia.

"You may speak," Micah informed her.

I cringed and waited for blowback that never came. She stood. "Yes, they have approached me since the cataclysm, mostly to say it was time for me to come home, whatever that meant. When I refused to comply, they focused on Cleyn. They've harmed him, kidnapped him, and made his life miserable."

"Not miserable, Mistress," he hooted.

"They've hounded you too," I reminded Alia.

Micah frowned leaving divots in his otherwise smooth forehead. "From what I remember about the Sumerians, they're an arrogant lot. I can see them taking credit for a disastrous event, even if it wasn't of their making. Perhaps they had something planned, but another entity got wind of it and jumped in with both feet."

"To what end?" I asked, genuinely curious.

Micah shot me a pained look. "Evil walks all worlds, Rhys. Or have you forgotten?"

I winced at the rebuke.

Alia raised her hand again. After a pause, Micah nodded her way. She was already on her feet and said, "If you're correct, then my plan to time travel and attempt to locate the Sumerians won't do any good."

"We are brainstorming solutions," Micah informed her. To her credit, she didn't mutter *duh* or anything else before settling back in her seat.

Morris stood—or perhaps it was Thos. "As you all know, I also serve as seer for our order. Has anyone tested the epicenter of the breaking?"

Once he identified himself as our seer, the speaker had to be Thos. "Not sure we know where that might be," I replied.

"If Alia—and the Sumerians—are bound up in it, you might start with where you were when the leading edge of the problem surfaced. Test for residue." He blew out a noisy breath. "Of course, it would have been most effective on the heels of the event, but concentrated seeking magic could still unearth clues."

I considered the suggestion. We hadn't stuck around long enough to assess anything. Returning to central Mexico wasn't impossible, but we'd need to travel backward in time, and then forward once we arrived.

Unless I hadn't totally burned through the Lemurians' goodwill and could continue to borrow their travel channels.

"Did anyone contact you prior to the event?" Morris asked the griffon.

Cleyn shook his head. "Nay, only after."

Such a simple question. Made me wonder why it never occurred to me. "Are any of you skilled with manipulating time?" I asked.

"If we were, we'd have moved the guild house back two hundred years." Micah snorted.

"Moving people and objects are different," I reminded him. Before he could rebuke me again, I hurried on. "I've developed a rudimentary skillset. My library research today focused on learning how to be more elegant and burn through less magic."

"Then you're likely ahead of the rest of us," Darius said.

"It must have been a talent we drew on long ago," I insisted. "Otherwise, why have source materials in the library?"

"You've been here almost since the beginning," Micah reminded me.

"Aye, but I missed the first couple of centuries. Before we actually formed the guild in its current configuration. Regardless, if we return to my retreat center in Mexico, this could play out several ways."

I paused to collect my thoughts. "We could travel backward in time and show up before the disaster. We'd be ready for it and better equipped to examine energy signatures."

"Or we could time it more closely," Alia spoke up. "It would save us waiting around. What about all the other retreat attendees?"

Micah shot her a look that clearly told her not to speak until called on. She refused to meet his gaze.

"I'd send them home," I said. "Cite some emergency and refund their money."

This time Alia did raise her hand. After a long-suffering sigh, Micah said, "What is it this time?"

"How about Karen, Moriah, and Nola?" she asked.

"Who are they?" Micah asked.

"Two shifters and a witch who traveled with us for a time," I replied. "We left them in reasonably safe locations at their request."

"Exactly," Alia went on looking right at me. "If you send them packing along with everyone but me, you're signing their death warrants. In fact, we should keep everyone there."

I huffed out a breath. "It's possible the half dozen I ran into during my last trip back are still living there."

Thos walked nearer. "This is precisely the issue with manipulating time. It puts you in the position of playing God. Perhaps you could return to a spot near your center but not exactly there? It would get you out from under decisions such as these."

"How long would it take to scope out the residue you mentioned earlier?" I asked him.

He frowned. "Not long. You'll either find something. Or not."

"Would it be all right if I left the others here for a short while?"

"Wait a minute." Alia was done requesting permission to speak. "I don't like that idea. At all."

"You haven't even heard what I have in mind." I kept my voice neutral.

"Yeah. And I already don't like it."

"Makes two of us." Cleyn clacked his beak twice for emphasis.

I held up my hands, palms out. "My plan is to return to the Lemurians' lair, make my apologies, and assess if they're still angry. If not, perhaps I can use their portals to travel near the retreat center."

"But you won't be at the right spot in time," Thos pointed out.

"I'll be close enough," I shot back. "This way, I can be there and return in less than a few hours' time. Any other method could take days. This is information we need to plot what happens next. If the Sumerians aren't behind the cataclysm, we need to know who is."

"Why not bring us?" Alia asked.

"If you run into trouble"—Connor was on his feet—"you might need our help."

I squared my shoulders; small bones in my back creaked in protest. "The Lemurians gave me permission to use their portals. If I drag all of us back, it will be like rubbing salt into an open wound. If it's only me, perhaps they'll bend a bit, particularly when I tell them why I need their travel channels."

Public displays of affection have never been part of life in my guild house. Despite that, I walked to Alia, kissed her briefly, and jumped to the spot the Lemurian's portal had spit us out.

Sticking around for further conversation was pointless once I'd made up my mind. The beach where we'd battled the kraken took shape around me. I got my bearings and located the spot we'd emerged. It took a bit of floundering about, but I stumbled on an incantation that opened this end of the portal system.

Relief streamed through me. I'd been concerned the Lemurians would have closed off all access once they determined where we'd gone. Girding myself for an outright refusal, which would mean I'd have to time travel to return to where I'd left Alia and the others, I told the channel to return me to Mount Shasta.

It didn't take very long before the cavern where we'd begun shimmered around me. I'd assumed I'd have to hunt for Akbar. He saved me the trouble. He and two of his kinsmen sat at a small table.

As soon as the transit spell spit me out, I bowed low and held the position as a sign of deference.

Someone snapped bony fingers. "Enough of that," Akbar clacked. "Where are the others?"

I straightened. "Bringing them into the channels with me violated your hospitality. It's why I returned on my own."

"For what purpose?" another of the Lemurians asked.

I sketched out the problem and why I hoped they'd allow me further access, so I could visit the place I'd been when the world broke.

Power flickered around them as they communicated privately. I kept my gaze downcast and prayed for a miracle. If they said no, my next request would be if they'd be kind enough to see me back to the Isle of Skye.

"What happens once you return from Mexico?" Akbar inquired.

I cleared my throat. "I would share whatever information I was able to glean, and then I would be ever so grateful if I could return to where I left my companions."

"Will they return here?" one of the others asked.

"Would it be acceptable if they did?"

"Our initial offer, which was you could remain for a

short period of time, is still on the table," Akbar said.

It was as close to a yes as I was likely to get. I didn't push my luck. "Thank you very much. You might be interested that our exit point held a kraken. We did battle with him, and he retreated to the sea."

Clicks and clacks swirled around me as they digested my news. No one had said I couldn't leave. They'd asked about my plans post Mexico. I took it as permission and turned to face the opening to their portal system holding an image of the countryside near my retreat.

No one said *wait a minute* or *hold on*. The channel sucked me into its maw. Had the Lemurians wished it otherwise, they would have stopped me. I gathered my power close, weaving a ward. I had no idea what I'd find at the other end of this journey.

Unlike the gateways I was used to, this one appeared to operate on its own timetable. It spit me out in high desert amid a forest of pinion pines in less than five minutes. Less time than it had taken to reach the Isle of Skye. Made sense, since it was closer.

Warm dry air surrounded me. I marked my exit point and assessed where I was. The stream flowing nearby was the same one providing water for the retreat center, which was perhaps a quarter mile to the southeast. I considered going there to see if anyone had survived, but it wasn't why I was here.

After checking carefully and ascertaining I was alone, I peeled back a corner of my warding, enough to shoot a blast of seeking enchantment in a wide arc. At first, I didn't sense anything, so I dialed up the sensitivity of my spell.

Eyes shut, I focused through my third eye and third ear, urging the gods to gift me with information. It was slow to come, but bits and pieces filtered in. Chaos monsters were part of the problem. Tricksters too. Had they joined forces? Knowing what I did about both, it seemed unlikely. But I caught a whiff of both, absent specifics.

I pressed the edges of my casting farther out and waited, hoping for more, but nothing came. What I failed to sense was Sumerian presence. It simply wasn't there.

Slowly, gently, I reeled in my spell to preserve the cosmic balance. As I did so, I reviewed what I remembered. Chaos monsters were primordial creatures who sowed disorder, turmoil, and destruction. They reveled in disrupting things. Tiamat, Typhon, and Leviathans came to mind. Tricksters are cunning, mischievous, and deceptive. They create damage through pranks and challenges. Loki, Coyote, and Anansi were prime examples.

Anansi was tied to Africa. Coyote to Central and South America. Had one of them initiated the idea and someone like Tiamat jumped on it? Seemed plausible. Loki, with his Norse parentage, was by far the most dangerous of the trickster lot, but no one had heard boo out of the Norse pantheon since before the Christian era. After a final scan of the region, I was satisfied no one had intercepted my presence or my magic.

A hasty retreat through the journey portals spit me out in the same cavern where I'd left the three Lemurians, except now they numbered seven. The space was growing crowded.

"That was fast," Akbar crowed.

Before they could grill me, I said, "Chaos monsters and tricksters are behind the breaking."

The space devolved into clicks, clacks, and hisses. I considered leaving, but it would have been rude, so I waited them out. It took long enough I rocked from foot to foot to avoid sinking to a crouch. It told me how tapped out I was.

At length, Akbar glanced my way. "You did well. We will digest this new development. And your kraken tale."

"Many thanks for allowing me access to your gateways." I bowed again. "May I take my leave? My guild house and the small group I traveled with also await news."

Akbar flapped a hand my way. I took it as consent. "Find me when you return," he said.

Excellent. Meant I was free to use their portals until further notice.

"I will." With a quick twist, I entered the portals again, this time with an image of my guild house firmly affixed in my mind. Perhaps the portal system was getting used to me because this trip was even quicker than the outbound leg had been. Magic is funny like that. So much for my misplaced theory about distance playing a role.

Rather than the beach, I emerged within sight of my guild house. My initial joy at seeing the ancient structure was tempered by low, growling, booming sounds rocking the earth beneath my boots. I hurried forward, tugged on the ornate front door, and found it locked.

What the hell? We employed magical locks, not physical ones. I hit the dead bolt with enough power to force it to withdraw into its slot. It creaked from long disuse. The door swung open on silent hinges. I started to step beneath the lintel, but some sixth sense stopped me.

Pushing forward with enchantment, I searched out my link with Alia. It pulsed weakly. She was within, but a barrier stood between us.

Wards dropped into place around me. Not as quickly as I'd have liked, but they heeded my summons. Better safe than sorry.

A broadsword materialized in my right hand, a hunting knife in my left. Prepared for anything, I marched inside. The door swung shut with an ominous *clunk*. I knew without testing I was locked inside. Would it be as simple to leave as it had been to enter? I didn't believe so.

Sudden understanding welled. The manor house had its own methods of dealing with invaders. It had sealed me within recognizing I was one of its own.

Determined to find everyone, I began a methodical search. When the main floor turned up blanks, I started up a nearby staircase. What could have happened? I hadn't been gone more than a couple of hours, if that.

In the same way I felt certain the front door had locked behind me, I was also sure everyone's fate was suddenly in my hands. I had to proceed with utmost caution.

No mistakes played through my head as I searched the eerily vacant guild house's upper floors. All the while, I maintained my link with Alia. It ebbed and flowed depending on where I was. After a *duh* moment, I retreated to where it had pulsed the strongest, separated my astral self, and followed her energy.

CHAPTER SEVENTEEN, ALIA

Rhys vanished, leaving me with my mouth hanging open, the feel of his lips still warm and real. How dare he take off like that? We weren't done discussing his idea.

Which was exactly why he left, my inner maven snarked. He'd already made up his mind and wasn't interested in further conversation.

"So are the rest of you just going to stand here and let him go off alone?" I demanded and winced. I sounded like a shrewish fishwife.

"Why would we intervene?" Micah arched a dark brow.

"Aye," Darius cut in. "Rhys has been on his own for hundreds of years. Like us all, I might add." He angled a withering look my way.

I reached deep, testing my power. Could I chance the regular teleport channels?

"You will not do that." Cleyn's tone was strident.

Somehow he was behind me, wings wrapped around my torso. I'd had no idea they bent that way.

"Won't do what?" Micah asked the griffon.

"Eh, knowing Alia, she's considering going after Rhys," Connor spoke up before Cleyn could answer.

Cleyn's power muffled my own. I could have fought my way out from beneath his wings, but he was so resolute I couldn't bring myself to raise power against him. Never mind he was essentially doing the same to me.

Many sets of eyes were focused on me. Were they thinking I'd morph into Medusa and run amok with snakes coiling and biting? This might be Rhys's guild house, but it was his comfort zone, not mine.

Mindful Micah and the rest could order us back to Rhys's apartment—or to their dungeon if they had such a thing—I wiped my mind as clean as I could and asked, "Would anyone mind if we returned to the library to continue our research?"

Connor's face scrunched as he puzzled through what I was up to.

"It would be allowable, but one of us must be with you," Micah replied. "Otherwise, the space will deny you entry."

I waited to see who'd volunteer to babysit us.

"Once they're inside, no reason for one of us to remain," Thos spoke up.

I peered at the healer who'd spoken. Might have been the other one—Morris—for all I knew.

No one contradicted him, so he started out of the room gesturing for us to follow. Cleyn folded his wings against his back and waddled after the healer with his peculiar rolling gait. I followed, with Joss and Connor behind me.

Leaving the crowded dining area and all those staring faces was a relief. I'd begun to feel like a carnival attraction. I tried to get my bearings as we followed Thos but was hopelessly lost. Sending out a thin beam of seeking enchantment, I asked it to locate Rhys's apartment.

The healer skidded to a stop and spun to face us. "Who did that?" he demanded.

It took a moment for me to connect the dots. "Um, me. I think."

"Why would you raise power within our walls?"

For fuck's sake. "I like to know where I am, so I was trying to figure out where Rhye's rooms were. Not like I focused untoward magic on you."

"Next time, ask," he snapped and kept walking.

Feeling like I was about ten and had been caught stealing the family car—something I'd done, but only once—I shrouded my ability. If outside was safe, I'd have chosen to wait outside the guild house walls for Rhys.

Rhys.

What if he got into trouble and didn't return? Would the Lemurians' channels allow us entry? If not, was I skilled enough to bounce back and forth in time with all of us in tow?

I'd worked my way around to a qualified *yes*, when Thos barked a couple of words. A section of wall to our right withdrew into a pocket door revealing the library. Our piles of source documents still littered the table.

After clicking his tongue against his teeth in what might

have been dismay at the mess, the healer motioned us inside. Cleyn glided to the head of the table. The rest of us took up the chairs we'd had earlier.

"The route to Rhys's rooms is a series of right turns," the healer explained. "Will you be needing anything else?"

"Thank you for allowing us access to your library," Cleyn squawked.

"Next time, put things away."

I didn't bother telling him Micah had given us permission to leave the library in its current state.

"Of course." Joss's voice was neutral. It reminded me I wasn't the only one who resented being patronized.

"If there's nothing else—" The healer's thought was cut short by distant rumbling that issued from beneath us.

"Damn it," Thos swore. The air around him took on a crystalline aspect. He had to be seeking the source of the noise that was doing nothing but growing louder.

Cleyn hustled to my side. He was taking his protector role way too seriously, but I didn't want to hurt his feelings.

"What is that?" Connor asked, his deep voice shriller than normal.

The healer didn't answer. He'd rebuked me for searching with magic before, but this was new territory. Perhaps I'd sense something the men missed. Didn't matter. Anything beat standing around like a damsel in distress waiting for some man to scoop me out of harm's way.

I stretched power downward toward the escalating noise. Dark, slimy strands tried to hitch a ride. Panic set in. I had to cut the connection before evil augured dead into me. Even though I had no idea what we faced, my metaphorical hackles stood at full mast. It wasn't elegant, but I grabbed hold of the near end of my seeking spell and yanked hard. When that didn't work, I visualized a saber and sliced through my working. The last strands tore. Could anyone else hear the ruckus?

I was so immersed in not giving darkness a free ride into the library, I couldn't split my attention. Not for a moment. Finally free, I fell into Cleyn's side.

"Do not waken what you cannot control." Thos's voice was deeper, louder, almost as if someone was speaking through him.

In a flurry of dust and vellum, the books and scrolls leapt from the table finding their places on the shelves. My stomach twisted into a knot. Cleyn curved a wing around me.

What was happening?

"Do not fight me," Thos instructed in the same multitoned voice. "I am removing us from immediate harm."

"Where are you taking us?" I screeched, worried Rhys would return and walk right into a trap.

The healer didn't bother answering. Power holding the feel of Rhys's surrounded Cleyn and me. I assumed it included Connor and Joss. The library walls imploded, replaced by dank stone. We had to be on a lower level judging from tiny windows set close to the ceiling.

Others from Rhys's guild milled about. Conversation ceased when we plopped into their midst. I took in a large rectangular room perhaps fifty feet long and thirty wide. Steam hissed from a corner vent but provided precious little in the way of heat.

"We are in a sub-basement." The healer finally answered my question. "We have sat out many a siege here. The building will protect us."

I listened, alert for the harsh booming, grinding noise that had filled the library. It was still present, but quite muted. Thos's words sank in. Meanwhile, his twin had joined him. Even looking at them right next to one another, I was damned if I could discern any landmarks to tell them apart. The telltale amulets weren't visible.

My questions wouldn't be welcome, but I couldn't help myself. "What do you mean by siege?" I asked. When no one answered, I disentangled my torso from Cleyn's wing and planted my feet in front of the twin healers.

"Tell me what's happening. Please." It went against the grain, but I tacked *please* onto the end. Anything to encourage them to talk with me, a mere woman and not part of their guild. Without Rhys, I was vulnerable. Perhaps they'd decide this whole thing was my fault because of my proximity to events.

I was wrapped up in it, but I'd been doing my best, and—

"She brought darkness into our midst," someone screeched.

Fuck. Were my thoughts about to turn into a self-fulfilling prophecy?

Cleyn leapt to my side, beak clacking ominously. Joss and Connor flanked us on either side. Their loyalty warmed me, but we were desperately outnumbered. And out-magicked.

I summoned power, intent on a jump spell to move the four of us outside.

"Foolish woman." Micah materialized between me and the twins. Where had he come from? Invisibility wasn't one of Rhys's skills.

I stood tall, eye to eye with him, and projected a bravado I was far from feeling. "If we're not wanted here, we shall leave. Perhaps we'll locate the source of the disturbance and deal with it."

Big words. Still, they had no idea the extent of my power. How could they, since even I wasn't sure.

Micah twisted until he faced the roomful of mages. "These travelers are under our protection until Rhys returns."

"What if he doesn't?" someone shouted.

"We shall deal with that eventuality should it happen." Micah paused, perhaps for emphasis. "But I have faith in Rhys. You should too."

Amid grumbling, the mages turned away. Apparently, the sideshow we'd turned into was over for now. Before Micah retreated to wherever he'd been hiding himself, I grabbed his upper arm.

He spun so fast, he nearly knocked me over. "You will not touch me," he snarled.

Oops. "Sorry." I withdrew my hand. Apparently, not talking wasn't the only rule. "I feel helpless. If you know what's happening, please tell us."

His harsh demeanor backed off a notch or two. "Best I can tell, one of the boundaries between the gods' worlds and ours has weakened. Energy is leaching through, and it's disturbing the warp and weft of Earth's magnetic field."

I racked my brain and borrowed a concept Rhys had told me about. "Do you mean borderworlds?"

"In a way. Each pantheon maintained a clean separation between their domain and Earth. Gods and goddesses would visit but always returned to their homes. Eons have passed since any have been sighted."

"Why now?"

His mouth, which had been set in a tight line, relaxed a bit. "You remind me of the days when we taught acolytes."

I didn't know if that was good or bad, but at least he was talking with me. The muted rumbling intensified briefly and then backed off.

"One thing is certain," Micah continued, his green eyes narrowed in concentration. "Sumerians wouldn't present this way. They walk through the front door rather than hiding their identities."

"I could have told you that," Cleyn squawked.

"So, we're just going to wait until whatever this is dies down or fades away?" I pressed.

"Do you have a better idea?" Micah thumped my breastbone with a stubby index finger.

"Um, yeah. Why aren't we out there fighting?"

"Because we don't harbor death wishes." Someone who'd obviously been listening to our conversation spoke up.

I winced. Neither did I, but sitting on my ass twiddling my thumbs didn't work for me, either.

"The guild house is sentient. It will protect us," Micah said before he turned away.

"Best to quit while you're ahead," Connor whispered very close to my ear. A couple of the mages nearby probably heard, but I didn't care. I've never been the holding-secrets type.

Where was Rhys? He'd been gone over two hours by my internal clock. On a worried whim, I reached for the link we shared. It pulsed weakly. I nearly choked on a squeal.

Cleyn, who rarely misses anything, backed me into a wall. *"I feel him too."*

"Why didn't you say something?"

"Didn't have a chance. This is brand new."

I rolled the information around. My first bent was to jump myself out of the dungeon or basement or wherever we were and join the man I was falling in love with.

What would happen if I told the other mages? Would they launch a rescue party?

Knowing what little I did about this group, they'd talk it to death first. Rhys was out there. He needed us. Or I convinced myself he did. Cleyn and I were a few paces removed from the others. We could leave fast enough they couldn't stop us.

I'd be damned if I'd leave Joss and Connor. We were a team. We'd started this together, and we'd stick it out until, well, until we found an endpoint. Using shielded mind speech, I called the two men over. My spell was ready. The second they were next to Cleyn and me, I punched it.

Our next stop was the huge hall next to the guild house's front doors. In the wake of our egress, I was pretty sure I heard a chorus of *don't bother* and *good riddance.* Could have been my imagination, though.

The grand entry hall took shape around us.

"What are we doing?" Joss asked as the dregs of my spell cleared.

"Rhys is here," I said tersely. "We're helping him."

"First we have to find him," Connor muttered. The shape of his hawk fluttered behind him, a sure sign he was distressed.

I latched onto my link with Rhys. It pulsed stronger here. Brighter. No reason to shield our presence, so I cupped my hands around my mouth and shouted his name. Telepathy might have bought me more.

I'd try that next.

Turned out I didn't have to. The sound of boots pelting down steps brought me at a dead run with Cleyn and the others right behind me.

Rhys cleared the last set of risers and swept me into his arms. "Thank all the gods," he cried. "I was heading for the basement. I've searched everywhere else."

"Why not start there?" Cleyn clacked his beak. "According to your guild kin, they're in the same spot they've sat out sieges."

"Wouldn't know. I've never been here through one." Rhys still held me tight against him.

Being in his arms felt heavenly, but we didn't have time for indulgence. I wrenched free. "What'd you find out?"

"Chaos monsters and tricksters appear to have their feet all over this."

"No wonder the Sumerians were so pathetic when we've run into them," Cleyn hooted.

The booming and crunching were back, louder than ever.

"I say we go out there and face whatever's determined to sow discord," Rhys suggested. "Only reason I spent time in here was to locate all of you."

"Your kinsmen are all hiding in the basement," Joss sneered.

The corners of Rhys's mouth twitched. "Be easy on them. Much like your kin, the Druids, we were never a warrior guild. The building is imbued with sufficient power to protect its inhabitants.

"Nothing like being cornered to bring out your inner soldier," Joss mumbled.

"Are we agreed?" Rhys looked from one to the other of us.

"I've been ready ever since Thos shepherded us to the dungeon," I said.

Rhys cracked a grin. "Dungeon is it? We won't bandy that term about where the others can hear. Okay, then. We'll march out the front door. Gather defensive magic, but only use it if we have to fight our way out of something."

It felt amazing to be doing something. For the first time, I said a quick prayer to the Sumerians, who'd created me to be something other than a shrinking wallflower.

We crossed the hall in lockstep. Rhys grasped the latch on one of two ornately carved front doors. Curved at the top, they were set into matching molding. I felt the shot of power he lobbed at the door when it didn't open the usual way.

Ready for damn near anything, I blinked stupidly when the courtyard came into view. It hadn't changed a bit. No one was in sight. The only disturbance was distant booming, as if the gods were engaged in a sprightly game of bowling somewhere in the distance.

"Stay close," Rhys cautioned and hurried down terraced stone steps.

The air around him glistened as he deployed energy. It must have given him what he needed because he said, "This way," and headed for the beach where we'd battled the kraken.

When we'd left the beach, I'd been unconscious, so the terrain wasn't familiar. We loped downhill until we came to cliffs that overlooked sand, rocks, and pounding surf. The noise grew much louder. Now that I was closer, it sounded more like a battle than an eldritch bowling alley. I crowded near the cliff's edge. Breath whooshed from me.

I'd been right about the battle part. Where we'd fought a single kraken, this time half a dozen were scattered along the shoreline. Their adversaries looked like giants.

"What are those?" I kept my voice low, which was stupid. No one could have heard me over the roar of monsters and the crashing surf.

"Refugees from Odin's realm," Cleyn answered me. "They have a land where giants live, Jotunheim."

"Makes sense," Rhys muttered. "Loki is the preeminent trickster, and at least one of them is behind the breaking."

"They're not fighting the kraken," Connor observed. "They're forcing them to serve as steeds in the sea."

I started to ask why, but it didn't matter. My heart goes out to all creatures, even those I assumed were our enemies. "We need to help them," I said.

"It could backfire. Badly," Rhys said.

"We have to try. Those Norse fuckers are interlopers here."

"Not the way they see it," Cleyn hooted. Something about that hoot drew one of the giant's attention.

Looking up, he pointed at us, bellowing his fool head off.

"Onto my back," Cleyn ordered. "We'll chase them back through the veil if it's the last thing we do."

I didn't understand any of it—except the fighting part. Leaving Rhys to marshal an offense with Connor and Joss, I straddled the griffon, readied lethal bolts of enchantment, and took careful aim. There were only four giants. If I did this right, I'd make them sorry they were ever born.

Wind tangled my hair. I gripped Cleyn's sides with my thighs. Despite everything, a pervasive sense of rightness raced from the tip of my head to my toes.

This is what I'd been born for. I loosed my first bolt of magic. It skewered a giant midback. He crumpled where he stood like an oversized tree crashing to earth. Encouraged, I readied myself to do it again.

Meanwhile, Rhys, Connor, and Joss had joined forces. From my aerial perch I both felt and saw their enchantment lasso another giant, bringing him to his knees.

"Duck!" Cleyn shrieked.

I flattened myself across his back. Reality crashed over me like ice water as a boulder whistled by. What? Had I assumed the giants would sit idly by while we decimated them?

More on my toes than before, I selected my second target. Adrenaline coated my tongue and throat with a coppery taste. No matter how this came out, being out here eclipsed cowering in the guild house basement.

Maybe my thoughts had an effect on those we'd left behind. Perhaps shame played a role. First, I heard bagpipes and drums and flutes, and then Rhys's guild brothers poured over the cliff where we'd stood.

I clapped my hands, delighted they'd chosen action over safety.

Another volley of rocks and sparks sailed uncomfortably near. Cleyn wheeled out of their path. I refocused on the field. When I'd begun, there'd been four giants. I'd taken one out. Rhys had nailed another. By my count, it should have left two, but four giants still stood bellowing and hurling small boulders along with magic.

"Must be a gateway open nearby," I told the griffon.

"Let's find it and close it." Cleyn banked and headed up the beach.

I shielded my eyes with a hand and then smartened up and augmented my hunt with my third eye. A pulsating incandescent spot lay immediately ahead. "There it is!" I shouted.

My trusty companion winged toward the center of a shimmering mass of light. I mixed fire into my casting and directed as big a blast as I could manage dead center into the writhing clump of enigmatic power.

CHAPTER EIGHTEEN, RHYS

My astral self wasn't helping me search for Alia. No ability to open doors and peer into rooms, so I returned for my body almost immediately and continued hunting. I was nearly done with everything but the basement when a miracle happened. One moment, I was clinging to a faint shadow of Alia's magic. The next, it bloomed brightly, and she was in my arms. I held on to her with everything in me, relieved beyond measure she was safe. Cleyn, Connor, and Joss drew near.

After we caught one another up with highlights of where we'd been and what we'd been doing, consensus was to leave the guild house and face whatever was causing the disturbance. Didn't take much for me to determine the noise was coming from the same beach where we'd met the kraken.

A handy cliff provided a vantage point. For the moment, no one paid us the least heed. Several kraken were locked in mortal combat with giants. It appeared they were attempting to harness the sea serpents as steeds, although I'd be damned if it made sense. Giants are crappy swimmers. Why they'd want to corral a kraken pod was tough to understand.

I poked and prodded with magic, keeping my touch light, but I couldn't tell if one of the giants was Loki or not. My vote was for not. The Norse trickster generally had others do his dirty work if memory served.

Alia took off riding Cleyn.

Something about the griffon's hoots drew the giants' attention. We'd lost the element of surprise. Most of it, anyway. Before anyone decided to deal with us, I gathered defensive enchantment, laced it with earth and air, and heaved it at the nearest giant. My blow hit him mid-back; he swayed before sinking to his knees.

Could it be this simple?

I followed my blow with two more. He fell to the rocky beach and lay on his side, motionless. Had I killed him? Too much to hope for. Loki was immortal, but the other giants from Jotenheim weren't. Didn't mean they were easy to kill, and I hadn't done that much.

Meanwhile, Alia flattened another of the giants.

Connor had shifted to his hawk form. I'd caught him stripping clothes off out of the corner of one eye. Joss remained near me at the top of the cliff. Kneeling, he had his palms flat on the dirt. Light shimmered around him. Perhaps he was asking Gaia or Danu for aid.

I'd been keeping an eye on the giant I'd felled. He still hadn't moved. Perhaps being so far from home meant he couldn't draw on Yggdrasill's power. Heart and soul of the

Nine Worlds, the One Tree was instrumental in keeping Odin's realm intact.

Bagpipes, drums, and flutes snapped my head around. My heart swelled; joy shot through me. Rather than trusting the manor house to protect them while they rode out the storm, my brothers ran forward. Some carried weapons. Others relied on magic jetting from their outstretched hands.

We've never been known for our fighting skills, but something had lit a fire under them. Possibly Alia and the others walking out had shamed them into action.

None of it mattered. I joined the throng as we ran downhill and into the fray.

More giants bellowed and lassoed lightning and thunder from the sky. I could have sworn we'd begun with four. Between the one I'd felled and Alia's victim, we should be down to two, but four remained. As I scanned the field, two more lumbered forward.

Fuck. Meant a gateway had to be nearby. Earth is one of the Nine Worlds, but I rarely think of it in that light. In much earlier times, easy access from the other worlds to this one occurred via a magical bridge that spanned the Norse kingdom.

Alia and Cleyn flew up the beach away from the battle.

"Where are you going?" I sent.

"To close the breach."

"You can't."

"Too late. Already started."

Aw crap. What would happen to the balance within the Nine Worlds? Could Earth survive independently if Alia shattered the connection? Backtracking, did the Norse realm still exist?

Parts of it must. Otherwise, where would this batch of giants have come from?

Darius grabbed my arm and spun me around. "The enemy is that way, mate."

I fell into line and wove power in with the brothers nearest me. Recognizing a gift from unexpected quarters, the kraken were slithering back into the sea. What looked like harness material clung to a few of them. They'd escaped today's onslaught.

My bet was they'd dive deep and remain for a good long while. No one had ever tamed one of the beasts or used them in any fashion that I was aware of.

As I heaved power, nicely augmented by the four guild members I fought alongside, my mind was a chaotic mess of competing priorities. Knocking the giants out of the game was a bare first step.

Why were they here?

It couldn't be accidental they'd chosen this spot in proximity to Alia. Had the kraken provided entertainment? An appetizer while they warmed up for the main event.

Clearly the manor house felt threatened, or it wouldn't have gone into defense mode. Alia had been within...

"Duck!" someone shouted. I pivoted in the nick of time. A boulder crashed where I'd been standing a moment before, a sobering reminder to keep all my attention on the battle.

Connor was agile in his hawk form. He divebombed the giants, pecking ears and eyes. Nimble and quick, he outmaneuvered our adversary easily as he flew between lightning bolts. I couldn't see Joss. Hopefully, he was still at the top of the cliff cajoling divine intervention.

I hadn't seen one of the gods in so long, I had a hard time convincing myself they gave a fuck about anything here on Earth. Rain pelted from leaden skies, probably a result of the giants creating an electrical storm.

Only one giant remained upright. He shambled up the beach, hell-bent on escape. "We can't let him leave," I screeched.

"Why not?" Darius asked.

"Don't you want to question him?"

He shook his head and mumbled, "Sorry. Rusty at this."

I reached for Alia. *"How's the gateway?"*

"Half gone. No one's tried to come through since I started tossing fire through it."

Relief sloughed through me. The Norse realm was more resilient than I'd hoped. *"Don't do any more until we get to you."*

I expected pushback but didn't get any. We were all blowing through magic like no tomorrow. Maybe she was growing tired. I sure was. I'd been going full bore ever since I left the guild house for Mount Shasta. It felt like that had been days ago, not a mere span of hours.

All my guild brethren ran after the retreating giant. We were far more maneuverable, so we formed a ring around him forcing him to shamble to a halt. He regarded us out of small reddish eyes. An axe reminiscent of the one Odin used to carry was strapped across his back. He didn't make a move to unsheathe it.

"Why do you disturb our peace?" Micah shouted.

"I am leaving. I shall not return." His words were deep rumbles.

"You didn't answer me." Light flared from Micah's hands. It circled the giant, holding him in place.

"Nor will I." He straightened and glared at us all. Close to eight feet tall, he had cropped dark hair and a Neanderthal look to his bone structure. Leather breeks covered his legs. A matching leather tunic stenciled with Norse runic markings hung from shoulders to hips. His arms were bare as were his feet.

Alia and Cleyn chose that moment to fly back to the rest of us.

The giant's eyes widened in surprise. "Griffon. What are you doing here?"

Cleyn circled. "They have asked you the same. Who sent you? Why harass the krakens?"

We could play at crumpets and tea for hours and get nowhere. I focused on the giant's thick-skulled head and drilled through it and into his mind. I didn't try to be subtle—or gentle.

He moaned and grabbed the sides of his head.

At first, nothing made sense. The creature's mind was almost as much a muddle as my own. Sensing what I was about, the feel of Alia's energy married with my own. We've always been more efficient as a team. Glowing golden ropes joined Micah's enchantment circling the giant.

Images of the Norse realm flooded my senses. Snow-covered forests, frozen lakes. I'd forgotten the giants' home remained in a state of perpetual winter. And then I saw an interlocking series of canals. One lone kraken broke through ice with his snout, keeping the waterway open for a longboat skimming along behind him. He looked sick and old and tired.

Were they trying to replace him with fresh blood?

It explained one part of the puzzle. That they'd chosen this place, this beach, might have been coincidental. But I don't believe in coincidences. Kraken swim in both the North and Irish Seas. No particular reason to choose this spot if they didn't have another motive.

"You bastard." Alia punched empty air with both fists.

"What did you see?" I yelled.

"Some dickwad wants me for his bride or mistress or something. Yeah. Good luck with that."

What in the unholy hell?

More power rode in on the coattails of ours, probing the giant's meager gray matter. He bellowed and lunged for where Cleyn hovered.

Except the latest incursion wasn't the griffon's doing.

"I almost have it," Morris or Thos cried. "One more— Got it. You can cut him loose."

"Piss on that," Alia shrieked. A circle of blue-gray barbs flew from her hands, impaling the giant from all sides. Rain, which began before we reached the beach, had done nothing but grow worse. It dislodged a couple of barbs; blood ran down the giant's arms and legs and soaked into the rocky beach.

Micah and the healer twins converged beneath Alia and Cleyn. "He has surrendered," Micah shouted. "You will allow him to leave."

"Why should I? He'll just come back with more exactly like him. The gateway is damaged but far from destroyed."

Cleyn plopped onto the ground. Alia vaulted from his back and raced to stand in front of Micah and the healers. Her whole body glowed with expended power. In that moment, she was so striking, looking at her made my soul ache with wanting.

"More might arrive anyway," one of the healers explained.

"The rules of engagement are quite clear," the other went on.

"I am not bound by them," she bristled.

"Och, aye, but ye are," Micah said in very old Gaelic.

She shot a sideways glance my way. I nodded and said, "Micah is correct."

Hazel eyes shooting sparks, she marched in front of the giant. "You go back to this lord of yours and tell him if he tries to kidnap me, I will cut off his dick and feed it to the kraken. Are we quite clear?"

I wasn't in the creature's mind any longer. I'd withdrawn as soon as Thos or Morris had said he had what he needed. The giant stopped moaning, but his slumped shoulders screamed defeat.

"Say something," Alia shouted. "My magic binds you. I will not sever it until you acknowledge what I said."

"I have no control over what he does or does not do," the giant said stiffly, "but I will deliver your message."

After glaring at the giant, Alia sliced a hand downward. Her segment of the spells around the giant exploded in a series of sparks. My brothers fanned out. Micah dismantled his enchantment.

The giant started up the beach one plodding step at a time.

"I cannot believe we're just going to let him leave," Alia muttered.

Joss joined us, a drawn look on his face.

Connor flew to where he'd left his garments, shifted, and proceeded to dress.

Scales scraping on sand were a slap in the face. Fucking krakens. Had they come to engage us now the giants were out of the way?

Fueled by rising anger, I took off toward the shoreline at a dead run. By the time I reached it, two krakens had hauled their long sinuous gray bodies out of the surf.

My hands were raised to rain hell on their scaled heads.

One coiled about three feet of his bulk above the sand. "Stand down, mage. We mean you no harm."

"Why should I trust you?" I snarled.

"We are here to thank you," the other kraken said. "The giants stole one of our kinsmen over five centuries ago. He has been bound as an indentured servant ever since."

"Your intervention"—the first kraken chimed in—"saved us from a similar fate. We are here to reassure you we will not raise fangs or talons against you again."

"Why did you before?" Alia said in between panting breaths as she joined me.

The right-hand kraken made a long hissing sound. "There is a price on your head, young woman. We thought to collect it."

Kraken were akin to dragons in that regard. They craved riches. The brighter and shinier, the better. "Say more." I crooked two fingers their way.

"We should not," the left-hand kraken hissed.

Patience has never been my long suit, and it had been a long, difficult day. I snared both beasts with a golden noose and drew it tight enough to drag them together. "Tell me. Everything." I seeded my words with the strongest compulsion at my disposal.

By now, everyone had joined us.

"Need a spot of assistance?" Micah eyed my hodgepodge magical bonds.

"Nope. Got it."

The kraken remained stubbornly silent.

Alia glided between the duo and where I stood. Hands extended like a supplicant, she said, "You do not know me, only what you have been told. The truth is probably quite different." She turned to me. "Release them. They will not leave."

"If they do, we lose a valuable source of information," I warned.

She shrugged. "They're not talking now. Perhaps they will once I'm done."

Force wasn't loosening their tongues, so I reeled in my noose. The creatures moved sideways so they were no longer squished together.

Alia scooted closer. "Test my words with a truth spell so you know them to be accurate. You said one of your kin has been a captive for a long while. I haven't been much better than one. The Sumerians shaped my essence and held it in abeyance until twenty years before the cataclysm. They told me nothing yet expected blind obedience.

"I had no reason to believe I was other than mortal until my fifteenth year. Once my magic manifested, I spent hours, days, years doing everything I could to get rid of it."

Both kraken hissed, tails swishing in the sand.

"If your world turned end over end," Alia went on, "you'd fight it as well. When the Sumerians finally showed up, they wanted to drag me off somewhere. I refused. They've been after me and Cleyn ever since.

"None of us"—Alia swung an arm wide—"believe the Sumerians are who broke the world. In the first place, I was an elemental part of their plans. I was supposed to serve as a sort of cultural intermediary. Since most of the mortals are dead, they created me for nothing.

"They might be my kinsmen, but I don't know much about them other than what I've gleaned from lore books. It doesn't appear they'd have gone to the time, trouble, and wasted magic only to cast me onto a slag heap."

She hunkered close enough to lay a hand on each of the krakens' heads. "There's an old saying about knowing your enemies. You could shed a great deal of light if you told us how you came to know about the price on my head."

The beasts swiveled their heads and looked at each other. Disturbances in the marine air suggested they were conversing.

I waited, hoping Alia's honey was more effective than my vinegar.

Micah moved next to me. *"She's quite effective."*

His words, although couched as a compliment, annoyed

me. I bit back a stream of rebuttals. He didn't know Alia. None of my guild did. They no doubt assumed because she'd been raised among mortals and was ambivalent about her skill, she wasn't worth much.

Mages can be snobs like that.

Alia was still stroking serpent heads. One had wound half a coil of his long body around her waist. She clearly trusted him to hold to his word about not raising fangs or talons against us.

"We will tell you what we know," the kraken who'd draped a few meters of scales around her agreed.

"Thank you."

"'Tisn't all that much," the other beast warned, "but you deserve the truth."

"Do you mind if we all remain?" Micah asked.

"Not at all," the kraken replied.

Good thing, since I wouldn't have left under any circumstances.

The krakens hauled the rest of their bodies out of the water and wrapped themselves in neat coils facing one another. Perhaps this was their usual position ahead of revealing information.

Regardless, I waited, both anxious and fascinated about what they'd have to say.

CHAPTER NINETEEN, ALIA

Usually, I come out with all my guns blazing, but I sensed it wasn't the right approach. Their explanation about trading me for the price on my head made sense. The kraken who'd attacked us hadn't counted on the violence we'd levied against him.

Not that it excused his behavior, but at least I understood more.

I fell back about ten paces until I was close to Rhys as both krakens formed tight coils.

"None of this is new," one of them intoned in a singsong voice.

"Relatively new, but not new-new," the other interrupted.

The first kraken hissed at his companion. "We agreed I would tell this tale."

"So we did. I am merely aiding where your memory may have failed."

A spate of hisses flew back and forth. I resisted the urge to tell them to just get on with it, afraid if I drew attention to myself, they might change their minds about revealing anything.

"News travels through the seas first." The krakens finally traded hisses for words. "Reason being water touches every part of Earth, flowing and replenishing. If anyone wishes to broadcast a message, they begin with whichever body of water is closest."

"If they are off world," the other kraken spoke up, "'tis a small enough matter to follow one of the mother streams."

Rather than chiding his companion, the first kraken ignored the interruption. "Shortly after the disturbance, a message drifted from shore to shore. Usually, we pay that type of thing little heed. Were it not for the deaths of so many, we'd likely have disregarded this one as well."

"When will you get around to the gold part?" The second kraken projected annoyance.

Gold, eh? I wanted to ask Rhys what earthly use kraken would have for gold—or silver or gems for that fact. I'd quiz him, but later.

Another round robin of hisses cut through the roar of the surf. At least it had quit raining. I was so wet, I hadn't noticed until now.

Both Thos and Morris detached themselves from the group. After bowing low, they approached the krakens. Once they were quite close, one said, "I believe we may have intercepted a variant of your message."

The kraken who'd been doing most of the talking

muttered, "Of course, you did. You are situated near this body of water."

"Aye, but we're not in the habit of culling through the waves for clues."

I started forward, intent on dredging information out of someone. Rhys grabbed my arm and hauled me back to his side.

"Let go of me."

"Patience. This will play out sooner rather than later."

I could have broken free, but the kraken had begun talking again.

"We are unsure who offered a reward, but the message was quite clear. A chest of gold doubloons to the first person who returned yon woman to any Sumerian stronghold."

"Mind you, they're not simple to locate these days," the other creature added as he swayed this way and that atop his pile of coils. "The rest of the message indicated not only would there be a reward, but that returning yon female to her rightful place would reverse the process that did so much damage."

"Never believed that part," the first kraken snarled. "Which is why I left it out."

I yelped with surprise before clapping a hand over my mouth. What a pile of hogwash. Since it was looking as if the Sumerians had merely claimed sovereignty over the cataclysm, no way would me returning to the fold do anything except curtail my freedom.

Probably forever.

Nope. My makers had jumped on a serendipitous event and attempted to bend it to their benefit. Hell, for all I knew, they'd planted seeds or rustled up a mix of tricksters and monsters to do the deed.

Rhys sidled to the two healers. "May I have leave to speak?" he asked the krakens.

"Don't see why not," the one on my right muttered.

"Many thanks for indulging me," Rhys told them. "This information is important, and perhaps you can distribute it via your channels. I am recently returned from a journey where I revisited the spot where I was when the cataclysm struck. The reason I went there was to sniff out what type of mage was behind the destruction."

Heads swayed closer to Rhys. Lidless reptilian eyes zeroed in on him.

"It became clear," he went on, "that the destruction was caused by a union of Chaos monsters and tricksters."

"Where do the Sumerians fit in?" a kraken hissed.

I'd actually given that more than a little thought. "Best I can tell," I spoke up, "is they like appearing more threatening and important than they really are. Widespread destruction was their original plan, though not nearly as widespread as what transpired. They may have joined forces with these Chaos monsters and a trickster or two after the cataclysm for the sole purpose of getting me back. Their earlier efforts along those lines yielded nothing."

Something else swatted me broadside. The giant who'd been hell-bent on dragging me off to the Norse realms. "Plot gets thicker," I added. "Before the last giant traversed their damaged portal to the Norse realm, he let slip I'd been promised to someone."

"Promised?" Morris looked askance at me. For once, I was fairly certain it was him and not his twin.

"Yeah, as a bride or indentured servant or some such thing."

"There's the trickster link," one of the kraken said.

"Aye, but which Chaos monster would be involved?" the other mused. "Surely not Leviathans. We'd have been alerted since we share the seas with them."

"We're still working on that problem," Rhys said. "Can we count on you as allies in days to come?"

Intriguing angle. Not a door I'd have thought to kick open. Judging from the expressions on other mages from the guild, it wouldn't have occurred to them, either.

Cleyn spread his wings and moved closer in little hops interspersed with spurts of flight. "It would be like olden times," he told the kraken. "When we used to work together."

One of the kraken tilted his triangular-shaped head to one side. "I had almost forgotten."

"See?" the other one pressed. "Your memory isn't flawless." He shifted his attention to me. "If we're to be allies, perhaps you'd allow us to deliver you to the Sumerians. Once we have the gold, we'd rescue you."

I choked on a wad of saliva. "Erm, not fond of that idea."

"Why not?" The other kraken jumped in.

"They consider her their property," Cleyn squawked. "They are as likely to unmake her as anything. Maintaining her safety would require guards, resources."

"But we would rescue her," the first kraken repeated. His tiny, deep-set eyes gleamed with anticipation.

Probably, he was already counting gold coins. I would become an afterthought once they collected the reward.

"I'm right here," I reminded the kraken, who was referring to me in the third person. "You wouldn't happen to know who promised me to some random Norse god."

"We do not." A shudder traveled the length of the kraken's coils.

Interesting. They were either prudes or easily shocked. Amounted to much the same thing. Were there male and female krakens? How did they procreate? Or did they? If they lived forever, they might not...

Rhys's voice dragged me back to the beach. "Time to leave." He slipped a hand around my upper arm. "Consider our offer to join forces with us," he told the kraken.

"Consider ours to collect the gold." The kraken on the left slapped his tail against the sand. Both creatures uncoiled enough to turn and slither back toward the waves.

"The two are unrelated," Rhys called after them.

I leaned against Rhys, aware of how weary I was. As we trudged along the beach toward the cliffs, I scanned the group for obvious injuries. "Amazing," I murmured. "No one got hurt."

"Not true. Morris and Thos are quick and efficient. They fixed problems as they arose." Rhys's deep voice was soothing.

"What do you make of all this?" I asked eager for his thoughts. Mine had developed a circular aspect.

We reached the base of the cliffy area. Most of the mages had disappeared, probably employing jump spells to return to the guild house. Connor and Joss caught up with us. We were last to leave the beach. The griffon was long gone.

"Interesting development," Joss said. "I didn't expect to ever see a kraken again once they fled from the giants, let alone two of them."

Rhys hadn't answered my question, so I asked one that was less global. "What do you know about kraken?"

He cracked a weak smile. If I was weary, he must be wrecked. He'd done a lot more than I had today. "They're ancient. Related to dragons and sea serpents. Extraordinarily long-lived."

"Are there females?"

His smile widened. "In theory. I've never met one."

"What were you thinking when you requested their support?" Connor asked. A long, jagged cut ran down one of his cheeks.

"The other side did their damnedest to co-opt them," Rhys replied. "I'd rather count them as loyal to us."

A pallid sun broke through the clouds. Its meager warmth was welcome. My clothes had been soaked for so long, I barely noticed their clammy feel next to my skin.

"As long as we're talking," Joss said, "which of the Chaos monsters might be involved? I'm figuring Loki is the trickster, given the giant invasion."

"Not necessarily," Rhys replied. "He usually snags others to do his dirty work. There are only three Chaos monsters that I know of, although we could ask Micah if he's familiar with others. He's always been our resident scholar. According to the kraken, the leviathans are out. Leaves Tiamat and Typhon."

Rhys exhaled loudly. "Typhon is unlikely. He lost a battle with Zeus and was either cast into Tartarus, buried beneath Mount Etna, or possibly beneath the Isle of Ischia."

"Any possibility he might have escaped?" Joss asked.

"Always a possibility," Rhys admitted, "but it would be unlikely after well over a millennium. Tiamat is Mesopotamian. She's the primordial goddess of the sea."

A rough map formed in my mind. "So she would have been close to where the Sumerians were."

Rhys nodded. "According to the lore, she bedded damn near everyone. I can see where the Norse gods would hold appeal. They're all comely."

"How would she have accessed the Nine Worlds?" Connor asked. "They're a long way from ancient Mesopotamia."

"There used to be many gateways," Rhys replied. "Earth, or Midgard, is one of the Nine Worlds."

"Of course. I'd forgotten. Stupid of me," Connor muttered.

"Humor me," I said. "Why would any of them have wanted to damage Earth? What's in it for them? Wouldn't the one in charge of the Nine Worlds have been invested in protecting all of them?"

"That would be Odin," Rhys told me. "He was never interested in Midgard. Norse legends only very rarely included Earth."

"Someone must know something," I pressed. "If we're to have a prayer of undoing this, we need to know why it happened in the first place. My initial plan of somehow sweet-talking the Sumerians into undoing their wreckage was naïve."

"We're all tired," Rhys said. "I'm going to jump us back to the guild house. We can kick this around after we've rested."

The familiar feel and scent of his power surrounded me. Moments later, the stone walls of the guild house formed a few feet away. Cleyn squatted at the base of the front steps.

"I was just leaving to look for you," he hooted. "Thought maybe the krakens came back."

"Thank you." I stroked a wingtip as I passed him.

"If it's all the same to you," the griffon squawked, "I will remain outside for a while."

"Of course," I told him. "Good hunting."

The guild house door stood open in welcome. We passed under the lintel and walked through the central hall spanning the lower floor until we reached a stairway. "You can find my rooms," Rhys told Connor and Joss. "Up two flights, turn left, and go to the end of the hallway."

"Where will you be?" Joss asked.

"We'll be along presently," Rhys replied.

Not exactly an answer. I waited until the men had disappeared up the stairway.

"Where are we going?"

"To soaking tubs in the basement. This way, Connor and Joss can use the shower in my apartment."

Hot water sounded ambrosial. I trotted down several sets of stairs after him. We were lower than the protected spot where I'd joined the rest of the guild to wait out the disturbance. The flooring turned from wood to stone to dirt before Rhys pushed open a door.

Clouds of steam billowed out, surrounding me with blissful warmth. A medium-sized circular room held two pools filled with clear, steaming water. I walked to a bench and levered off my wet footwear and socks. Once that was done, I stripped off my thoroughly soaked clothing.

"This one tends to be hotter." Rhys pointed.

I flopped onto the edge made of interlocking stones and lowered myself into the water. It was buoyant, which I hadn't expected. "This must be salt water," I said, immersed to my shoulders. Tilting my head back, I wet my hair and proceeded to pick grit out of it.

"It is salt water."

Rhys joined me, groaning as the water covered his body. "Damn but that feels good. We needed a break." Scooting closer, he plucked something that looked like an amber bulb from behind us and broke it open. The astringent scent of soaproot reached my nostrils.

"Face away from me," he instructed. "I'll work on your hair."

I turned and dropped my head into his hands. The feel of his fingers massaging dirt and grime from my tresses was a delight. "Does soaproot grow here?" I asked.

"Aye. It's native to the Highlands. Why would you ask?"

"I studied it when I took a course on native plants. Whoever wrote the book didn't mention it grew anywhere other than the southwestern United States."

"Amazing what passes for scholarly work these days." He

chuckled. "There. Scoot away and rinse it out. I'll work on my hair now."

I'd figured I'd find a shower somewhere to rinse myself. "Is the tub self-cleaning?"

"Water flows both in and out perpetually, so yes." Muscles flexed as he massaged another bulb into his thick hair. Such a gorgeous man. He steals my breath and then some.

Once my hair was squeaky clean, I asked, "Why'd you really want to come down here?"

"Asks the lass with her breasts bouncing in hot water." He shook droplets from his hair, pinched a nipple sending sparks to my nether regions, and opened his arms.

I moved into his embrace. Before he crushed his mouth over mine, and obliterated further conversation, I murmured, "Not so fast. I know you. Why are we really down here other than to clean up?"

"Tired of me so soon?" he teased and rubbed his chest against my breasts.

I gasped as sensation shot through me. "Not fair."

Taking one of my hands, he guided it to his shaft. "Can we have this discussion afterward? There's little privacy here. We should take advantage of it."

"But anyone could walk in," I protested.

"They won't."

"How can you know?"

"Because I spelled the door shut."

I snorted laughter. "What's the male word for vixen?"

"Does it matter?" He angled his head and silenced me with his mouth. His cock swelled in my hand. Every question in my mind fled in a flood of lust so primitive it left me raw and shaking.

Apparently, I wasn't the only one affected. He made a low, growling noise like a lion on the prowl. With his lips still glued to mine and his tongue painting the inside of my mouth, he moved one leg over his bent knees until I straddled him. The head of his appendage pressed into my sex.

I wriggled until he slid inside. Lust turned into a live thing ripping and tearing at me. I clawed his back, bit his tongue. His fingers dug into my ass as he plunged deeper and then deeper still. Shrieks and moans bounced off the walls as we grappled with one another, doing everything in our power to get as close as we could.

I wanted to turn off the rest of the world and spend every second of the rest of my life locked in Rhys's arms.

"Of course you do, darling. Come for me."

The water turned into magical streamers stroking my sensitive places. When he slipped a hand between us and rubbed my sex, I exploded into release. Rocking against him, I pushed higher still.

CHAPTER TWENTY, RHYS

The feel of Alia's body around me defied description. I've never wanted a woman with the intensity I craved her, but our opportunities had to be stolen. I hadn't exactly planned on making love—or maybe I had—but the proximity of her nude body proved too much to resist.

Perhaps I'd known all along that the soaking pools would buy us a few moments surcease from all our problems. In another time, another world, we'd have had the luxury of courting one another.

I sat on the shelf running all around the pool with Alia kneeling over me. Her breasts were crushed against my chest, their silver-dollar-sized nipples hard as agates. Between the steam and passion, blotches of color marked her fair skin. Tangled wet hair spilled down her shoulders. One of my hands stabilized her as she rose and sank over my shaft, each movement exquisitely delightful. With the other, I rubbed her distended sex.

I added enchantment to the mix, coaxing the bubbling water to tease and excite. Welcoming the diversion, I balanced on a knife-edge of desire, but I wasn't ready to give in to release.

Not yet.

Panting and moaning, Alia writhed against me. I rubbed harder, faster. She was like quicksilver in my arms. Reminiscent of the ancient goddesses who'd provided a prototype for her creation, she projected a timeless quality. Her beauty and strength and sheer animal magnetism overwhelmed my determination to make this last as long as possible.

I may have sealed the door, but anyone could undo my enchantment. So far, we'd been fortunate no one had decided the tubs would be perfect to soak away the stains of today's battle.

Vanilla, cinnamon, and lilacs tantalized my senses. Her hot, tight vault squeezed my shaft. Head thrown back, neck corded with passion, she crowed pleasure as she crested yet again.

My cock ached with desire; my balls were bursting. When she raked her nails down my back and bit my neck, it sent me tumbling over the edge. Semen burned as it spurted into her.

Panting and straining to be closer still, we clung to one another as the volcano in our bodies subsided. I stroked hair away from her face. "I love you."

"You're just saying that because you're overwhelmed by

my charms." She loosened her embrace and stroked fingertips down my arms. Her smile could have lit the world.

"No. I truly do love you, Alia. If the goddess grants us grace, perhaps we'll find a time when we can simply be together."

"I would like that."

Eventually, we disentangled our limbs, rinsed off in the water, and scrambled from the pool. Alia hefted her discarded trousers. "I had clothes that supposedly went to a laundry."

"They should be back in my rooms. For now, let's find you something from next door so you're not wandering the guild house halls naked."

"I can put these back on. Not that far to your apartment."

"If you're sure."

She giggled. "Look, dude. Your stuff is just as wet. I can man up too."

The modern nomenclature within our ancient walls struck a chord, and I laughed. For the next few minutes, we got dressed. My garments were clammy next to my skin, but they warmed quickly.

"I'm going to jump us to my place," I said, not wanting to get sidetracked by a chance meeting with one of my guild brothers.

"Fine by me." She grinned. "The sooner I get to those dry clothes, the better I'll like it."

I draped an arm around her shoulder and took us up several stories. We'd no sooner arrived than Micah's hearty, "Knew you'd show up sooner or later," drove stakes into my hopes we'd have a few more minutes more-or-less to ourselves.

Connor and Joss were sitting at the small table. Micah lounged against a wall. Everyone looked as if they'd cleaned up.

"What's going on?" I asked.

"You can figure it out," Alia said. "I'm after dry clothes."

She trotted across the room and pulled the bedroom door shut behind her.

"We've convened an all-mage meeting," Micah informed us. "It begins in about half an hour. If you didn't show up here, I was about to hunt you down."

I groaned inwardly. We'd already processed everything we knew. "What are we meeting about?"

He detached himself from the wall and walked close enough to slug my upper arm. "We took an informal vote. Everyone believes it's in the guild's best interest to join forces."

I waited, but no further information was forthcoming.

"For what purpose?" I probed.

"Seems awkward," Connor mumbled.

"What was that?" Micah's tone was sharp.

The hawk shifter shrugged. "Sometimes more cooks aren't better in a small kitchen. We've had challenges with our low numbers. Originally, we were seven plus the griffon. We're down to four. It's simplified some things."

"What would you expect with inferior magic?" Micah crossed his arms over his chest and narrowed his brown eyes.

Joss and Connor were out of their seats in a flash. I inserted myself between them and Micah. "Enough," I said.

"Our enemies would like nothing better than for us to turn against one another."

"Mmph," Micah growled.

Connor's hawk was visible behind him, wings spread.

"What are we joining forces to do?" I asked again.

"Why, get to the bottom of the cataclysm," Micah sputtered. "Once we do that, we might be able to fix it. Roll back the clock, as it were."

The bedroom door opened. Alia glided through. She'd pinned her wet hair out of the way behind her shoulders. "Heard most of that," she said.

Micah switched his focus to her. "We've had a bit of superficial discussion about the krakens' offer—" he began.

"Which offer?" Alia's pleasant expression faded. I felt her gather power.

"Why the one where they deliver you to the Sumerians." Micah held up a hand. "Before you pitch a fit, consider the benefits. You'd be installed in close proximity to those who created you. If you mind your manners, perhaps they'll let down their guard, trust you enough to let a few things slip.

"As it stands, we know precious little. That could all change."

A corner of her mouth twisted downward. "Have you hatched a plan for how to extricate me?"

"Still working on that part, but the krakens said they'd take care of it."

I'd had quite enough of this conversation. Rounding on him, I said. "This. Will. Not. Happen. Period."

"Why not, Rhys? Do you have a better idea for gathering information?"

Exasperation curled around my spine. "I'm not in the habit of sacrificing my own."

"Her magic is powerful. Do you not have faith in her?"

You bastard. My hands curled into fists.

"That has nothing to do with it," I shot back. "Your logic is flawed. No matter what she finds out, if we can't get her out of the Sumerians' citadel, we'll never know what she uncovered."

"Cleyn would be with me," Alia said.

"What? You're on board with his suggestion?" I made a grab for my temper. What I wanted was to tell her it was out of the question. The twenty-first century female who stood before me wouldn't take that well.

She shrugged. "Of course not, but it's not all that different from one of my original plans where I'd seek them out. This way, we can save oodles of time, since the krakens will know precisely where to deliver me. Perhaps they'd even honor their commitment to get me out of there, although I'm not seeing how once I'm no longer next to a shoreline."

"What makes you think the Sumerians would do anything other than chuck you in a cell?" I asked. "Or unmake you."

"Whole lot of unknowns," she agreed.

"We've burned up enough time to head for the meeting room," Micah said.

"Fine," I snarled. "You leave. We'll be along presently."

Once Micah was gone, Connor's hawk, which had been hovering, disappeared. "I'm kind of agreeing with Rhys," he told Alia.

"It does seem overly risky," Joss said. "Surely, there's a better way to accomplish the same thing."

"What if we asked the krakens if there was an agreed-upon meeting place?" Connor mused.

"What good would that do?" My tone was sharper than I'd meant, but I wasn't pleased with my guild brothers turning Alia into a sacrificial sheep.

"Maybe, if we were close, we'd be able to sense where the Sumerians are holed up. Then, we might be able to sneak inside."

I snapped my fingers. "If we could sneak in, we could also sneak out."

"Assuming they didn't catch us," Alia mumbled.

At least we had one alternative to toss out at the meeting. "We need to get moving," I said.

"I'll alert Cleyn," Alia murmured. "He'll want to be part of anything that involves me."

I hustled everyone into the hall. From long habit, I sealed my door. Not that I didn't trust my guild mates, but neither did I want anyone snooping around or leaving a listening device.

Cleyn was already in the meeting hall when we were the last to arrive.

"Tardiness isn't appreciated." Darius slammed the double doors once we scooted through.

"Do the same rules apply?" Alia asked.

"Unfortunately, yes."

She muffled a snort. *"I'll do my best, but if they annoy me, all bets are off."*

I grabbed a nearby seat at the end of the table nearest the

door. Joss and Connor sat next to me. Alia trotted to Cleyn and placed a hand on his feathered front leg.

Despite this being a special meeting, convened for a specific purpose, Micah and Darius went through our normal procedures, taking roll and noting the date, time, and who was in attendance. We could have skipped that thirty-minute time waster.

Micah strummed a lyre to indicate we were now formally in session. I'm as protective of ritual as the next mage, but I felt edgy.

"We voted earlier," Micah intoned. "The majority of the guild wish to assist Rhys and his company in their endeavor."

"Not as if we asked them," Connor mumbled, so low probably only I could hear him.

That was just it. We hadn't solicited aid other than temporary lodging. Perhaps the dustup on the beach had whetted appetites for further conflict.

I stood, indicating I wished to speak.

"Come forward," Micah invited.

I walked to the head of the table. "Not that we're unappreciative," I began, "but what on earth motivated the guild to take on a task like this? We are not a warrior caste."

"Do you believe you'd be better off alone?" Darius inquired.

Something about his tone bothered me. "Not sure I've considered it one way or the other," I told him. "We've been feeling our way through uncharted waters. It's better to proceed with caution rather than pressing forward with incomplete understanding."

He waved a dismissive hand in my direction. I ignored

the hint to return to my seat. After sending a penetrating glance at me, he said, "Exactly. We need data. Far more than we have. The krakens were kind enough to—"

"Krakens are many things. Kind is not one of them. I know them far better than you do." Cleyn waddled closer with Alia by his side.

"We did not give you leave to speak," Micah sputtered.

The griffon extended his wings, knocking into several of my guild brothers, who scooted out of his way. "I do not require your permission."

I sent up a silent cheer for Cleyn. Alia moved under the shadow of a wing.

With my gaze squarely on Micah, I saw spots of color light both cheeks. He was furious. And stuck. If he ordered Cleyn from the guild house, we'd all leave with him.

It shouldn't be the end of the world, but Micah was struggling to keep a lid on his temper. The question was why.

I tapped his upper arm. He spun to face me, upper lip curled into a snarl.

"What's really going on here?" I kept my tone neutral and had a truth net at the ready.

"We. Are. Attempting. To. Help. You," he gritted.

"How? By setting Alia up as a sacrifice."

The red blotches deepened. "Show some respect, Rhys."

"How about if you do the same?" I countered.

Something was definitely amiss. We rarely argued in these halls, and never in our meeting room. One of the benefits of our guild membership was a congeniality that appeared to have taken a hike.

"I can speak for myself. This isn't the Middle Ages." Alia glided to my side.

Micah's mouth opened and closed like a gutted fish. He was losing control of the meeting, and he knew as much. Hoping he wouldn't notice, I drilled into a corner of his mind.

So far, so good. He was upset enough by Cleyn and Alia, he wasn't paying attention to small pinpricks. Perhaps he chalked them up to an incipient headache.

I didn't have to dig very deep to find what I sought.

When I did, it was so atrocious, I withdrew immediately. My hands were still fisted, and it took everything in me not to drive both into Micah, pummeling him.

I opened my mouth to blurt my discovery, and then thought better of it. My crew were outnumbered and certainly out-magicked. Maybe. Alia was a wild card. If she was pissed enough, all bets were off. The same went for Cleyn.

Still, best keep my finding to myself. We'd play along just enough to wait out this meeting.

"Rhys?" Micah rubbed his temple.

Oh-oh. I aimed for an affable expression and said, "What is it, mate?"

"You were looking a bit green." He skewered me with his dark gaze; I felt him probing my thoughts.

"Probably just hungry and tired," I said and erected a barrier aimed to discourage mindreading. What in the hell had we been talking about before this segue?

Oh yes. "You were going to flesh out details about our collaboration," I reminded him. I've never had cause to distrust my guild brethren. Hell, I've known them for hundreds of years. If what I'd viewed in Micah's mind was common knowledge—except for me, of course—it made me more than a little sick.

"What's up?" Alia's mind voice was barely there.

"Tell you later."

Morris and Thos pushed through the double doors. I hadn't realized they weren't here. The twin healers hurried to the front of the room.

"Apologies for being late." Morris bowed. At least I thought it was Morris.

"We had good reason," Thos added. "I consulted my pool. Information was slow to form, but when it did, it didn't stop."

"Traitors live in our midst," Morris announced, his keen gaze scraping through the room. "At least two. Perhaps more."

"Don't be ridiculous," Micah snapped.

"You've been drinking again," Darius pronounced dismissively.

Undeterred, Thos continued. "Rhys. Please take your companions and leave. While I am fully aware you are one of us, this is not your affair."

"Why send him away?" Micah demanded.

"Aye, he might be the culprit." Darius stared at me. "Him or that woman of his."

"'Tisn't them." Morris's baritone rang clearly. "We determined that much."

I considered lodging a protest but didn't. What came next wouldn't be pretty. Certainly not something for Joss,

Connor, or Alia to witness. Let alone Cleyn, who was as likely to rip the traitor to shreds with his talons as he was to sit by squawking outrage.

I gripped Alia's arm and started for the door.

"But—" she began.

"We'll talk outside," I said firmly and motioned for Cleyn to come with us. Joss and Connor as well. Thos had provided an unexpected excuse. I'd been wanting to leave ever since I'd helped myself to Micah's thoughts.

Where to go? I considered my rooms. I could spell them so no one could hear what transpired within. The only other options were outdoors or one of the guild house's many empty chambers.

In the end, I led the way back to my apartment. Depending on the outcome of the all-mage meeting, this might be my last visit here, and there were a few things I wanted to take with me.

Familiar corridors flashed past. Even though I hadn't spent much time here since migrating to the New World, I still considered it home. The specter of never returning saddened me.

Alia pushed the door open. The rest of us walked through. I took my time erecting sound shields and securing the door with spells.

"Must be pretty bad," Cleyn squawked.

I put the finishing touches on both castings, walked into the kitchen, and set a kettle of water on the stove. Joss joined me and divvied up tea leaves in mugs. Once the water boiled —with a slight magical assist—I poured it over the leaves and added a jot of mead to each cup.

"Come get tea," I called.

Once we were settled in my living room, I said, "The Sumerians got to Micah. Probably Darius too."

A high keening whistle was followed by a series of beak clacks from Cleyn. He waddled to the door. "Release me," he demanded. "I will kill them."

"Hold up," Alia told him. "How do you know this?" she asked me.

A long burbling sigh pushed past my lips. "Something about his words or how he said them didn't sit right, so I snuck into his mind. He's met with the goddess with the lantern and was promised riches beyond measure once he turned you over to them.

"I was worried it was the whole guild. From Thos and Morris's account, now I'm thinking it's only perhaps Micah and Darius rather than widespread collusion against me."

"No. It's against me." Outrage bled through Alia's words. "Those fuckers. How could they?"

Cleyn buried his beak in my door. "Let me out!" he repeated.

"Not safe here, either," Connor murmured.

"May as well return to the Lemurians," Joss agreed. "At least they're not plotting our destruction."

"My destruction," Alia gritted. "None of the rest of you are implicated." She straightened from where she'd been leaning against a wall and placed her mug on a table. "I should go. The Sumerians will never leave me be. No reason to drag all of you down with me."

"Don't be ridiculous," I said.

She looked at me, her eyes brimming with sorrow and

determination. Before I could say another word, the air around her liquified, and she was gone.

An anguished cry burst from the griffon. Moments later, he, too, vanished.

"Fuck." Connor drove a fist into the wall, leaving a hole. "What do we do now?"

"Go after them." I forgot about the few keepsakes I'd hoped to salvage. The only important thing was finding Alia.

Before the Sumerians or the krakens or Micah did.

CHAPTER TWENTY-ONE, ALIA

I'd been threatening to leave for what felt like months. Walking out on Rhys and the others tore a gaping hole in my heart, but I couldn't continue to place them in danger. I loved them too much for that.

I considered a quick stop in the guild house meeting hall to curse them roundly. It was stupid. They'd never been my allies. Instead, I aimed my jump spell for the beach containing the Lemurians' portal system. There had to be other entry points, but I knew where this one was.

I'd return to northern California. From there, I'd bury myself so deep no one could ever find me. Or maybe I'd return to where we'd left the wolf shifter sisters and Nola. They'd said they were sick of moving from place to place, but I'd always felt guilty about leaving them.

I'd no sooner touched down on wet sand than the swish of wings told me Cleyn had tracked me. Or course, he had. Our bond transcended any magic I could toss at it.

"You don't need to do this," I told him as he circled above me.

"Aye, but I do. You're my responsibility. I understand the Sumerians far better than you ever will. I have no other family."

Okay, so he wasn't about to leave. The reminder he'd lost everything on my account stung. If he could locate me, Rhys could too. I ran toward the spot housing the gateway. When I drew near, it showed itself. Cleyn skidded into a landing, kicking sand high in the air. Some spattered me, but it was the least of my problems.

The griffon followed me through the portal. I held an image of the caverns beneath Mount Shasta and asked the Lemurians' enchanted byways to take us there.

"I am truly sorry about your lost kinsmen," I murmured.

"This will be harder on our own," Cleyn said, once we were underway. He ignored my condolences, but then he wasn't one to mourn spilt milk.

"Harder in some ways," I agreed.

"In all ways," he corrected me.

My eyes burned; I blinked back tears. Throwing my arms around Cleyn and sobbing would buy me less than nothing.

"How could you leave?" he asked.

"Because I love Rhys, and I value Joss and Connor. It's not their job to deal with my crap."

"Wasn't that their decision to make?"

His question was surprisingly gentle. "They never would have walked away from me." I snuffled. "Someone had to make a clean break."

"Rhys will drop everything and come after us."

A tear escaped and tracked down my cheek. "Tell me something I don't know," I mumbled.

"My point," Cleyn went on, "is he will find us. So you will have done all this, squandered scads of magic, for naught."

When I didn't say anything, mostly because I didn't have a response, he went on. "Have you thought what you will do once we reach Mount Shasta?"

"Sort of."

He poked my breastbone with a talon. "Tell me."

"I want to check on Karen, Moriah, and Nola. Leaving them on their own never felt right."

"It was what they wanted," he reminded me.

I shrugged. "We often don't know what we want."

A beak clack was followed by, "I rest my case."

"I didn't mean me," I sputtered. "I've known leaving was the right thing to do for a long while."

"For the wrong reasons," he hooted. "Our task is to turn the world around, right the violation. To accomplish that, we must travel backward in time and deal with what is looking like a coalition between the Sumerians, a Chaos monster, and a trickster."

"Never would have worked," I mumbled.

"With an attitude like that, you're right." Rather than snapping his beak, he poked me with it, but gently.

Fuck. "This isn't a replay of click my heels three times and end up in Kansas."

"What on earth do you mean?" The griffon's magic

delved deep into my head. Perhaps he was worried I was losing my mind.

Rather than explaining *The Wizard of Oz* to him, I tried another tack. "You are free to return to Rhys and the others. Perhaps the four of you can figure this out."

He shook his feathered head emphatically. "Your magic is the lynchpin. The element that draws everything together. 'Tis why the Sumerians are so anxious to kick your game piece off the board."

"Here I just assumed they were a bunch of soulless assholes."

Cleyn cackled laughter. "That too."

The cave system beneath Mount Shasta took shape around us. Akbar bustled toward us with his long-legged gait. "Where are the others? I do not understand."

Alien power circled Cleyn and me. I knew better than to batter my way through it. Not unless I had no choice. A truth net clanked into place around us.

"Was that entirely necessary?" I asked stiffly.

"In this instance, yes. Where are the others?"

"On the Isle of Skye," I told him. A clean, pure chime accompanied my words courtesy of the truth net.

"Why are they not with you?" Akbar pressed.

A deep, shuddering breath racked me. I was still distressingly close to tears. Not the image I wanted to project.

"Since we left here," I began, "Sumerians have infiltrated a kraken pod and Rhys's guild house in an attempt to force my return. They have promised untold riches to whomever turns me over to them."

"And?" Akbar spun one hand in a get-on-with-it gesture.

"Don't you see?" I blurted. "I'm a danger to those close to me. It wasn't fair to them for me to remain." Once the words began flowing, they wouldn't stop. "I've tried to leave before. Never had the guts. After those in charge of the guild house were proven to be in collusion with the Sumerians, my path grew far clearer. It was no longer a matter of maybe I should leave someday, but that I had to go now before anyone got hurt protecting me."

"Seems as if that should have been their choice, not yours," Akbar clacked.

"Same thing I told her," Cleyn squawked.

I shook my head. "Rhys loves me. He'd never have told me to go."

"Yon griffon loves you too," Akbar pointed out. "Yet he is by your side."

"He followed me."

"The others will as well," Akbar predicted.

"Which is why I must go, and quickly." I pushed against the circle of his magic. It didn't budge.

"Where will you go?"

"If I tell you, you'll just pass it along to Rhys when he shows up."

"We have discussed your predicament," Akbar went on. "The decision was to allow you to remain with the other displaced mages beneath our mountain."

"Perhaps the others will take you up on your offer," I said, "but we really need to leave."

Three more Lemurians trailed into the cavern where we stood. A conversation consisting of clicks and clacks followed. I only caught some of it. Meanwhile, Rhys would come bursting through the gateway at any moment. If I laid eyes on him, my resolve would crumple.

Damn it. I hated being so weak where he was concerned.

If my limited experience with Lemurians held true, this batch could burn through hours conversing. I couldn't bulldoze my way through Akbar's barrier, but nothing said I couldn't jump us out of here.

Maybe.

The Lemurians' magic was very different from mine, which is steeped in fire. Theirs relies more on earth, air, and water.

"Don't do it," Cleyn cautioned me.

"Don't do what?"

"Leave until they give us permission."

"By then, it will be too late."

"Do not discount Akbar. He must know things he hasn't imparted. His kind carry seer ability."

"Didn't help them save Mu," I pointed out sourly and hoped no one was paying attention to my thoughts. *"Awk. Do you suppose the Sumerians got to them too? Is that why we're trapped?"*

"Doubtful. Plenty of bad blood on both sides that dates back to the loss of their original homeland."

I wanted to know more about that, but leaving superseded my curiosity. Rhys should be here by now. Had something happened to him and Connor and Joss?

Worry for them ate at me. Had my actions, originally designed to protect them, had the opposite effect?

Time dribbled by. Hard to say how much. With each

passing minute, my concern grew, and I felt torn. Once the Lemurians gave us leave to depart, should we follow my original plans to locate the ones we'd left behind, or should we return to the Isle of Skye in search of Rhys?

"If the Lemurians hadn't held us here," Cleyn observed, *"you'd never have given Rhys's location a second thought. Except to worry he might catch up with us."*

"Your point?" Concern sharpened my tone.

"Merely that it's a wee bit late in the game to worry about those you left behind. I could say the same thing about Karen, Moriah, and Nola, but you seem hell-bent on checking on them. It's ironic you're focused on them rather than the ones who stuck by your side."

Ouch.

Once I'd left the group, but that time had been involuntary courtesy of Sedona's vortex. It had snatched me up and booted me fifty years into the future. I'd been on my own for several weeks, until Rhys found me quite by accident. He'd been looking, but he'd gotten lucky.

Or had he? Perhaps larger forces were in play. Forces I'd been a fool to ignore.

On the heels of that thought, a ruckus from the area housing the gateway snapped my head around. Something was coming. Question was what.

"Free us," I demanded, the sum total of my attention focused on the glowing, pulsing rectangle that served as an entrance to the Lemurians' journey channels.

The four Lemurians formed a line in front of the disturbance, almost as if they knew what would emerge.

Eh, they probably did.

First, the truth net clanked to the ground. Next, the enchantment holding us prisoner dissipated.

"You will not leave," Akbar told us. "Not until we have closure."

Closure? On what? No time for my endless parade of questions. Whatever was in the channel was almost here. Behind me, I felt air displace as the griffon extended his wings.

I raised my hands, balancing power between them as I prepared for damn near anything. A cursory scan of the channel didn't yield any clues since I couldn't sense shit over the gateway's powerful magic.

Micah blew through first. A long, jagged cut ran from shoulder to belly. Entrails bulged, some spilling out like ugly red worms. His brown eyes were wild with white showing all around the iris.

"This is your fault," he shrieked the second he laid eyes on me.

"Fuck you," I shot back and angled power at his already broken belly. "I didn't make you play nice with the Sumerians."

"Do. Not. Let. Him. Escape," Rhys shouted. I heard his voice before I laid eyes on him. Sheer joy lit my world. He was unharmed, or I assumed he was. He might be as damaged as Micah.

The Lemurians draped shielding around Micah, glowing cables that effectively trapped him.

Rhys, Connor, and Joss raced from the gateway. All were covered in blood. Was it theirs? I switched to my third eye, assessing damage. Mercifully, they seemed to be intact.

"We'll manage this one," Akbar told Rhys. The Lemurians laid hands on the cables surrounding Micah, who was shrieking his head off.

"Pull yourself together," Rhys told his former guild mate. "You're an embarrassment to our fellowship."

"All her fault," Micah howled just before he and the Lemurians vanished.

Rhys turned to face me. "Why'd you wait for us?" he growled.

I was so happy to see him, I couldn't stem the joy spilling through me. The tears I'd held back flowed freely but he didn't open his arms, nor invite me closer.

"We didn't," Cleyn spoke up. "Not on purpose. Akbar and his friends held us here. What happened? Why are you so bloody?"

"We stopped by the meeting hall to tell them we were leaving," Connor said.

"Micah, Darius, and one other were loudly protesting innocence and weaving nine kinds of spells to lull their brethren into believing them," Joss added.

"They'd done something to Morris and Thos. They lay on the floor unconscious." Connor picked up the tale.

"I cut through their spells," Rhys announced. "Once they were revealed as traitors, they thought to fight their way out of the hall." He laughed hollowly. "I'm still not sure how Micah made it to the gateway with a mortal injury, but we followed him. Darius and Johan are dead."

"That was the other one's name," Joss muttered.

"I can't do this any longer." Rhys addressed his words to me. "I'm done looking over my shoulder expecting you to bolt at any moment. I get it that times are difficult, but it doesn't give you permission to ride off into the sunset on your high horse leaving the rest of us to pick up the pieces. Either we're in this together forever, or not.

"Make up your mind."

The joy I'd felt curdled, leaving a painful place in my guts. He'd moved well beyond anger to controlled fury. I read the bottom line in his message well enough. If I was determined to go it alone, he wouldn't stop me. Neither would he chase after me.

Excuses battered against my throat. I refused to sink to that level. What I'd done might have had noble motives, but it had been the wrong choice.

"What do you want me to do?" I couldn't bear to look at him, at the pain and disappointment streaming off him in waves.

Rhys shook his head. Ice-blond hair cascaded down his shoulders. It had blood in it too. "I am not going to make this easy for you, Alia. Besides, what I want doesn't matter. If it did, you'll never have left in the first place."

Tears threatened to spill over again. I blinked them away. Time to be a woman, not a child. Everyone was watching me. I'd never truly wanted to be alone, but the others had been in constant danger because of my presence.

None of that had changed.

Why was it so hard for me to spit out a simple sentence? One that said I'd strike out on my own.

I sought cracks in the steely veneer of Rhys's face but didn't find a one.

Closing my eyes, I dug deep. Had my desire to run been

planted by my makers? Surely, I'd be simpler to capture that way.

When I found words, they were cracked, broken. "All I was doing was trying to protect you. You and Cleyn and Connor and Joss are the only family I have. I couldn't bear it if you were harmed on my account."

"What if we feel the same way about you?" Connor's hawk was visible behind him.

"I won't run again," I murmured. "That's a promise."

Rhys turned away, maybe to hide his reaction.

"The Lemurians said we can remain here with the other displaced mages," Cleyn squawked.

"Yeah, but I want to know why," I tossed out. "Cleyn thinks it unlikely the Sumerians got to them, but I'm not so sure."

"We have time to figure it out," Rhys said. He faced me again with a neutral expression. The touch of his power brushed over me once and then again. His blue eyes widened.

"What is it?" I demanded.

"Check for yourself," he said gruffly.

Except I didn't know what I was looking for. Cleyn grazed a wingtip from the top of my head to my feet and dissolved into a bevy of hoots that made him sound like an owl on steroids.

"Will someone please—" I began.

The griffon's hoots turned into a single word. "Hatchling. Hatchling. Hatchling."

It took a moment before I connected the dots and

clapped both hands over my stomach, reaching deep. The barest flutter of a life other than my own bloomed.

"Congratulations," Joss wrapped me in a hug. Once he was done, Connor did the same. The griffon was still hooting, interspersed with the occasional squawk.

"You carry a son," Rhys said. "Our son. Before today's events, I'd have welcomed such an occurrence."

I laced my fingers together. "I am sorry I disappointed you."

"Disappointed?" Rhys rounded on me. "This cuts far deeper than disappointment. I love you, Alia, and you tossed me out like yesterday's trash."

It hadn't been my intention, but I accepted his interpretation.

Before I could craft a response, Akbar trotted back into the cavern dusting long-fingered hands together. "He'll not bother anyone again."

"What'd you do with him?" Rhys asked.

"He's in one of our dungeons with a couple of ravens. They will peck at his innards, which will be perpetually renewed by magic. His suffering will never end."

"Good," Rhys said, followed by, "Thank you. It's far better than I could have done."

"Follow me. I will take you to where you can clean the blood of your brothers off yourselves and find fresh garments."

We filed out of the cavern after the Lemurian. My mind and heart were wounded; joy jockeyed with fear. A baby. How on earth would I manage a helpless infant when I could barely keep body and soul together?

Rhys was still furious. Angry and upset. He'd do the right thing by me and our group because it was who he was.

Would he ever forgive me?

I had no idea, but I had to keep moving forward. It wasn't only me any longer, perhaps it never had been just me and I'd deluded myself. Cleyn certainly thought so.

We left the men in a space with heated pools that reminded me of the one beneath Rhys's guild house. Akbar ushered Cleyn and me into a small dining room. "I am lifting the prohibition against talking with other residents since you will be here for as long as you wish."

Other mages sat at tables. The griffon waddled to a platter someone had placed on the floor for him and began pecking at globs of raw meat.

"Come sit with us, dearie," a witch invited. Maybe the same one I'd met before. My mind was too big a muddle to sort through anything.

I fell into the indicated chair. A plate plopped in front of me.

"Hard day?" the witch inquired.

"You have no idea." Not in the mood for idle chitchat, I picked at my food. I wasn't especially hungry, but the babe needed nourishment even if I was sunk in self-pity.

I'd win Rhys back somehow, but it couldn't be my sole focus. Nothing had changed. The world was still a shambles. How had I lost sight of our duty to do what we could to fix it?

Easily, an inner voice mocked my query. *If Sumerians held a presence in the guild house, they probably manipulated my thoughts,* Holding a ward in place twenty-four/seven was impossible.

Had they known about the babe? Probably, which would have made them up their game. My plate was empty. I pushed it aside, folded my arms on the table, and laid my head atop them.

Sleep refused to come, but then I hadn't expected it to. I heard the men's voices when they entered the dining room. The witch who'd invited me to sit got up and motioned for the men to join me.

I raised my head and regarded them with bleary eyes. Clean and garbed in Lemurian robes, Rhys, Connor, and Joss were digging into overflowing plates. Cleyn had tucked his head under a wing.

"Go back to sleep." Rhys's voice was gruff but not as icy as it had been earlier. "We'll wake you when we're ready to find our quarters."

"Thank you." I repositioned my head and shut my eyes. This way I didn't have to worry about sticking my other foot in my mouth.

Questions zapped from one side of my head to the other, resistant to my efforts to quiet them. The one place I kept returning to was what a rotten time this was to bring a child into the world. It was a huge stumbling block, one I couldn't get past.

"Rest, Alia. Everything will work out." Rhys's soothing baritone caressed my mind.

If he was still culling through my thoughts, it must mean he still cared. Or maybe he was worried I'd destroy the child, as if I'd be able to do such a thing. With a great deal of effort, I quieted my restless inner landscape.

Sleep came as a surprise, dropping me into darkness.

. . .

You've reached the end of *Conjuring Chaos*, second of the Sanctuary books. Look for *Conjuring Promises* soon. Read on for the first chapter. While Chaos is fresh in your mind, please take a moment to leave a review. They mean so much to authors and are an opportunity to let other readers know what you're loving about this series. Until next time, dear readers.

BOOK DESCRIPTION, CONJURING PROMISES

Despite the best of intentions, I've managed to alienate everybody. Soon, a baby will be dependent on me. I've never felt quite so unprepared for anything.

Never planned to be a magnet for trouble, but danger has dogged my steps ever since the Sumerians—my makers—decided they wanted me back. In single minded pursuit, they've done a bang-up job turning mages against one another. They won't stop until they've curtailed my freedom permanently.

It never occurred to me to find out why I'm so important to them, but I'm working on that angle now. Meanwhile, our small group has been ripped to shreds by my actions.

Perhaps they weren't truly mine but the product of magical suggestion. Not that it matters. The endpoint is the same. Remaining warded 24/7 isn't possible. Best I can do is lick my wounds and soldier on while I patch rifts I've created.

If we gather enough allies, we might have a fighting chance to undo the enchantment that spawned the cataclysm. It's the only way Earth will be whole again. And it needs to be. Raising a child in the midst of chaos—a child who will be hounded right along with me—will be damn near impossible.

I have the motivation and the magic. Time to trim my pride, apologize all over the flipping place, and go for the win.

CONJURING PROMISES, CHAPTER ONE, RHYS

After Alia jumped her way clear of my guild house, I figured she was headed for the beach in search of fresh air. The conversation had grown heated, good reason to leave for a bit. Still, I needed to go after her, soothe her ragged spirits.

Cleyn, her bonded griffon, had departed on the heels of her exit.

"Any idea where they went?" Connor asked. A hawk shifter, he's tall and broadly built with dark shoulder-length hair and blue eyes.

I shook my head.

"Hope the krakens aren't back on the beach," Joss mumbled. He's a druid with flame-red hair that falls to midback and the pale-blue eyes common to redheads. About as tall as Connor, but far more slightly built, he was steeped in earth magics.

Damn it. I hadn't forgotten about the sea beasts, not

entirely, and I did not want Alia dealing with them on her own. The Sumerians who'd made her, and who were hellbent on luring her back, had offered rewards all over the fucking place, including gold to the krakens.

Much like dragons in that regard, krakens cherish precious metals and gemstones. They'd offered to deliver Alia to the Sumerians, collect the reward, and then rescue her, but the rescue part always felt sketchy. I'd coaxed an agreement from them to ally with us. How far it went was anyone's guess.

Meanwhile, we needed to get moving.

"First stop is the meeting hall," I told Connor and Joss. "I want to make certain they know I've left the premises."

"Pfft." Connor arched a dark brow. "What you really want to know is which of your guildmates is guilty of treason."

"That too," I admitted.

At the point when we'd been asked to leave the meeting, Thos, our seer and one of our healers, had announced traitors walked in our midst. Of course, I'd known as much because I'd seen the treachery in Micah's mind. I hoped to hell it was only him and not the entire guild.

Looping a quick jump spell around all three of us, I moved us to the broad hall in front of the meeting room.

Raised voices battered my ears. The doors stood open. Thos and his twin, Morris, lay face down on the floor. Micah, our self-styled leader, Darius, and Johan were weaving compulsion spells as fast as they could utter words. The other forty-something mages who comprised my guild wore shell-shocked expressions.

I motioned for Joss and Connor to stand behind me. They ignored my orders and flanked me, one on each side. So far, no one had noticed us. I grabbed the opportunity and scraped the surface of Micah's mind. He was so preoccupied, he didn't appear to notice.

I'd done the same previously and discovered his perfidy. Was I hoping for a different answer? Probably so. He and I go back more than a millennium. Evidence of his treachery turned my stomach. I didn't bother repeating my actions with Darius or Johan. That they stood with Micah told me all I needed to know.

A quick scan revealed Thos and Morris still lived. I chopped through the spell holding them in place. Relief carved a deep path. So far, we hadn't sunk to murdering one another in our own halls. Not yet, anyway. That was about to change in a heartbeat.

Goddess damn the Sumerians from here to Faery. Were it not for their incessant meddling, we'd never have been at this juncture.

Connor nudged me asking how to proceed. The shape of his hawk hovered behind him, clearly ready to spring into action. Moving quickly, I shaped lethal magic into darts and sent them zinging at Micah's midsection.

He whipped to face me, his brown eyes wide with outrage. "How dare you?" he shouted.

I didn't bother to answer and sent another volley at his chest. It ripped open, spilling entrails in its wake.

Connor apparently thought better of shifting. He leapt on Darius, drove him to the ground, and buried a dirk between his ribs. Joss squared off across from Johan. In a gutsy move, he filched a blade from a sheath hanging from Johan's waist and sliced neatly through his large neck vessels. Blood shot skyward painting us all with crimson.

The other mages were shaking themselves, waking from the compulsion casting that had immobilized them. Clutching his ruined belly in both hands, Micah slithered around me and lurched into the hall.

"Come on," I shouted at Connor and Joss intent on giving pursuit. Once we reached the corridor, Micah was nowhere to be seen. Had he retreated to his rooms? Unlikely. His wounding was mortal absent immediate healing. Thos and Morris would probably rather die than aid the one who'd sold our guild down the river.

Alia hadn't returned. Had she run into the kraken pod?

Crap. I was spread far too thin. I summoned a jump spell and moved the three of us to cliffs overlooking a barren stretch of beach. We'd parlayed—and fought—with krakens there.

"Look!" Connor pointed.

"Why that slimy fuck," Joss shouted and started down the cliff face.

Micah had somehow moved himself into proximity to the Lemurian portal we'd used to travel here. I hadn't told anyone about it, but Micah must have explored on his own.

Scrambling was too slow, so I employed a shot of magic to land me next to Micah, who was frantically cycling through spells to coax the gateway to life. Nothing he did had any impact, but once I showed up, the portal sprang to glowing life.

Micah shambled through with me right behind him.

Pounding footsteps announced Connor and Joss, who crowded in behind me.

"Alia was here," Connor panted.

"Yes, she and Cleyn used these channels," Joss said between gasps as he worked to catch his breath.

Alia. I hadn't forgotten about her, but I'd been so gutted by my guildmates' betrayal, she hadn't been at the forefront of my mind. She should have been.

Goddamn it. Micah, Darius, and Johan weren't the only ones who'd fucked me over. Alia had actually followed through on her threats to abandon the rest of us and strike out on her own.

How could she have done that? I loved her, for fuck's sake. And I thought she loved me. *Thought* being the operative term. Her presence in my guild house had drawn the Sumerians. Although my brethren's betrayal wasn't exactly her fault, had she not been there, the Sumerians wouldn't have infiltrated our ranks.

A dull ache lodged in the vicinity of my heart. I stopped chasing Micah. If blood loss didn't do him in, the Lemurians at the other end would heed my request once they knew details.

"Why would she leave us?" Connor was saying, clearly as distraught as I felt.

"She didn't want to put us in danger," Joss said. "But her reasoning was flawed. Badly."

I didn't join the conversation. I had to sever my caring. It eroded my judgement and got in the way of, well, of everything. No more holding her in my arms. No more passionate clinches.

It wouldn't be easy, but I was done. I couldn't spend the rest of my life wondering if she was about to bolt at any moment. Subtle clues suggested we were nearing the Mount Shasta end of the travel channel. I cupped my hands around my mouth.

"Do not let him escape," I yelled, gratified to hear an echo of Micah screeching that everything was Alia's fault.

The next words to reach me were Alia's "Fuck you. I didn't force you tp play nice with the Sumerians."

Why hadn't she kept right on running? If her plan was to wait for us, why not wait on the beach? Hope burned bright; I tamped it down and stomped on it. No matter what she did, I had to be done with my ill-advised attraction to her. Leading my people in a last-ditch effort to salvage Earth had to take precedence. Over everything.

By the time I raced through the portal, the Lemurians had draped shielding around Micah, glowing cables that effectively trapped him.

"We'll manage this one," Akbar told me. He's one of the Lemurian elders. Like all his kin, he's tall and sylphlike, coated with fine gray-green scales, and garbed in robes that fell to ground level. He and a couple more Lemurians laid hands on the cable surrounding Micah. The craven was wailing piteously.

"Pull yourself together," I gritted. "You're an embarrassment to our fellowship."

"All her fault," Micah howled. Clearly, as sick as him as I was, the Lemurians hauled him out of the cave.

It cost me, but I faced Alia. "Why'd you wait for us?"

"We didn't," Cleyn, her bonded griffon, explained. "Not

on purpose. Akbar and his friends held us here. What happened? Why are you so bloody?"

"We stopped by the meeting hall to tell them we were leaving," Connor said.

"Micah, Darius, and one other were loudly protesting innocence and weaving nine kinds of spells to lull their brethren into believing them," Joss added.

"They'd done something to Morris and Thos. They lay on the floor unconscious." Connor frowned at the memory.

"Long story short, I cut through their spells," I said. "Once they were revealed as traitors, they thought to fight their way out of the hall for all the good it did them. I'm still not sure how Micah made it to the gateway with a mortal injury, but we followed him. Darius and Johan are dead."

So much for small talk. Truth time had arrived. I girded myself and took a deep breath, blowing it out slowly.

"I can't do this any longer," I told Alia. "I'm done looking over my shoulder expecting you to bolt at any moment. I get it that times are difficult, but it doesn't give you permission to ride off on your high horse leaving the rest of us to pick up the pieces. Either we're in this together forever, or not.

"Make up your mind."

Damn it. I hadn't meant to offer a choice. Why in the hell hadn't I stopped after saying I was done?

"What do you want me to do?" Alia's voice was small, broken.

I ached to open my arms and draw her near, but I couldn't let my feelings hound me into backing down. I pushed my shoulders straighter. "I am not going to make this easy for you, Alia. Besides, what I want doesn't matter. If it did, you'll never have left in the first place."

"All I was doing was trying to protect you. You three and Cleyn are the only family I have. I couldn't bear it if you were harmed on my account."

"What if we feel the same way about you?" Connor asked.

"I won't run again," she murmured. "That's a promise."

Her words hit me squarely in the solar plexus. I twisted away so she wouldn't be able to see my face. I might have talked big, but I still loved her, not that it had served me especially well.

"The Lemurians said we can remain here with the other displaced mages," Cleyn squawked, breaking into my scrambled thoughts.

"Yeah, but I want to know why," Alia tossed out. "Cleyn thinks it unlikely the Sumerians got to them. I'm not so sure since they seem to have coopted everyone else."

"We have time to figure it out," I said, grateful the discussion had moved to more global topics. I had myself under better control. When I faced Alia, I traced power the length of her body to reassure myself she was unharmed.

And found something completely unexpected. So unexpected, I repeated my actions to make certain I wasn't deluding myself. When the same answer surfaced, joy spilled over. I did my best to conceal my reaction, but she picked up on the unrest coursing through me.

"What is it?" she asked.

"Check for yourself," I said, my tone sharper than necessary.

Cleyn brushed a wingtip from the top of Alia's head to her feet. Hoots filled the air. Guess he hadn't known before, either.

"Will someone please—" Alia began.

Hoots morphed into a single word. "Hatchling. Hatchling. Hatchling."

Alia clapped her hands over her lower abdomen, a look of abject shock stamped into her features. Joss and Connor rushed to her extending congratulations.

I cleared my throat. This changed nothing—and everything. "You carry a son," I said formally. "Our son. Before today's events, I'd have welcomed such an occurrence."

"I am sorry I disappointed you." Alia's gaze was glued on the ground.

"Disappointed?" I rounded on her. "Oh, please. This cuts far deeper than disappointment. I love you, Alia, and you tossed me out like yesterday's trash."

Spots of color bloomed on her pale cheeks. Before she could reply, Akbar joined us. "Micah won't bother anyone again."

"What'd you do with him?" I asked.

"He's in one of our dungeons with a couple of ravens. They will peck at his innards, which will be perpetually renewed by magic. His suffering will never end."

Breath hissed from between my clenched teeth. "Thank you. It's far better than I could have done."

"Follow me. I will take you to where you can clean the blood of your brothers off yourselves and find fresh garments."

Akbar led Connor, Joss, and me to a room with steamy pools in it. Robes hung from hooks. Once he shepherded Alia and Cleyn away, we proceeded to clean up.

"Are you happy about the babe?" Joss regarded me through shrewd blue eyes.

"I will do right by him," I said stiffly.

"Not what I asked," Joss said.

"I don't want to talk about it," I growled.

"Better if you do," Connor pressed. "Here where it's just the three of us and safe."

Nice illusion. Nowhere was actually safe any longer, but he meant well, so I didn't jump down his throat.

"Not sure what I feel," I admitted as I rinsed blood from my hair. "If it had happened before she ran this last time—"

"It did," Connor said.

"Aye, but none of us knew about it. Certainly not Alia. She was as shocked as the rest of us," Joss chimed in.

"Not seeing how I can pick up the pieces and pretend she didn't try to leave me behind," I murmured.

"Not so much leave as protect," Joss corrected me.

"If she didn't care as deeply as she does, she'd never have left," Connor added.

I shook my head and hauled myself to a sit on the edge of the pool as water streamed down my body. "Not sure I agree," I told him. "When you care, you stick it out. Find ways to make things work."

Joss nodded. "Sure, but she's barely twenty. She doesn't have hundreds of years of life experience to draw on."

"She'll need all of us more than ever," Connor said.

"Emphasis on all," Joss agreed and smiled. It lightened

his gaunt features. "Did you see how excited Cleyn was? Warmed my heart."

A reluctant smile formed on my face too. Cleyn had lost his kinsmen. The specter of a new pack member would delight him.

Connor clambered out of the pool and reached for a towel. I got to my feet and did the same. He slugged me lightly in the shoulder. "Cut her some slack, man. Imagine how she must be feeling."

"I was thinking the same," Joss said and grabbed the last neatly folded towel.

We slipped into robes hanging from hooks. I left our garments in a stack. At some point, I'd ask Akbar about cleanup facilities. No one materialized to guide us, but someone had left lighted beacons. Following them led us to a dining area. Plenty of food was piled on serving trays. Cleyn squatted in a corner, his head under a wing.

We helped ourselves before a witch motioned us to the table where Alia sat with her head on her crossed arms.

Perhaps the commotion of us sitting woke her; she regarded us through eyes bleary from exhaustion. I told her to go back to sleep. A quick trip through her mind yielded guilt, shame, worry, and protectiveness over our child. Connor's words about cutting her some slack played through my head.

"Rest, Alia. Everything will work out." I aimed for soothing and might have come close. She made a small murmuring noise.

I hadn't realized how hungry I was until I started eating.

Nothing like trauma ripping your guild house apart to spur the appetite.

"Where do we go from here?" Joss eyed me.

It was a good question. "I need to return to the guild house long enough to ensure everyone is all right."

"Do you?" Connor asked softly.

"What are you getting at?" I asked him.

He set down his fork. "Seems to me like we have a laundry list of problems, a long one. Your guild mates are capable of caring for themselves."

"They weren't doing all that well before we showed up," I noted dryly.

"Aye, but they should be fine now."

"Where do the two of you think we need to focus our efforts?" I asked.

"For starters, determining how Chaos monsters, tricksters, and the Sumerians are linked," Joss said.

"Getting the Sumerians to back off and stop offering rewards for Alia's capture has to be another priority," Connor added.

"And then there's the link with the Nine Worlds and all those giants. Never did figure it out," Joss mumbled.

I nodded. They were right. Returning to the Isle of Skye and my guild house could wait. Perhaps for a good long while. The farther we moved out from the cataclysm, the tougher it would be to undo, which was one more argument for focusing all our efforts on how, what, and why it had occurred.

"Sold. Thanks for a solid redirect."

"What are friends for?" Connor grinned.

I didn't mention I hadn't had many outside my guild house. And Micah, who I'd always counted as a companion, had turned on me without a second thought.

Akbar glided to our table. When I looked up, the dining area was empty save for us. "Leave your plates. I will show you to your quarters."

Alia, who'd either been asleep or pretending, raised her head. "That would be lovely. Thank you."

He offered a hand. She grasped it and rose to her feet. I tapped the griffon as I passed, gesturing for him to follow us.

Things between Alia and me might never be the same, but I'd been serious when I'd said I would raise and protect our child. How that would look amidst the dregs of civilization remained to be seen.

We needed to talk, she and I, but I wasn't quite ready. One truth battered me. If she'd truly loved me, valued me as much as I did her, she'd never have fled.

Inconvenient, but true nonetheless. I'd have to absorb it and move forward.

"Here we are." Akbar pushed a door open. "We will meet tomorrow and craft plans."

Plans, eh? What he like as not meant was the Lemurians would tell us what they wanted us to do. Whether we complied would determine the length of our tenure beneath the magical mountain. I shielded my thoughts, hoping for the best.

We entered yet one more cavern with pallets scattered on the floor. I waited until Alia chose one and picked another on the far side of the grotto. The griffon glided next to Alia and draped a wing over her.

Jealousy pricked. *It should be me next to her, protecting her,* but I'd abdicated that role when I'd chosen a distant pallet.

Weak suck, bastard, an inner voice chided. *Make up your fucking mind.*

ABOUT THE AUTHOR

Ann Gimpel is a USA Today bestselling author. A lifelong aficionado of the unusual, she began writing speculative fiction a few years ago. Since then her short fiction has appeared in many webzines and anthologies. Her longer books run the gamut from urban fantasy to paranormal romance. Once upon a time, she nurtured clients. Now she nurtures dark, gritty fantasy stories that push hard against reality. When she's not writing, she's in the backcountry getting down and dirty with her camera. She's published over 100 books to date, with several more planned for 2024 and beyond. A husband, grown children, grandchildren, and wolf hybrids round out her family.

Keep up with her at www.anngimpel.com or www.anngimpelbooks.com

If you enjoyed what you read, get in line for special offers and pre-release special reads. Newsletter Signup!

Broken Line

Circle of Assassins

Shira

Quinn

Rhiana

Kylian

Grigori

Coven Enforcers

Blood and Magic

Blood and Sorcery

Blood and Illusion

Demon Assassins

Witch's Bounty

Witch's Bane

Witches Rule

Dragon Heir

Dragon's Call

Dragon's Blood

Dragon's Heir

Dragon Lore

Highland Secrets

To Love a Highland Dragon

Dragon Maid

Dragon's Dare

Dragon Fury

Earth Reclaimed

Earth's Requiem

Earth's Blood

Earth's Hope

Elemental Witch

Timespell

Time's Curse

Time's Hostage

Gatekeeper

Shadow Reaper

Rebel Reaper

Untamed Reaper

GenTech Rebellion

Winning Glory

Honor Bound

Claiming Charity

Loving Hope

Keeping Faith

Ice Dragon

Feral Ice

Cursed Ice

Primal Ice

Magick and Misfits

Court of Rogues

Midnight Court

Court of the Fallen

Court of Destiny

Rubicon International

Garen

Lars

Sanctuary

Conjuring Fate

Conjuring Chaos

Conjuring Promises

Soul Dance

Tarnished Beginnings

Tarnished Legacy

Tarnished Prophecy

Tarnished Journey

Soul Storm

Dark Prophecy

Dark Pursuit

Dark Promise

Underground Heat

Roman's Gold

Wolf Born

Blood Bond

Wayward Mage

Hands of Fate

Jinxed

Hunted

Salvaged

Tiana

Wolf Clan Shifters

Alice's Alphas

Megan's Mates

Sophie's Shifters

Wylde Magick

Gemstone

Lion's Lair

Unbalanced

STANDALONE BOOKS

Branded, That Old Black Magic Romance (paranormal romance)

Edge of Night (short story collection, paranormal and horror)

Grit is a 4-Letter Word (nonfiction)

Heart's Flame (post-apocalyptic romance)

Icy Passage (science fiction romance)

Marked by Fortune (post-apocalyptic coming of age story)

Melis's Gambit (historical paranormal romance)

Midnight Magic (paranormal romance)

Red Dawn (post-apocalyptic paranormal romance)

Shadow Play (historical paranormal romance)

Shadows in Time (Highland time travel romance)

Since We Fell (contemporary romance)

Warin's War (paranormal romance)

www.ingramcontent.com/pod-product-compliance
Lightning Source LLC
Chambersburg PA
CBHW071353300726
48976CB00006B/1866